DIPTERA

JIMMY YU
VICKY HANEY

Disclaimer

This book is a work of fiction. Any references to historical events, real people, or real places are used fictitiously. Any resemblance to actual events, places, or persons, living or dead, is purely coincidental.

PROLOGUE

It was eight minutes past eleven pm in Kyiv. All the government workers on ground level had long gone home and were probably snug in bed by now, but not Boris Shevchenko. Boris hoped the next generation of flies would be larger and more voracious than the last. Delicately, he placed a specimen under the microscope. Adjusting the scope with one hand and holding a set of calipers with the other, he meticulously took measurements of the specimen's legs, wings, eyes, and beak. Then he jotted down some notes in his journal and logged the measurements into his logbook.

This had been the thirty-fifth generation of specimens since the project was launched, a top-secret priority which began ten years ago when rumblings in Crimea prompted the Ukrainian government to think creatively. Selectively breeding and keeping generation after generation of the experimental flies was starting to wear on Boris. Seven days a week, fifty-two weeks a year, he would secretly descend to this bunker-like lab and patriotically serve his country, certain his efforts would change the course of the war. He poured over the multiple statistical projections provided by his American counterpart, aiming to address any anomalies that could derail the time sensitive project. He took care to separate the male flies from the females while keeping a constant watch over the health of the swarm. He'd been relegated to this secret lab thirty feet below ground for the last nine years and was so close to their mission objective but could not grasp the final piece of the puzzle.

Now, the threat of a wider war was at his doorstep and Boris feared his time may be running out. His only distraction from this fear were the thoughts of his beautiful wife, Olga, who had stuck with him faithfully for the last seven years.

Before the COVID pandemic broke out, he and Olga took extravagant trips to Europe; places they both dreamt of going as children but did not have the means to do so. Since starting this lucrative job, Boris and Olga have climbed a few rungs up the socio-economic ladder. Suddenly, places like Paris, Santorini, and Monaco were within reach and they took full advantage of their new-found wealth.

CHAPTER ONE - BORIS AND OLGA

A top entomologist who taught at the university, Boris Shevchenko never dreamed he would be called to duty in this way. *Better this way than in the actual throes of battle*, he thought. He could never survive as a warrior, and he knew it. His frame was long and slight, and his skin pale and sickly. Boris was what they called "book smart" wisdom in human nature or worldly matters often escaped him. After all, he'd been in school for better than half of his adult life. The only son of a hardware storekeeper, he was brought up by modest means. The redeeming qualities of his intellect and industriousness earned him a PHD in entomology from the National Technical University in Kyiv and a comfortable life as a professor. He was a professor by day and a fly keeper by night.

It was at the university where he met Olga. Boris had walked past the salon at the edge of campus many times in the past to stretch his legs or to grab lunch before his next class. Sometimes peering through the shop window, he made out the undeniable shape of graceful femininity standing over smiling college age boys. The line of university boys, and some girls, had up until this point discouraged his patronage; however, this day was different.

It was a slow autumn day for the salon, and his curiosity lured him inside.

His heart leapt as she approached. Clad in a white, low-cut, cashmere sweater her bosom drew attention in the most flattering way. A tight-fitting, long, black skirt adorned her tall slender frame revealing a figure befitting a tech billionaire's mistress – not a 300 hryvnia per cut hairdresser.

"How would you like your hair styled today?" she said smiling.

When he raised his eyes from his initial sitting position, she delivered a sultry look with her stunning blue almond-shaped eyes.

"I'm not looking to change my hair style, just trim it nicely in the back with clippers and shorten it a bit in the front so I can see," he said with his eyes firmly affixed on her bedazzling gaze.

"Sure ……., can I see?" Olga playfully bit her full and shapely bottom lip, smoothly moved between Boris' manspread, and gently ran her long supple fingers through his hair.

Her skin was a light buttery cream color accentuating her long strawberry blonde hair. She lingered there long enough for him to take in her womanly shape and for her perfumed hair to softly graze his face. Boris fell into a dreamlike trance and closed his eyes, unaware of his involuntary reaction. A minute or so later….

"Sir…. Sir? Are you ok?" Olga asked, smiling sheepishly.

"Yes… Yes, I'm fine." Boris replied, embarrassingly awakened from his enchanted state.

"Let me get my new clippers from the storeroom," she said softly, as she elegantly strode away.

A year after his failed marriage, Boris felt ready to explore new possibilities. Based on their engaging glances and her gentle touch, he considered the possibility of love and companionship.

Another minute or so later, Olga returned from the storeroom with the clippers.

"Shall I begin?"

The sound of the clippers gently grazing the back of his neck reminded him of the Robber Fly and the time he and his ex-wife Natalie spent in Florida studying them. Boris married soon after landing his teaching position at the university. Though the marriage lasted only a little over a year, he fell to pieces when it abruptly ended, surprised that he hadn't seen the early signs of trouble.

Boris had been fascinated by insects since childhood. As an only child growing up by modest means, he occupied his time collecting them, playing with them, and even naming them. He was fascinated by them. Their anonymous yet essential existence prompted him to major in entomology at university. After gaining his bachelor's degree, his thirst for knowledge didn't wane. He competed for and won fellowships on the subject and earned his way to a PHD.

When the U.S. Army and Ukrainian Secret Service commissioned a research project in Florida on the aerial hunting abilities of the Robber Fly, they tapped Boris to lead the project. He, of course, made Natalie, his wife at the time, his project assistant. Natalie was a star pupil in Boris's class, and quite ambitious. The marriage was seen as a matter of convenience rather than true love, at least according to Natalie. Having the opportunity to leave Ukraine and do research abroad was plenty of incentive for a twenty-five-year-old research student to marry her professor. Although Boris was seven years her senior, she found his innocence and naivety somewhat attractive. Boris once told her he admired the "efficient" mating traits of flies. For those uninitiated, when a male fly wants to copulate, he simply jumps on the females back, pins her wings down with his hind legs, and does his business. And, if the amorous object of his affection happens to be in the air, well, he just charges head on like a kamikaze pilot and knocks her out of the sky.

An odd choice of words for two people supposedly in love, but being an entomologist herself, Natalie knew exactly what Boris meant, and quickly dismissed his bookish sentiments.

Olga, as it turned out, was also driven by motivation that was not entirely honorable. She was only seventeen when she realized she had a special gift, an asset most women would do anything for, a natural beauty men could not resist. Olga's long hair showcased her flawless ivory skin and pale blue eyes. Her slender frame was highlighted with curves in just the right places. By the time she was in secondary school, she was turning the heads of her male classmates as well as some of her teachers. Unwitting to this gift, she perceived it as a handicap and an annoyance; the girls shunned her, jealous of the amorous attention from boys. Then she started to notice their bashful smiles when they were caught stealing glances, how their pleading eyes invited her presence in the seat next to them in the lunchroom, and how quickly they offered to pay for a sweet treat at snack time. She quickly learned how to perfect her smile, tilt her head in just the right way, and throw her pretty hair back, revealing her enchanting visage when the occasion was warranted. She quickly learned that timing was everything.

Olga was the only child born to hardworking parents in Kyiv. Her mother was a pre-school teacher, and her father worked as a tailor. The family survived on the meager wages brought in by her parents and whatever financial help the government provided. Olga decided early on she wanted a better life outside of Ukraine and with her coming of age, she knew exactly how she would achieve that goal.

While her classmates were studying Russian as a second language, Olga spent hours on YouTube learning American English, hoping, one day, to travel to the wealthiest country in the world. Although her parents couldn't afford to send her to the University, Olga thought her best chance of meeting a wealthy future husband was her alluring presence there.

Fortunately, those cosmetology courses she took in secondary school prepared her for serendipity when she saw a "stylist wanted" sign on the window of the nearby campus salon.

CHAPTER TWO – THE ROBBER FLY

While Boris sat patiently amongst a densely wooded patch of forest in the Ocala National Forest, Natalie decided to take a daytrip to the beaches of St. Augustine. It didn't bother Boris that his wife of only eleven months had decided to tan herself instead of helping him, after all, they were still considered newlyweds and vitamin D along with her nicely tanned body would only enhance their carnal pursuits. Boris started the day around five a.m. Already with six varieties of Robbers in his mesh sack, he decided to pack up and head back to camp, eager to set some experiments in motion.

The research project was well funded. Boris quietly reveled amongst the high-tech video equipment and the ambience afforded by the shade of massive oak trees surrounding the campsite. There was a powerful generator with enough fuel to last a couple of months. The refrigerator was well stocked with food, water, and libations of all sorts, even champagne for the newlyweds. Wooden shelves made from plywood held an ample supply of canned goods, complimented by a small gas stove for heating its contents. A couple of hammocks hung between trees and two standard army-issue cots sat under the tin roof of the well-constructed camp. Even though the camp could sustain two entomologists in outdoor luxury for a couple of months, Natalie insisted that their project budget included line items for hotel stays and fine dining. Though not entirely sincere, Natalie eagerly introduced Boris to the adage...happy wife, happy life.

Boris walked through the door of the large ten-foot by ten-foot butterfly cage enhanced with mesh netting to keep his study subjects inside. The confinement was overgrown with tall grasses and flowering bushes, providing cover and natural habitat for critters to hide, and more importantly, to hunt. With a gentle tug on the bowtie around the mesh sack, he released twenty-five or so flies into one corner of the cage. In the opposite corner of the cage, Boris held a second mesh sack containing small beetles, grasshoppers, bees, and other flying insects. He loosened its drawstrings, opening the sack, and held it at shoulder height, but nothing came out. It was as if the insects sensed danger nearby. Boris then flipped the sack upside-down and after a couple of gentle shakes, a mass of fluttering wings, prickly legs, and wagging antennae spewed from the bag opening into the air. He then hastily flung the sacks aside and swiftly exited the cage, closing the door behind him.

After a period of frenetic flight, the insects blended into their surroundings quickly vanishing from sight. Boris walked around the outside of the enclosure to the side where the high-speed video equipment was set up. A sturdy wooden stool placed Boris at eye-level with the camera lens. He'd forgotten to pull up and hang the white tarp on the opposite side of the cage for better video contrast, but it didn't matter, Boris was ready for carnage to ensue...

The Robber Fly is also known by another name, the Assassin Fly. Its feeding instrument is often described as a beak-like proboscis. In simple terms, a sharp straw capable of piercing insect armor. But calling it a straw would suggest only one way traffic, trivializing mother nature's ingenuity. These flying vampire aces use that same beak as a syringe – injecting a lethal dose of neurotoxins into their victim, immobilizing them. Then, the carnivore fly injects a dose of caustic digestive enzymes melting their prey's inner flesh, allowing them to enjoy the unfortunate insect like a chocolate milkshake. Robber flies are voracious feeders that prey on juicy beetles, unsuspecting grasshoppers, and other Robbers too. But flying around with a hungry mouth hardly makes you any more lethal than a hungry toddler with wings. These flies have vision specifically adapted for predation. Relatively speaking, it can spot its prey a football field away if measured on a human scale. Sitting prominently on top of their head, their compound eyes encapsulate thousands of lenses in assorted sizes allowing them to track other flying insects with deadly precision.

After twenty minutes of calm, mayhem began. Boris had a front row seat at the macabre alien freak show. The innocent and unsuspecting prey had no chance against the flying aces. Each time one flew within range, the Robber easily intercepted its flight path ensnaring the victim with its long prickly legs and wasted no time piercing its head or armor-plated parts with his hungry dagger-like mouth. Sitting behind the high-definition camera, Boris could in his mind hear the cracking sound of broken armor as fluids spew from each victim. He could practically feel the convulsions of each dying animal from neurotoxins coursing through their bodies, paralyzing them. Then, as the Robber discarded the lifeless empty shell that was once a succulent, living, life force, Boris felt small and insignificant. For several hours and from various angles, Boris captured the spectacular display of the fly's voracity and hunting prowess.

The research project centered around the acrobatic flying capabilities of this incredibly special fly because the US Army imagined it would supercharge their drone technology program.

Well, not the whole army, just Colonel Wesley Walker. The Colonel drove up from Cent-Com right after lunch. Cent-Com is short for "Central Command," where all significant active military campaigns are led. It was the Friday afternoon of a long weekend, and Wes, as he likes to be called, didn't expect that the holiday weekend traffic would start so soon. What normally would have been a two-hour drive from Tampa to Ocala took him four hours when he arrived at the campsite. In his younger days, he would have been enraged the whole drive up; some creative expletives may have even blurted from tightly clenched teeth, but now, only ten years from retirement and a full pension, he knew when to get excited and when to save his energy for the golden years. Those years, he hoped to spend boating and fishing in the panhandle beaches of Florida, or as native Floridians know it – *The Redneck Riviera.*

Daylight beckoned dusk when Wes stepped out of the SUV. The whole vehicle rose about eight inches, relieved of the weight of a rather large man. Boris surmised a black SUV with tinted windows was likely to be official, probably relating to his employer. Boris had already packed up the expensive video equipment before the boss arrived. He had only met Colonel Wesley Walker once during the interview process in Kyiv. All the other administrative details were taken care of by the Secret Service of Ukraine, simply referred to as the SSU. Adorned in full military uniform, the Colonel looked even more impressive than his six-foot five-inch stature already projected. Medals and ribbons crowded the left side of his chest, and four shiny brass buttons ran down the middle of his uniform coat. Atop his head sat a rigid peaked cap decorated with gold rope and shiny accessories.

"Enjoying a cold one I see, good for you Boris!" shouted the Colonel, as he saw Boris from afar, enjoying a non-alcoholic beer, seated on a stool under the roof.

"Hello Colonel Walker, it's good to see you again," said Boris, greeting him stiffly.

"Call me Wes! Please! The sooner we get on a first name basis, the sooner we can get down to business. Besides, I can't quite pronounce your last name – Pacheco, is it?"

"It's Shevchenko." Boris said, sheepishly, silently laughing inside.

"How did you both like the champagne? It's the real stuff you know, imported from France. I wanted to make sure you and the missus enjoyed your time here, you know.... being newlyweds and all. Where is the pretty lady?"

Boris had been studying Wes since he stepped out of his vehicle. His anemic right brain was struggling to grasp how this high-ranking official could be so affable yet hold the key to top secret military initiatives of the most powerful country in the world. Boris made some excuses to placate the Colonel's curiosity as to Natalie's whereabouts and handed Wes a thumb-sized SSD card.

Boris enthusiastically reported: "You have approximately three hours of footage here. I was lucky – I captured all six varieties in flight."

Playing along with Boris's diversion, the Colonel nonchalantly replied, "Hey, that's wonderful Boris! I'm sure the boys at DEVCOM will appreciate your excellent work."

The Colonel didn't really know where Natalie was, but being part of an intelligence agency and living in a State surrounded by water gave him a hunch, he continued, "Well, I best be on my way. Got a ways to drive to meet my better half. Oh, and I just gotta warn you about the sun out here in Florida; it's brutal on pale skin. Make sure you lather up with that bottle of sunblock over there. I'll check up on you in another week."

Standing under the shade of giant oak trees, even Boris realized the Colonel wasn't referring to his pale skin. Wes hopped into his SUV and began his drive up to the Panhandle to meet his wife, daughter, and grandbaby.

Colonel Wesley Walker is a Christian man who often struggles with his less than pious profession as a weapons developer. Sure, they called him Colonel on base; but Wes made no bones about his true role. To be good at his job, he must use his imagination, his ingenuity, and his God-given talents to develop munitions, drones and bombs that maim, kill, and destroy. Like the standard operating procedures of the US Army, the Bible also gives everyday guidance for warriors of the Christian faith: love thy neighbor; do unto others as you would have them do unto you; and avenge not yourselves. The juxtaposition of his job and his faith had plagued him for years.

After graduating from West Point with degrees in mechanical engineering and statistics, he served in the Gulf War. Shortly thereafter, he was promoted to Captain and a permanent change of station moved him to what is known today as DEVCOM, just outside of Baltimore Maryland. The Combat Capabilities Development Command or DEVCOM is tasked with developing cutting-edge technology, or in other words, more efficient killing machines for soldiers on the front line. The promotion and move to a more stable environment after the war helped Wes grow roots. He met his wife Sharon, and they started a family in a suburb just north of Baltimore. They raised their daughter in that neighborhood and all the while he was helping the Army integrate innovative technology into its weaponry.

As military drones continued to evolve globally, the U.S. fell behind, so Wes was assigned to lead a task force to catch up to the rest of the world and in the process *"think outside the box."*

Better drones meant less need to risk real lives in combat; as to the targets of those drones, well, that was a matter for God to sort out. When an entomologist at DEVCOM introduced him to the Robber fly's uncanny ability to adjust their flight in midair, Wes was eager to learn more about the fly and commissioned a research study. The U.S. also needed a battle testing ground for any innovative technology, so they partnered with the Ukrainian Government, anticipating that conflict had a good chance of erupting in Eastern Europe after Russia's annexation of Crimea in the Ukraine.

After serving twenty-eight years at DEVCOM, Wes's daughter had grown up, married, and moved to Florida. When news came that he had become a grandfather to a baby girl, he pulled some strings at the highest levels and received a transfer to CENTCOM in Tampa, Florida. Afterall, he was now a Colonel with some clout. He promised the Army he would continue to shepherd the project from Tampa, but he would relinquish his task leader role to someone else at DEVCOM.

Wes made a couple more visits to the campsite to check up on the newly-weds before the two-month Robber fly research concluded. Natalie and Boris were eager to get back to Kyiv and university life. They agreed to make a final trip to DEVCOM with the Colonel to transfer the fruits of their research.

CHAPTER THREE – THE UNNATURAL

The Colonel was anxious about the meeting. He and the SSU had a sister project in motion at the same time as the drone enhancement project. One that involved a team of geneticists. Now that the two separate phases were complete, it was time to sell the final phase to Boris. They had done their homework on Boris; his history, his character, and his naivety. Their psychological profile concluded, among other things, that he was a patriotic man made with good moral fabric, would work hard for the right cause and ask little questions. But Wes knew full well the parallel experiment was immoral and abhorrently unnatural. He took issue when he learned about it a year ago. He had to square things with God; so, he went to church, talked to his pastor, and prayed God would intervene directly and in the most personal way. But God didn't. Throughout his career, Wes had to tell himself half-truths while ignoring the half that carried unconscionable consequences. His time with Boris amounted to only six months from the interview process until now, but in that brief time, he had grown to like Boris in a sort of paternal way. Now, he had to leave him with the SSU. Wes was somewhat melancholy about leaving his friend even though he didn't want to be involved any further in the next phase.

What would Boris do? How would he react? he thought to himself, as the three of them strode through the sterile hallways of the secure building. As they passed a lavatory door marked with a unisex emblem, Natalie excused herself and stepped inside. Ten seconds later, as Boris and Wes turned the corner, she poked her head out making sure the coast was clear. Then, she quickly made her way back in the opposite direction and found an office door with the number eighty-one on it. The door cracked open, and she hastily stepped inside leaving the door half open.

"What the hell Denys! I was promised a plane ticket back to Kyiv!" Natalie blurted, practically screaming.

"Shh......" quickly closing the door "Don't worry Kateryna, my pet. We have to make flexible plan; this is not so simple like kissing boys," Denys chided in a heavy Ukrainian accent.

Denys Boyko was affectionately known by his colleagues in the SSU as "The Fixer." A former identity thief, Denys, was recruited by the service at a very young age. He can steal your identity with just a few keystrokes or fabricate it out of thin air. He oversaw all security clearances domestically and internationally for the SSU and was assigned to this project by the higher ups.

Lowering her voice a little, Natalie said "Easy for you to say, it wasn't you who sacrificed three years of your life."

"And you will be paid handsomely for it, mousy" Denys said with a patronizing grin "I see the Florida sun has treated you well Kateryna..."

He reached out with his right hand to touch Natalie's toned and well-tanned left arm, only to quickly withdraw it after noticing her reactionary scowl.

"Don't call me by my real name, ever!" she snapped. Then somberly, she said "You promised me as soon as I got home you would unwind this marriage."

"Already in the works my dear; your graduation documents, your divorce papers, and even your 'Dear John' letter," he reassured.

Natalie could not bear the thought of someone else writing such a personal letter. Silently, she resolved to accept that burden herself.

"And...what about the money?" she asked shamefully.

"Two-hundred fifty-thousand dollars, U.S. as agreed will be in your bank account. Thank you for your service to your country."

Denys handed Kateryna her plane ticket and passport and she left in a cab for Baltimore-Washington International Airport.

The SSU's use of psychological profiling is much more prolific than the West. You could say mind control sits at the top of an extensive list of preferred tactics in the clandestine community akin to the old USSR. Based on the profile worked up during Boris's interview process, they knew how his mind worked. They predicted that, for him, love and companionship would enhance his enthusiasm for life and positively affect his research, while heartbreak would lead him to focus intensively on the final critical phase of his work. Like a puppeteer on steroids, the SSU was pulling all the strings. Besides, two-hundred fifty-thousand dollars was well below the project budget for the line item of temporary bride.

Colonel Walker and Boris entered a windowless room with bright fluorescent lighting. Heavy duty metal tables lined the right side of the room. Crowded atop were test tubes and beakers of various shapes and sizes, heating elements, microscopes, and square metal boxes with doors and precision gauges affixed to them. On the left side of the room sat a long conference table with ergonomic office chairs surrounding it. Only cinder block lines adorned the drably painted walls. Directly opposite the entry door was another door leading to an interior room.

Shortly after the two men sat down at the table, the interior door opened, and three men walked through. Boris immediately recognized Denys as the man that arranged for his security clearances and administered the in-depth psychological evaluation, but the other two faces were foreign to him. Wesley was puzzled as to why there were no other American representatives in the room. Denys greeted Boris and the Colonel warmly, then formally introduced the two men as General Mikkael Valarie and Dr. Francis Bartosh. The General was dressed in official uniform and the doctor wore a lab coat over his plain clothes. After some exchange of pleasantries, they all sat around at the conference table and the General spoke.

"I want to give many thanks to our great American friends. Without their support and partnership, we could not come so far today in our goals," he said diplomatically, looking directly at the Colonel.

After an approving nod from Wes, he continued "Many did not belief Pushkin would take Crimea. Many lines were drawn in the sand, but Pushkin doesn't play well in the sandbox. He took our land, he killed our leaders, our children, their mothers, and their fathers."

Out of the corner of his eyes, the General caught a glimpse of Boris with a tear tracing down the side of his nose. He continued...

"Russia has nuclear missiles, big guns, many fighter jets, and, still, many more soldiers than Ukraine. And what do we have?" he asked rhetorically "We have a two-thousand-kilometer border with the world's biggest bully; we have patriots like Boris; we have friends in Europe and America, but most importantly, we have freedom."

Wesley secretly peeked over at Boris wondering how Boris would react to the details of the next phase. Was he sufficiently moved by Valarie's words to even consider the forthcoming proposition? Tears welled up in Boris's eyes as Valarie's words stoked a sense of national pride inside him. His anticipation grew as he awaited words about the success of the drone enhancement project and about the positive impact his research may have had over the last two months. Boris had his observations notes, drawings, and diagrams in his briefcase just ready to be showcased and discussed.

"We must outsmart a bully and catch him with surprise... and when we strike....We must do it so swiftly and with such force, he cannot react. Today, Dr. Bartosh will discuss the next phase of our plan, he is a geneticist who study at Cambridge and his English is much better than mine."

Bewilderment registered on Boris's face, *next phase? Geneticist? When he was introduced to Bartosh earlier there was no mention of his field of study. Why would the SSU need a geneticist?* He looked over at the Colonel only to catch a glimpse of him, quickly averting his eyes.

Dr. Bartosh was a small-statured man standing just over five feet tall. His black plastic spectacles held lenses so thick they distorted the shape of his eyes. He wore a hairstyle reminiscent of the bowl cut made popular by the Beatles in the 1960s. But despite his peculiar appearance, the most beautiful sound of the Queen's English came from his mouth.

"General Valarie, the brevity of your summation was admirable, and the facts are nothing short of sobering; but I am inspired by it and our resolve is equal to the task!" Bartosh exclaimed.

Wes and Boris turned to each other with slightly puzzled gazes. Denys, noticing the soliloquies playing out in their heads interjected in his thick Ukrainian accent "what he means is we have special something for Pushkin," and followed up with an awkward wink.

A visible eye roll from the General preceded his reprimand "Denys, please let Dr. Bartosh speak without interruption."

"Yes Sir..., Sorry," his apology was accompanied by an extended open right palm toward Bartosh as if to say – please continue.

Bartosh continued, "Gentlemen, we have been collaborating with DEVCOM for just over two years now. The United States has been providing our geneticists with gene sequencing data for the most workable candidates for genetic combination. Hundreds of combinations were tried..."

"What are you talking about? This is not drone-technology!" Boris said in an agitated tone. Turning to Denys, "Where is Natalie, we have to go back home."

Boris sprung from his chair and made a motion towards the door. Anticipating his reaction, Denys civilly obstructed Boris's path, a wry smile registered on his face "Boris, we made arrangements for Natalie to return to Kyiv first. But don't worry she will be waiting for you when you get back home."

"Boris, we need you to stay a while longer and hear what Dr. Bartosh has to say, please, your country needs you," General Valarie said in a conciliatory tone.

Reluctantly, Boris sat down with his arms folded in protest. Unfazed, even by the second interruption, the doctor continued, "Well, I don't want to be verbose; so, I'll let the tireless work of our team speak for itself."

The doctor reached into his lab coat pocket and revealed a small, ventilated plastic case no larger than a matchbox. Gently placing the case on the conference table, he slid it to the center where curious gazes fell upon the object. Unexpectedly, the box shook and shimmied, accompanied by bursts of a strong buzzing sound. Although Wes knew what was in that box, he continued to perpetrate a façade of ignorance. He knew the unholiness of the creature inside, yet he condoned its creation through half-truths he told himself: "We can control the breeding environment...This is a single use trump-card...We have a fail-safe contingency plan...This is my final hand-off."

"What is it?" Wes said, while a nervous smile crept across his face.

Immediately, Wes felt Boris's dubious gaze burning the right side of his face. His silence this whole time had fed a suspicion within Boris; a suspicion that the Colonel was not such a righteous man, that his stately uniform was earned through guile rather than honor. Even so, his impression of Wes as a "good" man was not in complete upheaval. Boris still considered the kindness the Colonel had shown thus far to be genuine.

Turning his attention to the center of the table, Boris picked up the case and stared intently at the specimen inside. He then raised it above eye level so he could inspect the underbelly of the strange fly. Curiously, and to everyone else's surprise, the fly seemed to calm down, the frenetic buzzing of wings paused. Carefully, Boris placed his thumb over the plastic tab to open the box.

"I wouldn't if I were.........!"

The doctor admonished but paused mid-sentence as a strange prickly creature crept out onto Boris's palm. Hues of sunset orange, charcoal black, grizzly bear brown and metallic green covered an insect about an inch in length. Adorned with iridescent wings, it reflected pink and purple from the bright fluorescent lighting. Bending his elbow, Boris tepidly brought the animal in for a closer unobstructed inspection. Upon doing so, the fly crept towards the edge of his palm and fluttered its wings drawing an anxious gasp from the audience around the large table. Boris instinctively rotated his palm inward, allowing the creature more room to roam, as its six bristly legs tickled the back of his hand until coming to rest on his second knuckle. He stared at the unholy spectacle which appeared irreverent of any natural order and millions of years of evolution. Its very existence disgusted Boris and brought a queasy feeling to his gut.

He immediately made out the marquee attributes of the Robber Fly – large orange compound eyes sitting prominently on each side of its sleek narrow head; two protruding mini-antennae forming a perfect "V"; a sharp beak below its eyes protruding downward from bristly brown hairs; and a pair of long regal wings sprouting from the thorax draping down the length of its body. And then, he spotted the anomaly. A bulbous metallic green abdomen weirdly joined to the thorax of the fly. Boris expertly identified the body part as that belonging to the common green bottle fly.

The queasiness in his gut intensified as he visualized hundreds of maggots feeding on rotting flesh. *Why would they create such a Frankenstein creature?* He thought. Boris quickly returned the fly to its case, closed the lid, and abruptly slid the case in Bartosh's direction. A complex mix of emotions was now brewing within him.

"Why?" he blurted across the table where the Ukrainians sat in silent repose.

Upon hearing his cue, Bartosh called for assistance in the direction of the interior door. Two men in white lab coats hoisting a seventy-five-gallon terrarium staggered through the door. General Valarie, Denys, and the doctor moved aside to allow the glass enclosure to be placed atop the large conference table. The terrarium had two small interior compartments inside. In the bottom right-hand compartment, a white lab rat spun around frenetically looking for an exit; while in the top left-hand compartment, Boris noticed three of the genetically modified flies resting side by side, their compound eyes fixated on the animal below. Boris looked over at Wes in disbelief only to find him staring stoically through the glass of the terrarium. Denys's eyes grew to the size of silver dollars, his face wore a maniacal grin. Bartosh stood up, walked across the room to the lab tables and retrieved a pair of rubber lab gloves. The two lab-coats stepped aside, ready for additional instruction from Bartosh.

When he came back, the doctor pulled out a needle and syringe from his other lab coat pocket and held it at eye level, extending his arm for everyone to see. He stood proudly to address the room – all five feet one inch of his unimpressive stature.

"Gentlemen, this syringe holds synthesized neurotoxins identical in chemistry to that of our Robber fly friend in the wild. Except! It is 150 times more potent due to the volume inside the syringe. Our genetically enhanced subjects in this corner here have neurotoxin potencies fifty times more than their natural state in the wild. But what is even more impressive is the amplified potency of their digestive enzymes at one hundred times more."

Disbelief morphed into shock as Boris pieced together the general's inspirational speech and the doctor's tedious words, revealing the goal of this insane and unnatural plan. The temperature in the windowless room crept up as body heat emanated from the group in anticipation of the gruesome spectacle.

Before Boris could raise his objection, Bartosh gave the rat a jab of neurotoxin and released it among the ornamental grasses, shrubs, and stumps occupying the center of the terrarium. The effects of the poison were exhibited instantaneously. The rodent's eyes became transfixed and unblinking as if they were staring inward through the window of its soul. Its muscles and joints suddenly tensed up as it fell on its side. Uncontrollable tremors ensued sending micro-vibrations through the air evoking a natural feeding response from the genetically engineered flies.

Sensing wounded prey, the voracious flies flew wildly inside the small confinement, smacking the plexiglass so hard it reminded Boris of large bugs smacking his windshield at eighty miles an hour, while driving down a country road in Florida.

The same maniacal smile Denys had now appeared on the doctor's face. He pulled on a handle from outside the terrarium which opened the small trap door, and the ghastly creatures flew a beeline towards the compromised prey. Though the toxins coursing through the rat had immobilized it, the pain receptors in its brain were unaffected.

Two flies landed on each side of the rat's head while the third claimed its abdomen. With their bristly legs dug into the animal for leverage, the two on the rodent's head impaled the cornea of each eye with their sharp beaks injecting digestive enzymes one hundred times more caustic than nature intended. The suffering animal let out a high-pitched traumatized squeal amplifying the harrowing show playing out for the audience. Using its last modicum of energy the rat shook its head violently in pain trying to dislodge its attackers while tiny beads of blood stained the glass walls of the terrarium. The cornea melted like hot butter frying within the eye sockets, then quickly disappeared as the flies hungrily slurped it up through their straw-like proboscis. The flies then burrowed into the rat's brain through its bare eye sockets to continue its smorgasbord of soft tissue. The third fly had melted a hole in the abdomen of the rat and crawled inside for its prized intestines. When the three assassin flies had satiated their hunger, they lethargically crept out of the rat and disappeared into the terrarium landscape while a defiled carcass laid in the corner reeking of burnt flesh.

Boris doubled over and threw up on his shoe. Although Wes was privy to the genetic modification phase of the assignment, this was his first demonstration. Clearly disturbed, beads of sweat poured from his forehead, prompting him to pull his handkerchief. After wiping the sweat off, he offered the hanky to Boris to clean off his shoe.

"How in the world did you turn these insect eaters into ravenous carnivores?" asked the Colonel.

In a prideful tone, Bartosh explained "well, technically they were already carnivores, Colonel; all we did was change their preference of protein. It's sort of like upgrading from fish sticks to filet mignon."

Smirks emanated from Denys and Valarie.

The doctor continued: "the Diptera Order includes many other insects besides flies. Mosquitoes, akin to what you Americans may refer to as crazy cousins, prefer mammalian blood. So, quite naturally, we included this genetic trait in our gene sequencing to change our flies' dietary preference. Additionally, to capture and digest larger prey, we amplified the genes associated with neurotoxin and digestive enzyme production…"

"And why the genes from the green bottle fly?" Boris interrupted the doctor mid-sentence.

Relishing yet another cue to brag, Bartosh continued: "Excellent! Mr. Shevchenko, you were quite impressive handling that female fly earlier. The ones we just witnessed in action were males – sleeker and more agile. As an entomologist, I trust you know blowflies are prolific breeders, laying 2,000 eggs in their short thirty-day lifetime. Compared to the Robber fly which takes two years to develop underneath the earth, it's quite obvious why they were the perfect species for genetic combination."

General Valarie was silent the whole time, observing and assessing each person in the room, internally strategizing the approach he would take to convince Boris to come on board. Now that the river card was revealed, he was ready to play his hand.

"Which is precisely why we need you, Boris."

With a nonchalant hand gesture, Valarie dismissed Denys and the two lab-coats from the room. Again, Wes wondered why there was no other U.S. Army representative present.

"So, you need me to breed these genetically modified assassin flies?" Boris asked.

The General looked over at Bartosh signaling he needed some technical help. Bartosh obliged: "There are one hundred specimens in a secret lab under heavy surveillance in Kyiv – eighty male flies and twenty females. We need these newly combined attributes in these specimens to be enhanced through selective breeding. We expect these traits to be naturalized in the lab by the ninetieth generation. According to our calculations, accounting for natural selective factors, after five years, a swarm of 50,000 agents of Ukraine will be ready to defend our country! But I must warn you. You must keep the female population down and separated from the males; only the males will be on combat duty to prevent breeding in the wild."

Boris knew deep down that the unscrupulous doctor had broken the moral code of scientific discovery, but his patriotic fervor overshadowed his concerns. The General's earlier speech had evoked a powerful sense of national pride within him.

"How many assistants besides Natalie will I have?"

An awkward silence fell over the room while Boris looked around pleadingly for an answer.

With a solemn tone, the General explained: "Boris, other than supply vendors sworn to secrecy, you will be alone in your service to your country. No one except the four of us in this room and Denys knows the details of our plan. Of course, it will be revealed to our brave commanders when we are ready. But, for now, no one can know; that is why you must do this at night after your work at the University so that there is no suspicion. There is a lab near the City's center and your workspace is in the basement away from other scientists working above ground during the day…"

After General Valarie laid out the logistical and security details, Boris waffled between patriotism and self-interest. After all, he was still a newlywed. He would essentially be giving up married life and how would Natalie receive the proposal?

The SSU's psychological profile on Boris had been dead on thus far, Boris's reactions were so accurately predicted that the General was inclined to deliver the coup de gras to seal the deal.

"And your country is prepared to reward you handsomely for your dedication; $300,000 U.S. per year."

Wes was momentarily stunned at the figure thrown out by Valarie. As the task force leader of phase one, he was not privy to the combined budget of all three phases, only his. His brain began to perform mental gymnastics trying to arrive at a reasonable estimate of the overall budget. His years of top-secret project management experience arrived at a figure around $300 million, but still, Wes wondered how tightly the Ukrainians were managing to budget.

Boris's outlook on the proposal suddenly improved. He thought about places he could take Natalie, things he could buy, the standard of living they could enjoy. His thoughts must have covertly seeped out of his head prompting the General to offer his hand to receive Boris's acceptance shake, but Boris surprised Valarie with:

"I will accept only if Colonel Walker agrees to stay on with me to help with the statistical modeling to meet our swarm population goal."

After a moment of initial surprise, Valarie and Bartosh turned to Wes who was speechless at first, then a passionate rebuke blurted from his mouth "Now, wait a second here. As far as I'm concerned, my work and my country's contribution are complete! I delivered the prototype drone to carry these flies..." Sensing his hasty words betraying him, he quickly rephrased "to carry the munitions within your specifications. I can't commit to working in a bunker in the Ukraine; that wasn't part of the deal!"

Boris confirmed his suspicion at that moment that the Colonel had been withholding knowledge of Bartosh's work from him; that Wes knew all along this was not a hand-off meeting; and, that the Colonel orchestrated this charade with the SSU to secure his employment. Although he felt somewhat betrayed, he was also flattered that his country would entrust such an important top-secret project to him and provide compensation that could change his and Natalie's life.

Dr. Bartosh interjected "Colonel Walker, your statistical background could help ensure we meet project timelines, and you wouldn't necessarily need to be onsite."

"I'm willing to offer you the same compensation and clear it with DEVCOM," Valarie added.

Wes started thinking about the way he would like to retire. His thoughts turned to the fishing waters off the panhandle of Florida. Why with one grandchild already here, there may be more on the way. A forty-two-foot fishing boat would accommodate six people much better than a thirty-two-foot one.   After some negotiations on the finer points, the four men shook hands after cementing a deal. Wes headed for Reagan National Airport to get back to Tampa, while the Ukrainians headed for Baltimore Washington International for a flight headed to Kyiv.

CHAPTER FOUR – TRUE LIES AND TRUE FLIES

On the cross-Atlantic flight back to Kyiv Boris was silently rehearsing his pitch to Natalie. Concisely reciting his speech in thesis form, he began: First, he would tell her how much she meant to him and how he appreciated their shared interests. Second, how he appreciated her youth and vitality. *Third, ...? Well, it will come to him before they land,* he thought. But most importantly, he would tell her about the generous offer, a sum beyond their wildest dreams and only for a part-time gig at that. He'd also add that they would be financially set for life in five short years and could enjoy eco-tourism in faraway jungles and travel to some of the most remote places in the world.

His train of thought was annoyingly interrupted by loud banter and unrestrained bursts of manly laughter emanating from behind. He peered back to the last row of seats in first class to find General Valarie, Denys, and Dr. Bartosh sitting in that very row of the 747 jumbo jet, each holding vodka tonics in their hands. Seeing them so carefree in their intoxicated state, Boris contemplated ordering a drink himself. The only problem was he had never consumed alcohol during his lifetime, except the occasional sips of obligatory champagne.

Recognizing Boris's eyes peering over the seats at them, the General drunkenly commanded the flight attendant to serve him a drink. A discreet eye roll and a couple of minutes later, she brought Boris a vodka tonic.

The handshake agreement made at DEVCOM compelled Boris to obey an order from his new boss. After a few sips, the effects of the alcohol crept into his head delivering a mild euphoria. Admittedly, the effects were surprisingly delightful. With his inhibitions and introversion adequately dulled, he found himself overtly looking left and right and eavesdropping on any private conversation that floated within earshot. At times he would acknowledge their conversations with a doubtful look or an agreeable head nod and laugh lightheartedly at private jokes he overheard, oblivious to looks of dismay from unwitting passengers.

The banter three rows back got louder as unwary words were slurred between the three drunken SSU officers. Even though slightly tipsy, a few repeated names and words were taken in by Boris; names and words like "Kateryna, John, the letter, the islands, and budget," but he couldn't make out any coherency from them. He figured he needed another drink; so, he ordered three more vodka tonics – to be efficient of course.

Boris woke with the mother of all headaches as the plane touched down at 1am Kyiv time. His inaugural hangover greeted him with utter indifference as he reluctantly pulled himself up off his airplane seat. Chuckles emanating from three rows back went ignored as he sluggishly retrieved his carry-on from the overhead compartment. Boris glanced at his watch noting the ungodly hour before deplaning and walking to the terminal to retrieve his checked bags. When the General caught up with him in the baggage area, he handed Boris a portfolio containing his access key card, blueprints, and top-secret specifications and protocols.

They shook hands and acknowledged their next scheduled meeting before parting ways.

At two am Boris rushed through the door of their modest one-bedroom apartment just outside of campus expecting to find Natalie asleep in bed. After flicking on the lights, he found the apartment in disarray; books, periodicals, and unopened mail were strewn across the living room floor, while patches of discolored walls and nail holes greeted him in place of framed artwork and photographs of him and Natalie.

Her personal items such as coats, shoes, and purses normally loitering about the apartment were oddly absent. He called out for her anxiously "Natalie?!" then walked through their bedroom door. His countenance fell when he saw her open closet empty. His panic-stricken heart raced as he rifled through the pile of dirty laundry in the corner of the bedroom, their shared dresser, and the bathroom cabinets, hoping to find some clue or personal item that would contradict the sickening feeling in his gut.

Boris fell to pieces weeping on the bedroom floor. He thought about their random chance meeting at the museum, their romantic first kiss on Castle Hill, and their whirlwind wedding in the campus cathedral. Thirty minutes later, Boris's logical mind wrestled with his emotional assessment of the evidence, dismissing it as gratuitous and premature. He got up off the floor and grabbed his coat determined to find Natalie as he headed for the apartment door. Upon his approach, he discovered an envelope lying inconspicuously atop the kitchen counter. His hands were trembling as he picked it up, noticing his handwritten name on the front of the envelope. He recognized Natalie's handwriting having graded so many of her essays from class. Tears welled up in his eyes.

"Dear Boris,

Where do I begin? I have committed a cowardly act, and I am ashamed. You have every right to hate me, and, in fact, if it would absolve my transgressions against you, I would gladly receive your wrath a thousand times over. Please know that my fondness and admiration for you as a mentor and as a person were genuine, but I cannot continue living a lie as your wife and soul mate. I envy the strength of your moral compass and the fortitude and determination within your character, for I have none of those qualities that define what is unique to you. I was raised with less regal qualities; self-preservation and survival are more prominent in my list of self-descriptors. I could never live up to the title of Mrs. Shevchenko and I pray someday you will find someone worthy.

I have learned much from you, and I will always cherish the genuine moments we shared.

Much love,

Natalie"

His expectations of a weekend spent in marital bliss with Natalie had now turned to feelings of heartbreak and despondency. The handwritten letter had decidedly spawned more questions than the writer's intent. During that sleepless weekend, Boris kept retracing each memory, each interaction, and each conversation in their brief courtship and marriage, trying to pinpoint the reason she abandoned him.

Before his first class on Monday morning, Boris stopped by the registrar's office to inquire the whereabouts of his wife. No change of address form, no transfer papers, not even the existence of Natalie Shevchenko could be found in University records. Boris tried to be impartial, but after reading her letter, and now, observing her apparent attempts to cover her tracks, he found it hard not to suspect duplicity on her part. Heartbreak turned to anger, and he steeled himself to discover the truth.

At five pm, Denys Boyko answered an anxious knock on his office door.

"Boris, I'm surprised to see you here. Are you having access issues to the lab" Denys asked sincerely.

"I haven't been to the lab yet; I need to speak with you in private. May I come in?" Boris blurted, walking hastily past Denys and planting himself in the guest chair facing the desk.

After closing the door and returning to his desk seat, Denys listened intently to Boris's account of his woeful discovery, asking for details that projected empathy and amity. Boris shared with Denys personal interactions that would normally be kept private between man and wife. He was distraught and emotionally vulnerable, but confident about the SSU's ability to find missing people. He included every detail of their two-and-a-half-year relationship. With the utmost sincerity in tone and manner, Denys vowed that every resource available to the agency would be deployed to find her so that Boris could find closure. Then, he benevolently suggested that the best way to keep his mind occupied and away from heartbreak would be to pour himself wholeheartedly into his work.

Which is exactly what Boris did. Every night after his day job, Boris entered the back door of the research building and descended fifty feet below ground to his office by a hidden elevator. The space was partitioned into four separate rooms; a general storage room with a dumbwaiter; a specimen room where the flies were fed, bred, and kept; a laboratory where precision equipment was used to measure and record; and his office with elevator access to exit the building above ground. An access card was required to operate the elevator and enter the other three rooms from his office.

The specially designed specimen room was cavernous, boasting a thirty-foot ceiling and housing an elaborate screened enclosure to contain the flies. Inside the enclosure were live trees, shrubs, and flowering bushes planted in natural soil. The concrete floor had been cut out. Hanging near the ceiling from wooden beams were grow lights of various shapes and sizes. Though it currently contains one hundred flies, the enclosure was designed to accommodate a swarm of 50,000. The room was outfitted with powerful HVAC equipment, allowing Boris to change the temperature of the room fifty degrees Fahrenheit in a matter of minutes. This allowed him to leisurely work with the swarm at his own pace. When he needed to count the swarm, separate the male flies from the females, or select the perfect specimens for mating, he donned a heavy coat and turned down the temperature setting to forty degrees causing the swarm to lay obediently at his feet. Feeding and breeding time temperatures were set at a balmy eighty-five degrees. Boris provided the essential needs for life and for all intent and purposes Boris was their God.

During his first month of work Boris failed to pair the right flies for propagation. His meticulous observation of each fly under the microscope should have identified the best candidates for breeding, but his valiant efforts failed each time. Heeding Bartosh's words, Boris understood that he needed time for the newly combined genetic traits to naturalize, and breeding the flies too quickly meant shortened lifespans and weak neurotoxin and digestive enzymes but breeding too slowly meant a protracted process. With eighty male flies and twenty females, 1,600 combinations were statistically possible, but time was not on his side. The genetically modified flies had an estimated adult lifespan of ninety days and Boris just used up thirty. He needed a fresh perspective and help from his friend and partner in Florida.

Wes Walker was in the Florida Keys when his satellite phone rang. When he saw twenty digits jumble across his caller ID, he knew it was Boris calling. It was four pm in Key West, so he knew it was midnight there in Kyiv and Boris must be calling from the lab. Wes had secured a bar stool around a quaint beach bar with the best view of the water. He was early, but competition for bar stools were fierce. Like everyone else gathered around the bar, he was preparing to partake in the local time-honored ritual of ushering the setting-sun into the shimmering orange sea. His preparations included sips of frozen margaritas while a certain iconic song played in the background.

When Wes answered the phone, Boris told him about his unfortunate marital situation and the continuing search efforts by the SSU. Although Wes was unwitting, he had a hunch Boris was being snookered by his own countrymen.

"Well, Dang! Boris, I am truly sorry to hear that," he said in a consoling tone.

"I've been working very hard to try to keep my mind occupied," Boris somberly added.

"Well, you know what they say Boris; idle hands are the work of the Devil," Wes naturally expressed.

Somewhat confused by the expression, Boris continued: "The reason I'm calling Wes, is the project is in great jeopardy. I am one month behind our target population goal."

With one eyebrow raised in a questioning manner, Wes speculated aloud: "Seeing that I just received my first month's paycheck, sounds like Bartosh stuck us with a bunch of barren critters."

Just as he uttered his thoughtful conjecture, a large mosquito bit his neck.

"Ow!" he cried into the phone, followed by an audible SLAP! "Goddamn mosquitos down here are downright ravenous!"

A light bulb went off in Boris's head. His mood suddenly lightened, and he felt a tinge of excitement "I have an idea! I think will work!" he exclaimed.

Puzzled by his sudden mood swing, Wes asked "Was it something I said?"

"Yes! I have to go Wes. I will send you some data soon" he blurted.

Boris had suddenly recalled Bartosh's genetic description of the lab created flies, that some genes belonging to the mosquito were infused to change its feeding behavior. *What if some genes relating to reproduction were inadvertently introduced?* He hypothesized. As an entomologist he knew that both flies and mosquitos prefer humid climates but that mosquitos required higher levels of humidity to be prolific breeders. That would suggest that the humidity levels produced by the current HVAC system were inadequate to induce a strong mating response. Granted by the powers at the SSU without hesitation, Boris's request for a humidifier was fulfilled three days later.

The industrial sized apparatus had to be assembled piecemeal below ground. When the installation was completed, the humidifier occupied a twenty by eight-foot space in the specimen room and stood impressively ten feet tall.

That very night of its installation, Boris flipped a large switch affixed to the monster machine and plumes of humidified air billowed from its bowels. Combined with a temperature of eighty-eight degrees, sweat collected on his eyebrows in a matter of minutes.

Having lost seventy-two hours of precious time from the installation of the monster humidifier, Boris decided to shortcut the propagation timeline. Instead of pairing three sets of flies in the conjugation compartment, he would flood it with the entire swarm – eighty male flies and twenty females.

But before doing so, Boris wanted to pay homage to that iconic song he heard while in Florida, and when he heard it again on the satellite phone call with his partner Wes. When the breeding conditions brought on by the powerful equipment resembled that of fabled Roman bath houses, he turned the equipment off, hit the play button on his boom box and took a seat in his comfortable observation chair. Boris felt his anxieties melt away as the famous lyrics transported him to a far-away tropical island. Sensing the smooth vibrations of soothing vocals emanating from the box, along with the hot steamy conditions in the air, the insects engaged in an orgy of epic proportions.

CHAPTER FIVE – THE GRIND

Wes received his first set of data over encrypted email three months later. The first generation of naturally bred, genetically modified, assassin flies had developed from maggots to adult flies. Images, measurements, attributes, and gender population data flooded his computer monitor. Wes hadn't considered the infinite combinations of statistical data he would need to model when he accepted the assignment, and now, he had to make sense of the voluminous data and provide a set of statistical estimates and recommendations in short order.

He worked over the weekend at his future retirement cottage in Pensacola Beach. A weekend planned for fishing and relaxing on the beach suddenly turned into exhaustive mental gymnastics performed behind a computer. When Sunday afternoon rolled around, Wes knew he could catch Boris working in his basement lab. The satellite phone rang twice before Boris picked it up.

"Hello Wes."

"Hi Boris, you've been quite busy with critter mating I see," the Colonel kidded.

"Yes, thanks to you Colonel, I was able to identify the problem," Boris said in a straight-forward manner.

"Is that song playing in the background what I think it is? Cause I could sure use a drink after the last two days," Wes declared, lamenting over the lost weekend.

"Maybe we can share a cold one to celebrate the good news," Boris replied, smiling coyly.

"I'm gonna shoot straight with you Boris. The birth ratio of females to males is just too high and the potency of the neurotoxin was 2 percent lower than the original swarm. Making some assumptions on mortality and metamorphosis, the timeline has just been extended seven years" Wes soberly announced.

"So, you are estimating I have to do this for twelve years? I don't have the strength. I must talk to General Valarie," Boris dejectedly declared.

"Tell you what Boris, you go and talk to the general and I'll call a few of my Senator friends and see if I can get the scoop on the total project budget. You and I have already been paid over $100,000 each, so this could be a budget buster. Once we get some information, let's circle back up and chat," the Colonel relayed in a southern accent.

After taking a couple of minutes to search the internet for the meaning of random American idioms used by the Colonel, Boris understood the plan and confirmed another call with Wes.

When Boris barged into the dimly lit office of General Valarie, he was surprised to find an attractive female officer sitting in the General's lap. Startled by the intrusion, Valarie peered over her shoulder making out the long lanky figure of the nerdy scientist. He gave a gentle pat to her behind and she sprung spryly to her feet, nonchalantly adjusted her disheveled uniform, and strode past Boris and out the office without so much as a passing glance.

The General's office bore more resemblance to a college dorm room than a distinguished command center. It was small and dingy. Faded posters of European supermodels were crudely plastered on one side of the walls. The ladies were clad in skimpy bikinis and posing provocatively over sports cars. On the other side, high quality prints of modern tanks and fighter jets were housed in polished wood frames. Behind the General's desk, and in between two windows, hung an oversized print of a pink-sand beach. Gentle lapping waves caressed the secluded stretch of sand. The photo was reminiscent of a distant tropical island found in a travel brochure.

General Valarie was a ladies' man and a silver-tongued devil. This potent combination of charm and cunning had elevated him to the highest heights of military rank and, at times, had sunken him to the deepest depths of depravity. Cloaked in a studly chiseled physique, Valarie exuded a brash and unapologetic persona.

Slightly perturbed by the intrusion, Valarie barked "What can I do for you Boris?"

Sensing the General's agitation, Boris apologized "I'm Sorry General…the door was open, and I was in a hurry."

Valarie softened his tone "That's OK, we were just finishing up a 'heart to heart' discussion," he teased.

"I wanted to share some good news and give you a progress report," Boris excitedly declared.

Up until this surprise encounter, Valarie hadn't seen or spoken to Boris since his pitch at DEVCOM four months ago. Still clouded by stubborn images of the female officer's buxom bosom, his mind froze, and he stared blankly at Boris.

The General's vacant stare gave away his hazy recollection prompting Boris to remind him "about the flies."

Without skipping a beat, the General quickly admonished "Of course about the flies! Only the most important top-secret initiative in Ukraine – please, go on."

Startled by Valarie's emphatic response he continued in a respectful tone "Yes, of course sir. I am pleased we were successful in breeding the first generation, however…"

While Boris continued to provide his boss with technical facts and details about observations and outcomes of the project, Valarie was mentally formulating another patriotic speech like the one he delivered at DEVCOM four months ago. Recalling the psychological profile notes on Boris, he knew Boris would need a booster shot of nationalistic pride to overcome these immerging challenges currently coming from his mouth.

After Boris delivered his inordinately lengthy report with his long six-foot six-inch frame standing over Valarie's desk, the General popped up from his chair and commanded Boris to take a seat, reversing the appearance of authority in the room.

With a ceremonial posture and ardent tone, the General began: "Boris, every civilized country in this world was forged from struggle; struggle between opposing ideologies, between faiths, or between the haves and the have-nots. Our country is no different; each man, woman, and child living peaceably by these forged ideals. But now, like thieves shrouded in the darkness of the night and the darkness in their heart, they are coming to steal our freedom and test our resolve to defend our beliefs. A crucible of truth awaits the hearts of every countryman; each one will be tested. Will we cower to our enemies in the face of evil? Or will we emerge from the crucible as a stronger force to be reckoned with and repel the enemy from our land. No amount of money is too much to pay, and no amount of time is frivolously spent to reclaim our land! Your country needs you, Boris. Don't let her down."

Boris sat contemplating the General's inspirational words when Valarie added: "And, to show our country's commitment and belief in you, the President has authorized me to offer you an advance of one million U.S. dollars. In exchange, you must resign your professorship and dedicate yourself fully to the project. The President wants you to lead a more normal life."

A beaming smile graced Boris's face. *The President himself had a personal concern over his long hours,* he thought, *only the President could authorize such a generous sum.* Since Natalie's abrupt disappearance, Boris felt distant and uninspired in his professorship. In fact, her nagging absence as his assistant and wife had heightened his insecurity and dejection each day since. He'd already thought about resigning soon after her disappearance but couldn't handle the guilt of abandoning his students halfway through the curriculum. But now, this was different; the President had sought his full dedication to his country and offered a thoughtful path without financial worry. How could he refuse?

Boris requested and Valarie agreed that Boris would resign in three months' time at semester end.

With a renewed sense of purpose and one million dollars enroute to his bank account, Boris returned to the lab. He was so anxious to hatch the next generation of flies and prove his worth to the President that he had forgotten all about the follow-up call with his partner Wes. Back in the Sunshine State, Wes lobbed several phone calls to his senator friends who served on the Armed Services Committee and left messages with their aides. Given this was an election year, he wasn't surprised when none of them returned his calls. Their concern over the cost and length of the project faded away and both went about their business of hatching flies like the dependable movements of a fine Swiss timepiece.

Having perfected a breeding environment replete with dripping humidity, ambient mood lighting and music, the mating response it created was palpable. Over the course of one year, each generation improved over the prior generation, exhibiting stronger than anticipated outcomes. Although the flies still required their prey to be compromised by a lethal shot of neurotoxin to elicit the feeding response, their own neurotoxin and digestive enzyme potencies had doubled. Their Frankenstein-like appearance revealed during the initial introduction meeting had morphed into graceful lines with complimenting colors. And the size of their wings, beaks and legs were all proportionately larger than the original swarm.

After Boris resigned his professorship and completed the final semester of his brief teaching career, he dedicated more daylight hours to his work in the secret bunker-like lab. His schedule became more in-line with the normal working hours of the general population, but he missed seeing the many faces of university life above ground, like the elegant, angular visage of the hairdresser in that salon on the edge of campus. In fact, he had gotten over Natalie's disappearance, and with Denys Boyko's help, completed the final paperwork for divorce.

Boris needed a break from the daily grind of fly keeping. He had his swarm and his music, but even his introversion could not deny him his craving for human interaction. He started to think about where he'd go and what he'd do on a mundane Thursday night in Kyiv, his thoughts waffling between activities and venues. Then, he remembered how those vodka tonics made him feel on that long flight home.

CHAPTER SIX – THE SEDUCTION

Olga sat expectantly atop a barstool at a swanky rooftop bar overlooking the Dnipro River. It was a mild summer night with refreshing sea breezes drifting up from the river below. The rooftop bar was adorned with classy modern neon lighting that emitted cool hues of pink and blue. Bottles of expensive liquor rested on mirrored shelves beckoning the most discerning tastes.

A German exchange student had invited her to meet him for cocktails and a late dinner at the five-star hotel located on the outer edges of the city. He was a graduate student who had happened to be at the salon a couple of weeks ago and fell enchanted by her beauty. After an hour-long haircut and some probing conversation, Olga collected enough information on Sven to indulge him in a second encounter. Sven was completing his graduate studies in August and returning to Stuttgart to work for his family's business which exclusively supplied automobile parts to the likes of Porche and BMW.

It was eight twenty pm and twenty minutes past the agreed upon rendezvous time the little shit so emphatically insisted upon, Olga thought. She'd been stood up. Olga had an innate ability to classify the truly enchanted from those acting on fleeting whims, but tonight she was second guessing herself; maybe it was her apparent eagerness in accepting his invitation, or perhaps he reconsidered the viability of a long-distance relationship, or most disturbingly, perhaps she was losing her seductive appeal to father time.

Just as she finished her sobering thought, she noticed a portly man ogling her from across the bar. He had noticed her stepping off the elevator when she arrived at the rooftop bar, taking in her svelte shape with well-placed curves. Dressed to the nines, Olga wore a sleeveless red blouse adorned with shimmering sequins and a plunging neckline that showed off her tantalizing cleavage. A form fitting black skirt scarcely covering her mid-thigh showcased her long sexy legs that were perched atop four-inch heels. With her strawberry-blonde hair worn in a bun, her elegant visage and stunning blue eyes captivated the men who were graced with her presence.

The ogling man across the bar wore a Hawaiian shirt unbuttoned halfway down to his bulging mid-section. A gaudy gold chain rested on his burly hairy chest. His face was craggy and loose from years of indulgent vices. Calling the bartender over, he gestured the age-old motions of ordering a drink be brought to a beautiful woman. Hoping to put off his gratuitous advances, Olga diverted her eyes away from her unwelcomed admirer when she saw Boris Shevchenko wandering through the bar door. She rose to her feet and made a beeline to him, greeting him with a warm smile and an affectionate hug.

Dumbstruck by her actions, he started to mutter something when she took his hand and led him to a table an earshot away from the bar. Neither Boris nor Olga recognized the other at first, until they paused long enough for a second glance. A bashful smile radiated from Olga while Boris wore a giant grin.

"Wow! What a greeting, do you always greet your customers that way?" Boris asked in a playful rhetorical tone.

"Depends on the customer" she replied smartly.

They both emanated gleeful chuckles and sat down at the table, curious as to each other's story. The unattractive man sensing his chances of an amorous encounter fading, slammed his beer glass on the bar, startling half of the patrons in the bar and stormed out muttering under his breath. The loud thud of glass hitting wood prompted Boris to turn and investigate the source of the intrusive noise. After witnessing the outburst, he returned his eyes to Olga.

"What was that all about?" he asked curiously.

Olga shrugged her shoulders coyly, then said, "maybe his date stood him up."

A moment later, feeling guilty about her evasive actions towards the unattractive man, she told Boris the truth about their abrupt meeting and they both laughed about her neurotic reaction.

Olga had not intended an impromptu date with a salon customer whom she hadn't properly vetted; and, it would have been easier for her to just apologize for a case of mistaken identity and walked away, but as fate would have it, Olga's conscience and curiosity beckoned her to stay. They began with the obligatory small talk about their hometowns, their histories, and their circumstances. When the conversation evolved into each other's occupation, Olga's interest piqued. Even though crawling or flying insects weren't exactly 'a girl's best friend' she paid particular attention to Boris's comment about not having the time to spend the generous compensation he was receiving. He didn't give away any top secrets, but he did reveal that he had grown to love his work, doing exactly what his formal training prepared him for.

It had been three years since Boris had the company of a woman, namely his ex-wife Natalie. Having stepped inside a strange bar on a whim and accosted by a stunningly beautiful woman, he had to speculate that fate was at play. Boris was drawn to Olga like a moth to a flame and after a few drinks, Olga had forgotten all about the German exchange student who stood her up.

Genuine conversation flowed for a good hour before their chance encounter turned into amorous glances and light flirtation. After a few more drinks, the two adventurers, now rapt by each other's company, moved to a more private setting along the railing of the upscale rooftop bar. Both facing the Dnipro River, Boris and Olga looked out into its expanse, its banks quaintly illuminated by the lights of shops and businesses. Hues of orange, yellow, and purple captivated their visual senses while sensual jazz music emanating from the bar's loudspeakers roused romantic feelings. With his confidence rising, Boris boldly wrapped both arms around Olga's waist from behind and held her close to his chest, both still gazing out into the distance. The welcome warmth of Boris's embrace started her hips gently swaying to the seductive sounds of saxophone music in the background with neither in any hurry to move from their enraptured positions. When Olga felt his warm breath on her neck, she turned to meet his loving gaze, and they engaged in a tender first kiss.

The serendipitous evening filled with intrigue and enchantment culminated with an exchange of numbers and a mutual yearning for a second date. Boris called Olga the very next day, eager to rekindle the still smoldering feelings from last night.

"Hello? Olga, this is Boris, your unassuming date from last night" Boris greeted playfully.

"Boris who?" Olga retorted in a jokingly serious tone.

"That memorable huh? I'll work on a new hairstyle, I promise. With your help of course!" Boris gleefully proposed, evoking a flirtatious girl giggle.

Boris continued, "Do you like classical music? The Orchestra is in town, and I would love to have your company. They will be here for a couple of weeks and there are tickets for this evening's show. Can you come?"

Boris's flagrant violation of the sacred three-day rule of dating gladdened Olga's heart, validating the potency of her beauty. Although charmed by Boris's boyish enthusiasm, she made up a story to follow the time-honored rule "I would love to, but I have some friends coming to town this weekend, could we find a showtime for Wednesday night?"

Having memorized the entire schedule of showtimes for the next two weeks, he quickly proposed an agreeable time, confirming a second date with Olga.

Boris spent the weekend replaying that magical night spent with Olga in his head. Smitten by her physical beauty, he desperately wanted to find a way to impress her. He knew he could never compete aesthetically with the young university boys that lined up at the salon; and, of course, he had no idea Olga was more interested in the certainty of financial security than the fickle notions of physical attraction. Boris was racking his brains when an unexpected idea popped up, one that could jeopardize his future, but he quickly dismissed the concern for loftier aspirations. He had to work quickly though, his date with Olga was only three days away.

Boris got to work right away. After the janitors clean his office, the laboratory, and the storeroom, they usually just give the specimen room a quick once over, wary of the unknown creatures that lurked in the cages and the large, screened enclosure. It was usually up to Boris to ensure the specimen room was tidy enough to host the only four possible visitors – General Valarie, Dr. Bartosh, Denys, and Colonel Walker, whom have yet to visit even once.

Feeding his swarm, now 5,000 strong, was dirty business. Excrements from 700 pounds of live animals littered the bottom of the cages that lined one side of the specimen room. Rabbits, rats, and chickens made for a good variety of essential protein for the flies and their rotting carcasses hosted the maggots of the next generation of flies. Although a powerful ventilation system helped diffuse the stench, the odor of rotting flesh mixed with a variety of animal excrements kept the janitors from any honest effort to clean the room.

Lucky for Boris, the next weekly supply of live feed wouldn't arrive until Friday, which meant he could move the few remaining animals out of sight to the storage room and cover the cages with a tarp to hide their presence. He also cleared the screened enclosure of any dead carcasses, hiding the carnivorous nature of his swarm.

After two full days of arduous labor, the specimen room was ready but for a few finishing touches. Boris had to use his monthly allocated rainy-day fund to purchase a few enhancements to the room's lighting. Once they were complete Boris stood in the center of the room bursting with a sense of accomplishment and pride as he reflected on his hard work over the past year.

Olga's cell phone chimed when an encrypted text message appeared on its screen. A smile crept across her lips as she recognized it to be a message from Boris. After a few verification procedures, Olga was able to read the message:

"Meet me behind the building at 5, Hrushevsky Street at five pm, I have a surprise for you before the concert."

Olga had never received such a cryptic message from any of her suitors in the past. The message came across as bold as it was nonchalant, and she was drawn to this mysterious man who secretly worked for her country.

Just as the sun was setting over the city, Olga stepped off the city bus in front of a non-descript government building. She was wearing heels, so she was glad to see the number 5 prominently displayed on the building in front of her. She cautiously walked around the building towards its backside. It was ten minutes past five pm and Boris had been waiting twenty minutes for her arrival. When Boris saw Olga turn the corner of the building, he quickly walked up and greeted her with a light peck on her cheek, then without saying a word, he led her towards a hidden passageway in the back of the building. Although Olga surmised that Boris's work was not public facing, she hadn't expected this level of secrecy; first, receiving an encrypted message and now shuffling down a dimly lit passageway. Fortunately for Boris, Olga was feeling adventurous tonight, so she followed him through the heavy metal door at the end of the narrow passageway and down the secret elevator to his basement office.

She took a seat on a comfortable leather chair in the corner of his office and looked up expectantly at Boris.

In an enthusiastic tone Boris began, "You look beautiful tonight."

"Thank you, Boris, I'm not being kidnapped, am I?" she teased.

Acknowledging her question with a knowing smile, he continued, "No, quite the opposite. What I am about to show you is classified as top-secret and if you do not wish to go through that door, I would understand. Only a handful of people know the details of this operation, so you must swear to me that you will not tell another soul about any of this."

"Well, since you put it that way, I must see what is behind door number two! And I swear." Olga replied playfully.

With a few keystrokes on the access pad, Boris opened the laboratory door and led her into the impressive room filled with sophisticated scientific equipment. Olga stood for a moment to take in her surroundings, then casually strolled around the room, her gaze wandering from one piece of equipment to the next, at times gently tracing their features with her long supple fingers.

When she saw a square wooden cabinet hung on the wall, she reached up to open the doors expecting to find a dartboard hidden behind them. Boris caught a glimpse of her actions and blurted:

"No! don't open…"

But it was too late. Inside the cabinet were darts of a darker nature. A look of surprise registered on Olga's face as she saw twelve small needle-tipped syringes securely nestled inside the felt-lined cabinet. Affixed to the inside of the doors, were warning stickers with the iconic image of the skull and crossbones. Her eyes focused on the milky white substance filling each syringe as she uttered a question. A question so innocent yet so convicting and one that Boris had not expected to answer tonight.

"What is it?" She turned and asked him.

Boris quickly walked over to her and gently closed the doors. At the risk of insulting her intelligence he tried to minimize their significance.

"They are used for research and could be harmful to your health," he plainly stated.

"You mean deadly, isn't that what you meant?" she asked rhetorically.

Olga assumed that the syringes were a humane way to euthanize the study subjects. She was not an animal lover, nor was she opposed to the use of lab animals for research, what she did want to establish though, was her adroit ability to read men. When she felt vindicated by his conceding facial expression, she eloquently changed the subject.

"And what is behind door number three?" she asked with her bare arms elegantly extended towards the specimen room and a cute smile on her face.

Boris's face lit up with the anticipation of his big reveal. He pulled out a blindfold from his back pants pocket and made a circular gesture with his index finger suggesting Olga turn her back to him. When she obliged, he gently placed the blindfold over her eyes, then led her into the cavernous specimen room to a small café table accompanied by two comfortable chairs. After guiding her to her seat, he gently removed the cover from her eyes.

Speckles of soft refracted light encircled and rotated about the dimly lit room as Olga looked up to confirm its source. Hanging from a dizzying height, a large, mirrored ball reflected the colorful hues of stage lights shining in its direction. The warm colorful glow from the slowly rotating ball found every nook and cranny of the gigantic room, transforming its cold and dark ambiance into one that resembled an inviting dance hall. A delighted smile crept across Olga's face as she continued to gaze upwards at the glittering ball.

When her gaze returned to eye level from the spectacle above, Olga's ears met the festive pop of a champagne cork flying away from a bottle of Dom Perignon. Seated beside her, Boris poured the sparkling wine into two crystal champagne flutes sitting atop a white tablecloth that draped over the small table. Both beamed with joy as they lifted the flutes filled with expensive champagne to their lips. Neither Boris nor Olga had ever tasted the libation coveted by the rich and famous. Each rotation of the mirrored ball and each sip of the fragrant elixir transported them to an enchanted ballroom for two as they awaited the next musical dance piece to play over the loudspeakers.

"Oh Boris, this is fabulous. You really are full of surprises!" Olga gleefully declared.

"I'm so glad you are an adventurous person, because there is something else, I want to share with you," Boris said in a knowing tone.

"Something else? Now you are just showing off, but I love it! Please, share," Olga pleaded with excitement.

Boris rose from his seat at the table and strode across the room to a light switch affixed to the wall on the other side. He gave an upward shove on the industrial sized lever and turned on the grow lights inside the screened enclosure. Up until this point, Olga hadn't noticed the large, screened structure to the side of the cavernous room. Now illuminated by grow lights she could make out the features of live trees and shrubs inside the giant terrarium but the tightly woven mesh screen covering the structure concealed the subjects of Boris's research. The purple and orange hues glowing from the grow lights further enhanced the already festive ballroom atmosphere in the room.

Just below the light switch sitting on the floor was a boom box. Boris dropped to one knee and pressed the play button. The famous violin concerto, The Four Seasons by Antonio Vivaldi started to play. The vibrant sounds of the violin, viola, cello, and harpsichord emanated from the speakers, sending sweet harmonic tones floating throughout the enormous room. Even though the volume was low, the acoustics of the hollow space beautifully amplified each and every note.

Olga instinctively closed her eyes to enjoy the iconic piece with her head gently bobbing side to side in tune with the music; when suddenly, the music got a little louder. She opened her eyes expecting to see Boris bent over the boom box adjusting the volume, but to her surprise, he was seated next to her with a wide grin on his face. When Olga realized the added volume was coming from within the screened enclosure, she quickly rose to her feet and looked suspiciously at Boris.

"I thought we were alone. Are you hiding a string orchestra in that cage?!" she asked, with her voice loud enough to be heard over the music.

Still grinning, Boris got up from his chair, walked over to the boom box, pressed the stop button, and a silence filled the room. A look of relief registered on Olga's face only to be replaced by a look of shock when a violin solo erupted from within the cage.

Boris quickly walked back over to Olga and gave her a reassuring hug. With his lips near her ear, he whispered "shh…It's ok, we are safe."

"Who is inside that cage?" Olga whispered back nervously.

"Come, let me show you," Boris said calmly.

As they approached the enclosure, the violin solo was joined by the beautiful sounds of the other instruments in perfect time and pitch, and in accordance with the choral composition of the classic piece. Olga clasped tightly onto Boris's hand as she curiously followed him into the impressive structure. She peered around Boris to the right, and then to the left, looking for the source of the music, only to find shrubs and bushes neatly planted and trimmed. The beautiful orchestra music continued to play. Once they reached the center of the large space, they found themselves standing between two large trees. Boris turned around and faced her.

"I am about to show you something that no one else has ever seen, not even my research partner or my superiors, and they must not find out. Your presence here should also be kept a secret. Please, swear to me," Boris said in a kind but deliberate tone.

"I swear, but I don't see anything worth keeping a secret about," Olga replied smartly.

A smirk appeared on Boris's face as he raised an index finger upwards while still looking at Olga. Tepidly, Olga turned her gaze skyward.

Five thousand pairs of iridescent wings were fluttering energetically, throwing off beams of refracted light from the rotating mirrored ball. Orange and purple hues from the grow lights enhanced the visual effect of a miniature laser light show between the tall trees. Olga could now pair the sound of each type of instrument with the speed of the flickering light, confirming which sub-swarm was mimicking which type of instrument. The violins were perched high on the highest branches of the trees, while the cellos were playing just over their heads. Each time a violin solo ensued, a swarm would hover in the air between the two trees, feverishly vibrating their wings as if they were called forward by the conductor.

Olga was smiling and transfixed by the musical light show unfolding above her head.

Seeing Olga's reaction reminded Boris of the first time he discovered this hidden talent within these genetically modified creatures. It all started with that iconic beach bar song he heard while talking to Wes over the satellite phone. He decided to play it each time he mated the flies; it just seemed so appropriate with the room temperature at 88 degrees and the air dripping with ninety degree humidity. Besides, it served as a mental escape from the underground dungeon he was confined to for the past year. In fact, he set the CD on repeat mode each night on that very song for a month straight, out of sheer boredom. One night, he decided to listen to some classical music. To his astonishment, when he pressed the stop button mid-song, the song continued until its intended end.

He soon discovered that the tone of the human voice was more difficult to imitate by the swarm than that of a musical instrument. Human vocal sounds always came across like someone speaking through a giant turbine fan; but the sounds of violin music were always flawlessly emulated.

Olga felt a gentle tap on her shoulder. When she lowered her gaze, she witnessed an elegant bow from Boris, reminiscent of a seventeenth-century baroque dancer. She obliged Boris with a playful, stately curtsy of her own. Transported by the sights and sounds of their own making, they danced a Minuet to the last ten minutes of The Four Seasons beaming with joy and laughter.

After the classical piece ended, Boris glanced at his watch and realized that the human symphony concert they planned on attending had started over an hour ago. Before he could lay out their options to Olga, she made a suggestion of her own. Having forgotten all about the concert herself, she proposed:

"I'm hungry after all the secret oaths you made me take. Why don't we give your musician friends a break and find some food in town?"

After the astonishing events of the evening, she didn't want the evening to end without knowing more about this mysterious and charming man. They found a cozy café just a few blocks away from the secret lab and settled into a comfortable booth for some food and conversation.

By now Boris was enamored with Olga; so much so, he had little reservation showing his yearning for intimacy with her, hoping she had similar feelings for him. Olga was a savant in matters of the heart. Although she received Boris's amorous advances graciously, she considered him only figuratively rounding second base. Another date was necessary to consummate their relationship. So, when Boris bragged that the food they were being served couldn't possibly compete with his culinary creations, she opportunistically suggested he make her dinner this Friday night. And when Boris proposed a time of seven pm, Olga suggested he leave a key under his doormat for her, so she could get there a little earlier to prepare some appetizers for their intimate dinner.

When Boris arrived at the apartment around 6pm, he was surprised to find the door discretely cracked open, he peeked through the opening to find the shades drawn. As he reached up to push on the door, it curiously glided open on its own. Soon after stepping inside, the sweet scent of lavender caressed his nostrils while soft jazz music played in the background. As he turned to close the door, he found Olga standing there with a sheepish smile, her gorgeous hair shimmering in the delicate glow of candlelight.

Boris's face lit up as his gaze strolled downward to take in her long svelte shape. She was wearing a red satin robe which barely came down to her thighs, loosely secured by a half-tied knot. Adorned in white silk stockings, her long sexy legs were accentuated by four-inch red stiletto heels. When his gaze returned eye-level, she handed him a glass of red wine, glided to his left ear, and softly whispered *"I've been waiting for you."* Then, she gave his ear a gentle lingering nibble.

Boris was powerless. His knees almost buckled under the weight of those five simple words. The wine, the candle-lit room, the soft jazz music were all fibers of a deftly knit web spun to ensnare her prey, and Olga was mama spider.

He took her hand, and they both instinctively moved to the couch to enjoy their glasses of Cabernet and listen to jazz music while staring intently into each other's eyes.

"You are so beautiful. I didn't think you would come," he professed.

His sincerity and boyish innocence pleased her and stoked her ego. Sensing pheromone levels at its peak, Olga stood up facing Boris and allowed her satin robe to fall off her shoulders onto the ground. Boris's heart raced as the floral notes from her French perfume mingled with her personal scent rushed over his face from the falling garment. He lustfully took in her full womanhood; her voluptuous breasts held captive by a dainty pink push-up bra, skimpy sheer panties of the same color scantily covering her lady parts, and a lacy white garter belt adorned with pretty bow ties that held up her silk stockings.

Standing confidently over him, she seductively chided, "you have too many clothes on."

After kicking off her red stiletto heels, Olga smoothly straddled Boris still sitting on the couch, pulled his shirt up and over his head, and nonchalantly tossed it aside. While passionately gazing into his eyes, she reached behind her back and unclasped her bra, freeing her perfectly full and shapely breasts poetically heaving under quickened breaths. She hungrily planted a passionate kiss over Boris's open and waiting mouth sending waves of carnal adrenaline to his brain's pleasure centers.

With his eyes still closed in rapture and awash with the anticipation of lovemaking, Boris felt Olga unexpectedly pull away. Coyly, she unmounts Boris, picks up her empty wine glass, and turns towards the bottle of wine sitting on the kitchen countertop.

"Whew…, it's a bit warm in here, I need another glass of wine," she confessed with a sweet schoolgirl smile.

Shirtless and with his hair disheveled, Boris was confounded and lightly despondent. Unbeknownst to Boris, Olga was expertly navigating the waters of seduction. She was fanning the flames of desire she'd stoked within him, ensuring he was fully enchanted in her beauty.

As she sauntered over to the bottle of wine, Boris gave her curvaceous posterior a lustful gaze, taking in her scantily covered buttocks sashaying to-and-fro. She poured herself a full glass of wine, then, while holding the glass in one hand she leaned over the counter casually resting her elbows atop it, giving Boris a profile view of her full and perky breasts.

Sensing Boris's burning desire, she stood there topless in her centerfold pose and took a long sip of her wine prolonging the tortuous foreplay. Then, with her tawdry sheer panties barely covering her toned curvaceous cheeks, she shifted the angle of her seductive stance allowing Boris's wandering eyes to trace the folds of her womanly flower.

Turning her seductive eyes towards him, she sensually uttered: "Want some?"

Uncontrollable passion erupted within Boris as he swiftly rose to his feet, dropped his trousers, and rushed towards Olga like a charging bull towards the matador. Boris's ardent advance evoked a sudden vulnerability within Olga as she let out an audible gasp before Boris forcefully pulled down her silk panties and made passionate love to her right there against the counter.

The embers of passion remained lit as they retired to his bed where he made love to her twice more that night.

CHAPTER SEVEN – THE LAST STOP

After the night of intense passion, Boris considered proposing marriage the next morning. However, reflecting on his earlier decisions regarding his failed marriage with Natalie, he decided to restrain his impulse. The two lovers settled into an affectionate and steady relationship, each developing a wholesome devotion to each other. Six months of blissful courtship ensued before Boris proposed and Olga eagerly accepted. Olga also accepted that despite lacking the physical attributes of her ideal man, Boris could provide the comfortable life of leisure she sought. Boris's profuse adoration stoked her ego, making up for the rest of his perceived deficiencies.

They were to be married in the Spring, which was only three months away, so invitations were expeditiously sent to family and friends, and of course to General Valarie, Dr. Bartosh and Denys Boyko. Colonel Walker also received an invitation; after all, he was Boris's partner and friend, but Boris didn't expect Wes to fly halfway around the world for his wedding.

When Valarie opened and read the invitation, he stuck his head out into the hallway outside his office and called out irritably to

Denys in the next office over. When Denys stumbled in, ten seconds later, the General unleashed his frustration.

"Agent Boyko, were you aware our fly keeper had a girlfriend?!" he asked in an authoritative tone.

"Of course, General, every man needs earthly pleasure," Denys deflected with a factoid, not knowing where Valarie was going with his question.

"You haven't checked your office mail today, have you?" he continued, not willing to let Deny's off the hook just yet.

"The mail is yesterday's news and unreliable, Sir. What is this all about?" Denys relented.

Valarie casually flung the invitation towards Denys who adeptly caught it and read it mumbling under his breath.

He looked up afterwards, incredulous as to its contents and said pensively, "This is troubling development," with gears still churning inside his head, he continued, "we need to delay this wedding so we can better know this Olga."

"How?" Valarie blurted.

"We could have new information about Natalie's location…" he replied.

Denys was scheming to buy some time to work up a full profile on Olga. The divorce paperwork Denys forged over a year ago helped Boris get over his heartbreak, but Natalie's sudden reemergence could prompt Boris into delaying the wedding. It could reignite Boris's underlying need for closure on his abandonment.

It was ingrained in each officer's training at the SSU; every subject involved in the State's top secrets must have an in-depth psychological assessment to ensure secrecy and success. Both the

General and Denys knew that once Boris and Olga were wed, the clandestine nature of the project was more likely to be compromised. Secrecy was of the utmost importance to them – and to the Country, of course.

With the Russians stubbornly entrenched in Crimea, their ambitious goal of expelling the enemy by unconventional weapons was dependent on the will of a gangly, and now distracted, entomologist. The initial phase of the plan, which involved the design of super agile drones capable of evading enemy defenses and carrying the genetically modified assassin flies to the front line had already been achieved. The Ukrainian government had also begun production of the novelly designed drones with their partners in the United States. Now, it was up to this team of five to produce a swarm of 50,000 assassin flies that will attack soldiers indiscriminately within the proximity of their release.

Almost two years after Boris began his work thirty feet below ground in the secret lab; a comprehensive update meeting was called to order by General Valarie. Boris and the three SSU officers sat around a small coffee table in Boris's office with Colonel Walker on satellite speaker phone.

It was five pm in Kyiv and ten am in Tampa, Florida. Wes was drinking a cup of coffee in his office at Cent-Com waiting patiently to deliver his statistical projections and timetables. Dr. Bartosh was anxious to hear Boris's report on toxicity and feeding response, while the General and Denys sat silently scheming.

Boris began proudly "I am happy to report our swarm has grown from one hundred specimens to 18,000 in a twenty-three-month period. At last count, there were roughly 15,000 females and 3,000 males. Their initially primitive features have morphed into sleek lines and robust features."

He glanced over at Dr. Bartosh who was beaming. Bartosh and his team of geneticists had created the Frankenstein creatures only three years ago, and now Boris has taken these experimental flies to a self-propagation level of epic proportions.

Boris continued "Although the ratio of females to males is high, I am now better able to detect sterile female flies under the microscope and separate them from the breeding population. The focus on fertility will help us overcome this natural female-male ratio disparity."

While this information was all gobbledygook to Valarie and Denys, Bartosh's eyes widened behind his Coke bottle lenses, marveling at Boris's skill and tenacity. His enthusiasm could not be contained as he emphatically asked:

"What about toxicity and the auto-feeding response?!"

Sensing the Doctor's excitement, Boris framed his response fairly "Well, we're not quite there yet. The toxicity of the neurotoxins and digestive enzymes are sixty percent to goal and their limbs and proboscis size are seventy-five percent to goal. Their feeding response is still one hundred percent triggered manually by needle and syringe."

By this time, the General was ready to hear the bottom line, "Colonel Walker, could you please give assessment of time?"

"As I previously predicted, I believe our timeline will need to be extended six to seven years – all factors held constant. The most difficult estimation would be when we could gain the auto feeding response: there just isn't any correlation to anything we could tie this ability to," Wes said soberly.

After more salient facts were discussed between the five men, Wes congratulated Boris on his new-found love and upcoming nuptials, then excused himself from the meeting.

When Boris invited the group to take a tour of the lab, the three men eagerly followed him into the laboratory with Dr. Bartosh trampling over Denys's foot to be first in line behind Boris. He was also the first to peer through the microscope lens at his own creation. Standing on a step stool to get eye-level with the scope, the specimen brought a wide grin to his face.

The inch and a half long creature had a pair of orange compound eyes like the headlights of a collectible automobile and antennae between its eyes resembling a classic hood ornament. Its head and thorax were covered with plush brown fur and a pair of pixie-dusted iridescent wings ran down the length of its regal body. Its metallic green abdomen gleamed under the microscope light like a show car rolled out after a custom paint job. As beautiful as its bodily features were, its sharp, beak-like proboscis and talon-like legs reminded the doctor of the grisly intent of his creation.

Overjoyed at the prospect of temporarily assuming the role of "fly keeper" he asked Boris: "So, Boris, have you decided the length of time you will need for you and your bride to enjoy a proper honeymoon?"

The direct and unexpected question drew an awkward silence from the group. Valarie re-focused the team with his words: "Why don't we let Boris take us through the rest of the building so we can understand the whole operation."

The anxious thought of leaving his swarm to three strangers now plagued Boris; as a result, he took his time walking them through his routine, overemphasizing trivial matters like a helicopter mom dropping her toddler off at daycare. When the tour concluded, each of the three men gained a new appreciation for the painstaking work required and all three vowed silently to avoid cleaning the animal cages.

It was seven pm when Boris glanced at his watch, Olga would be expecting him home in a half hour. Sensing Boris's distraction, the General gave a facial cue to Denys, prompting him to take Boris aside and relay the news of Natalie's reappearance.

Denys ushered Boris to the far corner of the laboratory as Bartosh and the General retreated to the office. After the door closed behind them, Denys began.

"Boris, this may not matter to you anymore, but I wanted to tell you something" he said kindly and continued "We found Natalie in Lviv; she's living with an elderly woman."

A wave of nostalgia washed over Boris, but a pang of guilt kept his reaction subdued. With a monotone voice he asked, "Does she want to speak to me?"

"I'm sure she would Boris, but we didn't want to..." Denys replied enthusiastically before Boris cut him off.

"Good. Do not engage her on my behalf, I have come to terms with all of it," he said somberly.

The two men rejoined the others in the office where they discussed the details of each one's duties the two weeks Boris was to spend honeymooning on the French Riviera. Naturally, the General assumed the observation and recording duties. The doctor was ecstatic about the feeding and breeding assignment and Denys, being the lowest-ranking person, was plain pissed-off about stocking the storeroom and cleaning the animal cages.

Denys's efforts to delay the wedding failed, the couple married three months later. Prior to the ceremony, Boris and Olga had to agree to the SSU's rules and protocols for agent-spouse interaction related to the State's top secrets. Coupled with a stern lecture from General Valarie, both of them knew and feared the repercussions for any violation.

The wedding took place in a small Eastern Orthodox church in Kyiv. Wes surprised the team with his presence, bringing along his precocious five-year-old granddaughter Layla, who assumed the duty of ring bearer at the last minute. Layla wore a Ukrainian wreath displaying her worldly knowledge of Ukrainian tradition. Not willing to waste precious time off from the burdensome responsibility of fly keeping, the happily married couple skipped their own reception and were whisked away by jumbo jet to a seaside resort on the French Riviera.

Back at the secret lab, Dr. Bartosh was enjoying a glass of vodka while sitting at the break table in the storage room. It was ten pm on a Friday night and he was filling in for Denys who dubiously claimed he had an emergency, adding that he would be a couple of hours late. Bartosh was indignant after cleaning out mountains of animal excrement from all the empty cages at the end of the week. Plus, Denys didn't order enough livestock and Bartosh had to ration three days of remaining fly food over seven days. He felt well justified opening Denys's most expensive bottle of Ukrainian vodka while he waited for the delivery truck carrying live fly food for the upcoming week.

The service bell at the top of the dumbwaiter shaft buzzed after Bartosh had enjoyed half of the bottle. When Bartosh barked a greeting up the shaft in Ukrainian, the delivery man responded in kind, except in Russian. Sensing the man was probably deficient in Ukrainian, they exchanged subsequent words in Russian, and then, Bartosh sent the dumbwaiter skyward. Besides the elegant accent of the Queen's English, Bartosh spoke perfect Russian and Ukrainian, as most Ukrainians do.

As crate after crate of chickens, rabbits, and rats drifted down the dumbwaiter shaft, the five-foot-one inch man stacked them as high as his compact stature would allow. Though Bartosh was not a dwarf by genetic definition, he possessed the brutish strength of one described in folklore. After manhandling seventy-four crates and stacking them around the storage room, his thoughts turned to the tedious task of transferring the animals inside to the metal cages in the specimen room.

As the last crate of rabbits glided down the shaft, Bartosh called out to the delivery man above ground in Russian.

"Fine sir, you must be tired after loading and unloading that truck, do you enjoy vodka?"

What red-blooded Russian doesn't? he thought. This was his last stop for the night, and he had no family to go home to and no nagging wife to hassle him about drinking. Just like Bartosh, his partner bailed on him due to a family emergency.

Though Bartosh knew the rules against fraternizing with vendors, he needed a strong back and an extra set of hands to stock the cages in the specimen room.

As the heavy metal door at the end of the hidden passageway swung open, Bartosh met a six-foot-five-inch man with peppered grey hair. He looked to be about sixty years old with a sturdy build, pale skin, and blue eyes. He was wearing a drab company uniform with his name embroidered on his front pocket – Dimitri. As Dimitri stepped inside, Bartosh greeted him with a handshake, simultaneously peering around the large man ensuring no one else was witnessing his wanton violation of protocol.

Dimitri was astounded that a man of the doctor's stature handled seventy-five crates he himself had struggled with. In a fraternal tone, he complimented, "My God, you are quite strong."

A prideful smile crept across Bartosh's face as he relished any compliments of a physical nature.

Dimitri marveled at each well-designed room complimented with premium accoutrements befitting a secret government building. Over the last couple of years, he often wondered what all the secrecy was about after each delivery; but tonight, he was being personally toured by someone with authority. Although Dimitri surmised that the doctor would require a favor in exchange for the vodka, he had included the tour in his evaluation of a fair deal and concluded that the tour itself would be worth any favor Bartosh could ask of him.

The two men entered the gigantic specimen room on their way to the vodka in the storage room. Dimitri paused to take in the hollowness of the room, looking up at the thirty-foot ceilings, down at the polished concrete floor, right at the wall of steel cages, and left at the impressive, screened enclosure. He could see the outline of trees and shrubs through the tightly woven mesh screen but not the unholy study subjects lurking in the foliage. In his mind he postulated that the live animals he delivered tonight would be deposited into the large enclosure for some type of scientific study but couldn't quite grasp why they needed so many each week.

The two men sat across from each other at the break table in the crowded storage room. Bartosh poured a full glass of expensive vodka and slid it over to Dimitri who grinned widely, recognizing the bottle to contain libation of the highest quality. They made small talk about the weather and the latest local news topics, each enjoying the other's company. Sporadically, a chicken would cluck and flutter its wings in the crate creating a lively atmosphere in an otherwise lifeless space. Having sweated out his buzz from all the heavy lifting, Bartosh sloppily gulped down a full glass of vodka trying to regain his lost euphoria while drawing a modest chuckle from the delivery man. The new-found drinking buddies polished off the remaining half bottle of vodka, prompting Bartosh to open a second bottle from Denys's prized stash.

As the two men continued their carefree indulgence, their conversation waded into political waters. Dimitri revealed that he was sympathetic to the plight of ethnic Russians in Ukraine who were searching for a national identity and lamenting about the tragic dismantling of the former USSR.

To dilute any possible offensive effect from his statement, he quickly added that he opposed the forcible taking of any land by any country. But it was too late, he had unwittingly struck a nerve deep in the Cambridge educated Ukrainian. Bartosh held back the rage bubbling behind his still smiling façade and dismissed the foul sentiment with a patronizing nod. He raised his glass in a disingenuous toast:

"Of course, comrade! To the USSR!" he shouted and followed up with a boisterous laugh.

Too drunk to detect Bartosh's sarcasm, the service man raised his glass and gulped down his twelfth shot of vodka. Bartosh poured Dimitri another glass before excusing himself to the bathroom.

While standing over the urinal, drunken rage mixed with a maelstrom of other emotions churned inside the doctor's head. How could this lowly laborer possibly comprehend the complexities of Russo-Ukrainian affairs? And how dare he spout off fascist ideals so freely in my face – an agent of the SSU? He must be a Russian spy, Bartosh conveniently concluded.

On his way back from the restroom, Bartosh stopped in the laboratory. He filled a large syringe with neurotoxin from three smaller syringes, then he tipped it with an extra-large needle. Donning a lab coat he snatched off the wall, he gently placed the poison dart in his coat pocket.

Dimitri was still curious about the enormous enclosure in the specimen room, but he didn't want to come across as a nosy guest, so he grabbed a crate of chickens and staggered into the cavernous room. Just as he did so, Dr. Bartosh pushed open the door at the other end of the room, prompting a surprised look on both their faces.

"I assume you want these chickens in those steel cages over there?" Dimitri asked nervously.

A maniacal grin appeared on Bartosh's face, the same grin he exhibited when he showcased his flies for the team in Maryland.

"You are so helpful Dimitri. The chickens actually belong in the open terrarium, let me unlatch and open the door for you," Bartosh replied in an appreciative tone.

The six-foot-five-inch man entered the enclosure with Bartosh following closely behind. Still holding the crate in his large hands, he wandered around the spacious terrarium looking skyward, marveling at the tall trees without detecting 18,000 under-fed assassin flies lurking in every bush, shrub, and tree.

Suddenly, Dimitri felt a sharp, aching pain radiating from his backside, slightly buckling his knees. Releasing his grip on the wooden crate, it fell to the ground in a loud thwack as wildly clucking chickens threw feathers inside. When he flung his head around to investigate the cause of his pain, his eyes met the dastardly image of Bartosh squeezing the last drops of poison in the large syringe into his backside.

Dimitri's blood-curdling cry was met with the doctor's sinister cackle as his muscles began to convulse uncontrollably. The large man fell forward like a harvested redwood tree, his face careening into the wooden crate, sending wood slats flying and chickens fluttering away.

Still grinning, Bartosh casually took three measured steps back from his debilitated victim, not willing to give up his front row seat to the grisly fate awaiting Dimitri.

Triggered by the neurotoxins coursing through the large man's body, the swarm of 18,000 assassin flies took flight, darting towards the convulsing man with his face bloodied from the violent crash into the wood crate. One eerie "thuck!" after another pierced the air as the flies hurtled their bodies against fresh meat. The first arrivals focused their assault on Dimitri's head, melting his eyeballs into a gelatinous goo, then hungrily slurping it clean off the skull, leaving two bloody entrances to his brain.

Still half conscious, the innocent man let out an agonizing cry as hordes of ravenous flies burrowed into his bloody eye socket like sand through an hourglass, then feasted on his brain. When the abominable creatures crawled inside Dimitri's body through every orifice, involuntary spasms and twitches reverberated throughout his whole body as they melted and devoured his internal organs.

Like a time-lapsed video of a decaying dog, the flies consumed the live man from the inside out, quickly transforming him into a grotesque Halloween prop adorned in a service man's uniform.

Bartosh stood frozen and awestruck by the carnage he just witnessed as the satiated swarm disappeared into the foliage. The meandering chickens picked at the remaining scraps of flesh still hanging off the lifeless body that lay in a pool of crimson blood.

The door to the specimen room swung open once more. Denys entered the room as the pungent odor of burnt flesh wafted from the enclosure. He quickly clenched his nostrils and called out in a nasally tone:

"Dr. Bartosh! Are you feeding the swarm?"

"I'm in here," Bartosh declared calmly.

As Denys approached the screened enclosure, he heard rustling noises and saw the outline of the doctor dragging something across the dirt floor. As he opened the screen door, his eyes grew wide as a bloody skeletal carcass leapt in the air towards him landing at his feet with a lifeless thud.

Denys let out a horrified scream, his legs flailing wildly up and down in reaction to the macabre sight. When Denys looked up, Bartosh stood there covered in blood savagely laughing at his own depraved prank.

Horror and shock begot fear as Denys viewed Bartosh through a new lens. How could his expert evaluation of the doctor's profile fail to identify his proclivity to savagery? Was Bartosh afflicted with a multiple personality disorder? And how did this dwarf-sized man pick up and hurl a bloody carcass weighing well over a hundred pounds at him like it was made of straw? But the most obvious and important question was who's grisly remains lay at his feet?

Before these disturbing questions transmuted to words, Bartosh blurted without emotion "he was a Russian spy."

Though Bartosh had only conjured up this notion from an ultra-nationalistic bent earlier in the evening, the veracity of his claim was bolstered when Denys ran Dimitri Petrov's ID through the SSU's database and found ties to the Communist Party of Ukraine. The two men corroborated and embellished the details of the eventful evening when they met with General Valarie who awarded both men with the Cross of Military Merit for their courage in service to their country.

As coincidence smiled upon Dr. Bartosh by affiliating the innocent delivery man with a radical political group, Denys found no reason to vindicate the doctor's depraved actions that night.

Knowing now what Bartosh was capable of, he developed a learned aversion to the doctor's ire.

CHAPTER EIGHT – PANDEMONIUM

It took Boris several days to reclaim his workday routine when he returned from his honeymoon. The stand-in crew had done the bare minimum, ignoring many of the finer details he had written down for them in his instructions. The storeroom was left with empty vodka bottles strewn across the floor and scant supplies loitering on half-empty shelves. The specimen room reeked from decaying animals scattered about the screened terrarium; and the laboratory was littered with crumpled pieces of paper containing illegible notes. Nonetheless, Boris was glad to be home and back with his adopted swarm family. He worked hard over his first week back, restocking supplies, cleaning the cages, and catching up on his observation notes. He exhaled a sigh of relief as he counted the last fly in the enclosure; though there was no sign of maggots crawling inside carcasses, indicating successful mating, the swarm remained 18,000 strong in terms of numbers.

The three SSU agents were also glad to have their fly keeper back. After disposing of any trace of the suspected Russian spy, all three agreed that the details of that fateful night were better left classified, so as to minimize distractions to Boris. Although Bartosh wanted to remain on assignment as Boris's partner,

General Valarie was wary of the doctor's explosive temperament and quickly assigned him to something less interactive.

Olga was less enthusiastic about their return to Kyiv than Boris. If she had her druthers, they would have left everything behind and stayed in Monaco, or France, or even Italy. With Boris's education and experience and her cosmetology skills, she was certain they could start a new life in a European city. She'd related these exact sentiments to Boris after an enthusiastic love-making episode, but they both knew the SSU wouldn't take kindly to them acting on these frivolous fantasies.

Boris and his partner in the United States got back to the business of fly breeding in short order. As the swarm grew from 18,000 to 45,000 over the next five years, Boris had to alter their diet to larger prey. Chickens, rabbits, and rats were replaced with sheep, calves, and swine. A new incinerator had to be installed to dispose of the growing number and size of the carcasses left from each meal. Since the auto-feeding response of the flies had yet to develop, Bartosh and his team of scientists continued to produce and supply Boris with the synthetic version of neurotoxins needed to feed his swarm.

Over the five-year period, Boris had tried on many occasions to release healthy livestock into the enclosure hoping to trigger the elusive trait; but each attempt failed, leaving him frustrated and dejected. One afternoon, in between shipments of the poison darts, Boris bore an epiphany and acted on it. He filled a syringe with a harmless saline solution and walked into the enclosure hoisting a fifty pound juvenile pig. Sensing danger lurking in the bushes and foliage, the piglet let out a nervous squeal, garnering the attention of 45,000 pairs of compound eyes. Boris gave the piglet a hasty jab of the syringe causing the unharmed animal to startle and run wildly about the large, enclosed space. Nothing happened. Not even a hint of reaction from a single fly.

With his impromptu theory debunked, Boris was disgusted and waved his right hand in a gesture of utter dismissal in the direction of the still dashing pig. Just as he turned to exit the screened terrarium, a deafening buzz from 45,000 pairs of wings filled the air. When Boris turned back around, he witnessed a gruesome display of hunting prowess from 45,000 genetically enhanced assassin flies evolved over thirty-five generations of breeding.

Working as a team, the flies hurtled towards the animal in a staggered formation, anticipating the path of the scrambling swine. Each dose of neurotoxins sequentially delivered by a sub-swarm evoked a hair-raising squeal from the fleeing pig and caused its muscles to tense, slowing the forward speed. By the third dose, the piglet's wobbly gait sent it careening into the trunk of a tall tree, its muscles now convulsing uncontrollably, and its eyes rolled back in its head showing only the whites of its eyes. An ominous cloud of assassin flies descended on the quivering beast like a shroud of death. The smells and sounds of singeing flesh mixed with the labored squeals of the dying animal painted a macabre scene of an unholy, Sunday barbeque.

Boris was stunned by the monumental discovery. He had hypothesized that the swarm would eventually become conditioned to attack on the fearful reactions of its prey, but what he uncovered was beyond scientific explanation. He was confounded by their apparent obedience to him. There has never been a scientific case of communication documented between humans and insects at this level, but then again, these insects were created in a lab and bred generation after generation by man. One man – Boris Shevchenko.

Besides their loyal obedience, Boris was astounded by the phenomenal teamwork displayed by the swarm. It was well known that assassin flies in the wild are solo hunters, capturing their prey with their superior aerial agility and vice-like gripping ability.   What Boris witnessed today resembled a pride of voracious lions taking down spirited prey through a highly coordinated effort. Until now, the flies had never had to use their own neurotoxins to immobilize prey, making their measured approach in their inaugural attempt that much more amazing.

After relishing his newfound power, a pensive mood pervaded his consciousness. Boris turned his thoughts to the implications of possessing the sole and awesome power to direct an attack. *Could the flies be trained to obey an attack signal by a random soldier in the field of combat? If not, would the flies eventually gain a natural response to feed on human flesh? Probably,* he thought, *but that would take time – precious time.* He had already dedicated seven years of his life to this assignment, taking only two weeks to enjoy his honeymoon. Boris had worked tirelessly seven days a week, fifty-two weeks a year, motivated by what he believed could change the course of the conflict in Crimea.   After all his sacrifices, was he now prepared to offer his services on the battlefield as his ultimate sacrifice? Surely, that would be what his country would want, but he couldn't make that decision now even if he wanted to; his wife of five years would have to weigh in. Boris decided to keep this development a secret until he could wade through the morass of truths and their consequences.

When Boris arrived at their luxury apartment in an upper-class neighborhood of Kyiv, he found Olga sitting on the couch with her eyes glued to the television screen. His fond greeting was abruptly interrupted by her raised palm and an anxious shush. As Boris strolled around behind Olga, he witnessed occupied hospital beds crowding the sterile hallways of an Italian hospital. Doctors and nurses were frenetically meandering between beds and I.C.U.s wearing full, protective gowns and plastic face shields resembling those found in science fiction movies.

The Ukrainian newscaster was reporting on the scene, rattling off regional statistics of new cases of COVID-19 in Europe, then concluded the news clip by declaring 25,000 deaths in Italy alone. The Wuhan Virus had blossomed into a worldwide pandemic not seen in over a hundred years.

More concerned with the disruption of her consumerist lifestyle, Olga whined, "How am I supposed to go to the fashion show in Milan on Saturday? They have restricted travel, Boris."

"It's probably for the best, my love. Face mask designs should be left to medical professionals rather than fashion designers," Boris teased.

Up until this development, Olga enjoyed day trips to Lviv, and weekend stays in major European cities, shopping at the finest stores for the latest fashions. On the rare occasion Boris could convince Dr. Bartosh to stand in for him at the lab, he would accompany his wife on these shopping sprees, and they would dine at fine restaurants along picturesque waterways and boulevards. With almost two million dollars in liquid assets, the industrious couple had climbed a few rungs up the socio-economic ladder, enjoying the life of the Ukrainian upper crust.

Olga smiled, gave her husband a light peck on the cheek, and headed to the kitchen to prepare their dinner. Boris sat down on the couch and resumed watching the news. After a brief commercial break, the Minister of the Interior announced shutdowns of public transportation, bars, restaurants, and schools. Of course, salons and other personal services where social distancing was impossible were also ordered to shutter to slow the insidious virus. Boris never told Olga about that afternoon of revelation when the flies showcased their total obedience to him. He didn't want her to worry about the possibility that his country would call him to duty on the front lines, nor about the potential end to the lucrative assignment.

Boris was unaffected by these draconian measures since he spent most of his time alone and hidden away in the secret lab; it was a minor nuisance he quickly adapted to. For the next year, he continued to experiment with different hand gestures and body movements honing his communication skills with his swarm. He would expose the flies to different genres of music and sing along to familiarize the flies to his voice. It didn't take long before hand and voice signals were combined to direct the flies to feed, to mate, and to sing.

It wasn't long before Olga cried foul. For Olga, the pandemic brought about isolation, boredom, and jealousy. As the morning light crept over her bed, she let out a labored groan, then proceeded to pull the covers over her head. Just another boring day alone in their apartment. It had already been two weeks since the world came to a sudden halt and there was no end to the madness in sight. It was as if Covid-19 stranded the entire world on Gilligan's Island. Life had just started looking up for her; she was married to a successful man, she traveled and shopped to her heart's content, and she spent time at the spa with her friends on a scheduled basis. But now, she couldn't go down to the coffee shop to socialize with neighbors or even go to work at the salon. Every facet of her life had changed.

She wanted to share her frustration over all the government restrictions with Boris, but he was nowhere to be found. Boris spent most of his time at his secret underground lab with his precious flies. He didn't even come home for dinner some nights. Boredom and depression confined Olga to the devil's online workshop, searching the internet for relief and entertainment. She spent hours watching videos and following popular influencers online; she even dabbled in social media chats with friendly strangers, *it was harmless companionship, right?* she thought.

Olga started up her computer on a rainy Saturday morning. Boris had already gone to work, and she was left alone again, save for the vices dancing around in her head. The usual bleak and depressing stories popped up on her homepage; another epicenter of infection identified, another famous personality succumbing to the disease, a record number of new cases, hospitalizations, and deaths.

As she scrolled down the page to find any morsel of positivity, an ad for a social dating site popped up. The dating site was fittingly named "Unmasked for You" and advertised the broad spectrum of possibilities in the dating world; male and female, male and male, female, and female, and of course for the most discerning daters, the site advertised a personal chatbot customized with every imaginable trait one's heart desired. Olga couldn't resist the temptation for an ego boost. Excitement swept over her as she thought about finally showcasing the multitude of gorgeous outfits she had bought prior to the pandemic.

She quickly went to work building an alluring profile replete with photos of her in fashionable attire for every occasion, even a few photos she would have considered too risqué in normal times. That same night, after Boris returned to the lab after a brief dinner at home, she logged in to find thirty inquiries in her inbox. For the next three days, Olga amused herself reading the gambits of amorous suitors and flirting with men from the safety of her computer screen.

Just as she was about to log off the dating site one lonely Wednesday night, a new message popped up. With trepidation she clicked on the link directing her to Da-Mon-B's profile. The picture of a ruggedly attractive man in his early forties graced her screen. Olga quickly scanned the rest of his photos and read his profile. He declared himself to be six-foot-four-inches tall with an athletic build; single and looking for an online companion to get through this awful pandemic. His words resonated with Olga, showing a level of sophistication and charm worthy of further exploration.

Over the next six months, the two searching souls struck up a genuine friendship, both innocently commiserating with each other over how Covid restrictions had stolen their joy like a thief in the night. While their conversations were benign on the surface, each felt a budding fondness towards the other. As the awkwardness of first impressions faded over the months, their conversations gradually waded into impropriety, each expressing their forbidden attraction to the other. Not long after that, the attraction shamelessly blossomed into a scandalous infatuation that compelled the spellbound sinners to plan a future rendezvous.

Though Olga knew Damon was a wealthy and successful businessman, what Olga didn't know was Damon Blackwell was a third-generation hotelier. His grandfather was an innkeeper in south London for twenty years before immigrating to the United States and purchasing a small bed and breakfast in New York City. Damon's father, James, worked alongside his mother and father fervently learning the nuances of the hospitality business. James got his big break in the 1970's when he and his business partner caught wind of a failing "love-hotel" on a desirable corner near the city's center. His partner had connections within New York's financial district, helping the two fledgling developers secure a bank loan to purchase and redevelop the hotel. The project turned out to be a smashing success, squarely launching him into the hotel development and operations business.

In the 1980's, when competition for prime real estate heated up in New York City, James took his ingenuity and business savvy to south Florida and the underserved markets of Asia and Australia. His B-Well brand of luxury hotels became wildly successful at home and abroad earning him a place amongst hotelier royalty the likes of Hilton, Trump, and Marriott. Though he never went to college, James Blackwell had amassed a portfolio of forty luxury hotels and resorts worth billions across the globe by age fifty.

While James was globetrotting and building the family fortune, Damon and his sister Lydia attended some of the finest private secondary schools in the country. Often seen cruising the streets of Fort Lauderdale in his Ferrari, Damon was known to throw all-night ragers at his parents' mansion for his high school classmates. He attended the prestigious school of hospitality at Cornell University where he earned high honors and was befittingly named Vice President of Global Operations a year after graduation. His sister Lydia earned a fine arts degree from Yale and was appointed as Blackwell Hotel and Resort's Chief Creative Officer in similar fashion a year later.

With operations spanning the globe, Damon was invariably consumed by wanderlust, attending grand opening galas in exclusive vacation destinations around the world and rubbing shoulders with tycoons and world leaders.

Besides possessing earthly treasures of money and prestige, Damon was uncommonly handsome and robust. Standing six feet four inches tall, he wore his bison brown hair near shoulder length, pulled back to showcase his brilliant deep-set blue eyes. He had a chiseled jaw line that was accentuated with a prominent chin and light facial hair that projected an alluring mystique. Acclaimed by legions of adoring women, his good looks and charismatic style gave him unfettered access to high-society bachelorettes from all over the world.

Damon played the field of international beauties with fervor, juggling dates between international flights. His dutiful office assistant was also required to arrange his evening agenda, texting him his dinner rendezvous thirty minutes before touch-down.

It was a cold afternoon in the spring of 2021 when Boris received a call from his partner in the United States of America. Boris had just recorded his last count of assassin flies in his logbook and excitedly picked up the satellite phone in his office, eager to share good news with Wes.

Before Wes could extend a greeting, Boris exclaimed "55,000 strong! We did it Wes."

A deafening silence fell across the phone line, prompting Boris to reiterate "Wes, we are 99 percent to goal! The flies can be trained to attack, and I have developed the commands."

"Boris, listen to me carefully. I got a call from my senator friend who sits on the Armed Services Committee. The whole thing is a sham, and you are in great danger. Stay away from Dr. Bartosh!"

"What do you mean sham? Wes, have you been drinking?" Boris teased, unwilling to fall for another one of the Colonel's jokes.

"Boris, this is no joke. I am concerned about your safety!" Wes emphasized with a dead serious tone.

Boris took a minute to sort through Wes's curious words. After another minute of rumination, Boris engaged in an unsettling conversation with Wes that left him both incredulous and despondent.

Wes went on to explain that Congress had approved a two-billion-dollar defense bill aimed at deterring Russian aggression against Ukraine when the "rumblings" began in the Crimean Peninsula. Half of the funds were allocated to train 50,000 soldiers in asymmetrical warfare, and the other half was intended to improve drone technology. While General Valarie was officially designated by the Ukrainian Government as the administrative leader of the projects, Bartosh was really calling all the shots. They had used Valarie's stellar credentials and silver tongue to gain congressional approval while hiding Bartosh's involvement. Dr. Francis Bartosh was known by the committee to be mentally unstable and previously investigated for war crimes.

Like many top-secret military projects, oversight over the appropriate use of funds was scant and left to the discretion of the awarded country. But recent intelligence confirming Russia's movement of military equipment and personnel to the Belarusian border suggested a wider conflict was eminent, prompting the committee to take a closer accounting over the use of funds.

When his senator friend, who chaired the Senate Armed Services Committee, privately asked Wes for details of the project, he was mortified by what he heard and demanded Wes "sanitize" the project to avoid bringing shame and retribution from the international community.

"Boris, you must destroy the swarm," Wes somberly told to his friend.

"Do you even know what you are asking me to do?!" Boris retorted, fighting back tears.

"I won't pretend to know how you feel, but I know you to be a decent man, Boris. You and I both know this insane idea could have only come from a madman. We've both been manipulated by patriotism and honor and blinded by greed," Wes admitted.

"They are my family, just like you and General Valarie, and Denys, and even B…"

Before Boris could utter his name, Wes interrupted: "Would a true family member desert their family?"

"What are you talking about?" asked Boris, taken by surprise.

"Boris, I was working up to tell you, General Valarie and Denys Boyko have disappeared with $700 million dollars of

- 83 -

project funds and are probably on some tropical island enjoying the good life. Interpol has been activated to find them by both our country's governments. The certified 'nutjob' Bartosh has assumed the SSU's Ministerial position and intends to carry out his deranged vision."

When Wes revealed the brazen act of the two scoundrels, confusion and indignation flooded Boris's consciousness. *How could General Valarie, whom he placed in the company of the country's most distinguished patriots betray Ukraine with such a self-serving act? How could Denys Boyko, who helped him through heartbreak, desert the country that gave him a second chance at a normal life? Both raised their champagne glasses toasting his holy union with Olga, so how could this be true?*

Hurt and confused, Boris told Wes he needed some time to digest the unsavory bombshell unloaded on him and pensively hung up the phone with Wes who was still pleading his case on the other end of the line. Though Boris was hazy about what he would do with this disturbing information, he took heed of the Colonel's warning of danger.

He entered their apartment in an anxious mood, eager to share the disturbing news with his wife Olga. She was behind the computer monitor in their bedroom when he abruptly burst in. Startled by his intrusion, Olga quickly uttered "I have to go," and clicked off the video chat. When she stood up from her chair behind the monitor, Boris could see that she was elegantly made up. Her hair was drawn in a tight bun at the back, highlighting her beautiful face, an aura of seduction radiating from her pretty blue eyes. She was wearing an evening dress that hugged her curvaceous hips.

"Where are you going?" Boris asked curiously.

"You mean, where are we going? 'We' are going to Chez Francois, they just re-opened," Olga replied, adeptly diverting his attention away from her abruptly ended video chat.

"Great, I'll grab my coat, we can talk over dinner," Boris agreed.

Boris told Olga everything over a three-hour dinner. When he described the surprising discovery of his wide-ranging ability to control the flies, she feigned interest, while her mind wandered, conjuring up images of an idyllic meeting with Damon. He also expressed his dismay over the flies' inability to act on their own, adding his worry over the length of time it may require training someone else to direct an attack. To which, she blankly consoled "You can do it Boris, I believe in you."

Choosing his words carefully, he then proceeded to suggest the possibility of being called to duty on the front line.

A hint of excitement flashed across Olga's face before it was quickly covered with a veneer of consternation.

"Oh Boris, no!" she emoted, "Let's run away," she blurted with a gleam in her eye.

Boris's face beamed at her magnificent visage tenderly projecting concern for him. The romantic idea of the two lovers running away from peril and starting a new life together stirred powerful feelings of love and adoration for Olga.

When he told her about his conversation with Wes about how General Valarie and Denys Boyko had absconded with $700 million dollars of project funds, she added: "All the more reason to leave!"

After much deliberation, the couple concluded that an escape across the Atlantic to the great state of Florida was their best option. They had an ally and friend in Colonel Walker; plus, Wes was well positioned to help them navigate the path to asylum and access to green cards. Boris told Wes their plan the very next day, to which, he reminded Boris about the Senator's concern; adding that their path to citizenship would be that much smoother if he destroyed any and all traces of the diabolical project. So, it was settled, they each had their marching orders; Olga was tasked with finding temporary accommodations for them in Fort Lauderdale and packing up their belongings; Colonel Walker was to arrange secret transportation from Kyiv to the U.S. Army Garrison in Miami, and Boris was to destroy the swarm, the only true family he ever had.

That night, as Boris stood shaving in front of the bathroom mirror, a wave of nostalgia washed over him as he thought about the night he showcased his dipteran string orchestra to Olga. *What a magical night of enchantment!* His thoughts turned to the flies' miraculous evolution from crudely assembled building blocks to the sleek and elegant flying aces they've become. Against all odds, they became the beautiful creatures they are today, placing their trust and obedience in him, their true creator. Nostalgia turned into woe at the thought of betraying their trust, something Boris held dear in his heart. A teardrop escaped Boris's eye and traced its way down the outline of his nose.

Interrupting the poignant moment, Olga called out to Boris from the bedroom, startling him badly. Her abrupt intrusion on his thoughts caused the straight razor to stray, carving a nasty gash on his neck an inch deep. Wincing in pain, he quickly retrieved a face towel hanging on a ring on the wall and applied copious pressure on the wound. After an hour of agony and profuse bleeding, the wound remained open, requiring stitches. In their hurried state, the couple decided to continue preparing for their timely escape instead of seeking medical treatment for the wound. Boris opted to let the wound "air out", hoping it would scab up in its natural healing process.

The next morning, before his final act of betrayal, Boris decided to pay a visit to SSU headquarters and confirm for himself the absence of Valarie and Denys. As he pushed open the slightly cracked office door, he saw Dr. Bartosh sitting behind what was once General Valarie's desk, staring intently into the monitor screen and grinning maniacally. Without looking away, Bartosh invited Boris in.

"Come in Boris, I was expecting you," the wild-eyed doctor declared.

Startled by the doctor's second sight, Boris sheepishly entered the office and sat down in front of him as the new head of the SSU requested.

"Let me guess, you came here to see for yourself whether your American partner was telling you the truth!" Bartosh looked up and paused for any sign of a backpedal from Boris.

"Well, yes, it's quite unbelievable," Boris admitted nervously.

Dr. Bartosh let out a long sinister cackle that sent shivers down Boris's spine. After catching his breath, the doctor walked over to Boris from behind his desk. Looking directly into Boris's eyes, the doctor chided.

"What is so surprising about two quivering pussies running for their lives when they see enemies at their gates?!"

By his tone and demeanor, Boris was certain the doctor was experiencing a psychotic episode. He abruptly tried to leave when Bartosh's dwarf-like hand came to rest firmly on his shoulder, pinning him to his seat. Before he could object to his detainment, the evil doctor violently spun his computer screen around and shouted:

"WHAT IS SO SURPRISING TO ME, BORIS, IS WHY YOU WOULD CHOOSE TO HIDE YOUR TALENTS FROM ME!!!"

Boris's mouth fell agape as he gazed at the images flashing across the screen. Images of him and Olga dancing a Minuet in the fly enclosure, as the swarm serenaded them with Vivaldi's Four Seasons, was followed by images of him directing the flies to attack unsuspecting prey. Unbeknownst to Boris, Bartosh had secretly placed a hidden camera within the confines of the screened enclosure, watching Boris's every move.

An incriminating silence gripped Boris, as his mind raced to come up with a scientific explanation for the phenomena unfolding on the screen. But he couldn't; what he once considered to be a triumphant secret was now a devasting truth that could lead to his ultimate demise on the battlefield.

Unexpectedly, Bartosh demanded, "You will start training me your hand signals tomorrow."

The doctor's words jolted Boris out of his defeatist funk. *Of course, the sadistic madman would want to play a pivotal role in his own diabolical scheme*, Boris thought. Sensing his window of opportunity to escape detainment, he quickly replied.

"Of course, I will go to the lab and prepare for your training."

With a nonchalant wave of his hand Bartosh dismissed Boris. Boris hightailed it out of SSU headquarters and headed to the hardware store on a city bus. He picked up a case of aerosol insecticide with the highest potency of tetramethrin he could find, then headed for the underground laboratory.

Working feverishly, he collected all his research notes and logs and stuffed them into a brown leather satchel, then he collected the last remaining syringes of neurotoxin and hastily threw them in the bag as well. The screened enclosure reeked of dead carcasses from the last feeding, so Boris collected them in a wheel barrel and disposed of them in the newly installed incinerator. The storeroom was in disarray, so he straightened the stock on the shelves and picked up everything off the floor.

By the time 5pm rolled around, Boris was exhausted, he had done everything except for the one thing he subconsciously avoided – erasing ten years' worth of his life's work. As he lowered the temperature on the thermostat in the specimen room for the last time, an air of melancholy surrounded him. Although he acknowledged the iniquity of the project, he was willfully betraying his country, and his heart felt heavy with shame.

When the temperature dropped to forty degrees, the flies went dormant and fell gently to the ground. Boris entered the enclosure and delicately picked up a female fly cradling it in the palm of his hand. He wanted to behold the spectacular creature one last time, so he walked into the laboratory and gently placed her under the microscope. Boris stood over the microscope in silent contemplation of her ethereal beauty. The colors bursting from the dormant fly were stunning. He couldn't help thinking that though the creature was created by man, it must have benefited from some divine intervention; was he truly destroying something wicked or was he defying the will of God?

His emotions waffled between pride and despair when a teardrop fell on the lens of the scope blurring the enigmatic image below. The chilly air from the specimen room seeped through the cracked open door beckoning Boris to the dreadful task at hand. He hoisted the case of insecticide spray under his arm and went into the screened enclosure, grabbing two cans from the case, one in each hand. Taking great care not to trample on 55,000 dormant flies scattered about the floor, Boris systematically crab-walked from one end of the enclosure, releasing a cloud of insecticide fumes in his wake. When he emptied the two cans, he grabbed two more, until every inch of floor inside the cage was covered.

After a ten-minute break to let the poison take effect, he turned the temperature on the thermostat back up to 75 degrees. Guiding the wheel barrel and a shovel through the cage door, he started shoveling up the dead flies and dumping them into the wheel barrel. Making two trips, he then disposed of the dead flies in the incinerator one shovelful at a time until all the flies were gone.

Boris was both physically and emotionally exhausted. He glanced at his watch. It was 8pm, three hours away from his rendezvous with Olga and Wes at the secret airstrip just outside of the city. He set the alarm on his watch for nine thirty pm, planning for a much-needed nap and an hour and a half to walk to the airstrip. Boris made his way from the specimen room through the laboratory and to the much-welcomed sight of the couch in his office. He crashed headlong atop the comfortable cushions of the sofa, his sweaty body lying on its back.

Just as he fell into a deep slumber, the sole surviving assassin fly left under the microscope awakened from its own. Using its regal wings, the pregnant female fly flipped itself back onto its legs with a quick flutter. Appearing disoriented, she remained on the pedestal surveying the room for a minute. Suddenly, she took flight around the laboratory in a typical random fashion, then found her way to her sleeping master on the office couch.

Boris's sweaty body provided an attractive landing spot for the dipteran creature, but she sought more than just a surface to frolic, her urgency to propagate led her to seek a proper carcass to deposit 400 assassin fly eggs. The scent of blood mixed with sweat led her to the base of her master's neck where the inch deep flesh wound beckoned her urge. The fly stealthily nestled itself between the fold of his flesh and hid her eggs deep inside live human tissue. When she was done, she flew into the cavernous specimen room looking for her swarm and disappeared amongst the natural landscape of the open terrarium.

The distinctive chime emanating from Boris's wristwatch roused him from his deep sleep. He rolled off the couch clutching his aching back and turned off the alarm on the digital timepiece. A slight tingling sensation from the bad cut he suffered shaving the night before prompted him to cover the open wound with a bandage he found lying around in his desk drawer. As he hastily covered the nasty gash, he suddenly remembered leaving the dormant fly on the stage of the microscope.

He rushed back into the laboratory, only to find the stage of the scope starkly empty. As he swiveled his head from shoulder to shoulder looking for the airborne specimen, an uneasy feeling washed over him when he noticed both doors to the adjacent rooms were cracked open. The fly could be anywhere between the wide-open space of the specimen room and the nooks and crannies of his well-appointed office.

Boris was torn between looking for the sole surviving fly or making haste for the rendezvous. As he grabbed his leather satchel and his coat to leave, he whirled around and gave his office a nostalgic gaze, then rode the elevator to ground level and made his way to the secret airstrip by moonlight.

CHAPTER NINE – THE RUBICON

As the military plane took off on its transcontinental flight, Boris sat in silent contemplation by a window seat aboard. The city grew smaller as they gained altitude, evoking a melancholy and an acute sense of emptiness. He had just destroyed ten years of toil that could have helped his country defeat the barbarians that opposed their way of life; but now, it was he who felt defeated. Now that the enemy had ominously amassed thousands of troops and weapons at the northern border, Boris grew concerned about his aunts and uncles who resided in that region. He started to question his decision to abandon the project on the account of transgressions committed by the two scoundrels. Was money really more important than country? Or were the sadistic ideations of the madman guided by Satan himself? Maybe Wes was right, after all, pride and greed as Boris was taught in his Christian upbringing were among the seven deadly sins, and he had likely been swayed by the sinister allure of both.

A burst of boisterous laughter from the cockpit shattered Boris's pensive mood as he looked up to find Wes exchanging war stories and banter with the pilot. When he did so, he caught sight of Olga's beautiful profile next to him. She wore a hopeful smile and a faraway look in her eyes. Her expression gave him a warm feeling of reassurance that he had made the right decision. *She had to put up with his willful absence nearly their entire marriage and now he had a chance to right the ship, maybe start a family in America,* he thought. Boris turned his thoughts to the future and his desire to return to teaching at a university once again, then, he fell fast asleep next to Olga.

Although Olga had only forty-eight hours to gather their belongings and find temporary accommodation until they found a permanent home, she had the help of her billionaire suitor. When Damon learned about the serendipitous news of Olga's immigration, he quickly mobilized his team to help her every step of the way. His chauffer was ordered to pick the couple up from the Army Garrison in Miami and transport them to the B-Well Resort and Residences on Fort Lauderdale Beach, where an oceanfront suite awaited them well stocked for their extended stay. A luxury rental car was ordered by his office assistant to be delivered and parked in the VIP garage of the resort for the couple's use. And his real estate agent was on standby with a list of properties for sale bearing the amenities Olga specified over the internet the night before. Since every detail of their relocation had been meticulously planned, all there was to do was fantasize about her anticipated affair with the princely hotelier.

Wes, on the other hand, had less complicated thoughts on his mind. Rescuing the couple and organizing their defection was his last assignment in his long and distinguished military career. All the paperwork was submitted to Army administration and his transition to civilian life was only days away. Wes thought about his retirement cottage on Pensacola Beach and which marina to moor his new fishing boat. Overjoyed with the nest egg they'd built; he had already set aside a healthy sum for his granddaughter Layla's college fund. He and his wife can finally enjoy living out the rest of their years near family and Wes could rekindle his passion for fishing.

When the plane landed, Wes gave the couple their applications for green cards and the name of the administrative officer they were to see at the immigration office in Miami.

As the limousine pulled under the grand porte-cochere of the five-diamond hotel, two porters smartly dressed in pressed uniforms and white gloves greeted the Ukrainian couple by name. Strolling through the airy marbled lobby, Boris marveled at the spectacular opulence on display. Modern crystal chandeliers hung from soaring ceilings and stylish contemporary furniture was astutely arranged over luxurious Persian rugs. The walls were tastefully adorned with high-definition photomurals of Fort Lauderdale Beaches and landmarks, while tropical plants and elegant abstract sculptures occupied the wide-open passageways throughout the grand resort.

In his native Ukrainian tongue, Boris declared, "My God Olga, just look at this place!"

"I have a friend in the business, he gave us a great deal. Just wait till you see our suite!" Olga replied.

Boris sensed the excitement in her voice and decided that whatever the price her "manager" friend charged them was worth the joy exuded from his wife's heart.

Arriving on the twentieth floor, Olga pushed open the double doors to their oceanfront suite and ambled through the well-appointed living space and out onto the sun terrace overlooking the Atlantic Ocean. Boris walked through the luxurious bedroom and spacious ensuite admiring the soothing elegance.

When Boris glanced at the two suitcases sitting next to the closet in their bedroom, a panic washed over him as he noticed the stark absence of his brown satchel. It wasn't until he saw it lying on the bed that he breathed a huge sigh of relief. One of the syringes filled with experimental neurotoxin had rolled out of the bag and laid innocently in plain view. As he walked over to the bed to conceal its existence, he heard Olga's voice over his shoulder.

"Boris, weren't you supposed to destroy that? Why did you bring that all this way?" Olga curiously asked.

After securing the syringe snugly in the satchel, he turned to face his beautiful wife and explained in a loving tone, "I will darling, eventually. The research and development that created the compound is priceless, and it would be a shame to destroy it without analyzing it some more."

Staring intently into her beautiful eyes, he leaned in and gave Olga a tender kiss on the lips. The couple had not been intimate for a couple of weeks and both felt a simmering passion building up amidst the beautiful backdrop of the Atlantic Ocean just outside their suite. Olga reciprocated his loving intimation with a more passionate kiss, before the couple hastily stripped off their clothes and fell onto the bed succumbing to their carnal desires.

The next morning, they found their way to the VIP garage and hopped into the courtesy car provided by Olga's generous friend. They drove to the electronics store and purchased prepaid phones to coordinate their whereabouts and facilitate a divide and conquer strategy. Boris was to head south to the immigration office for their green cards and Olga was off to hunt for permanent housing.

"I'll call the realtor to pick me up from here darling," Olga told Boris.

Although Boris wondered why Olga was dressed so elegantly and in heels to go house hunting, he chalked her decision up to the cultural norms of a foreign country. He headed south on I-95 towards the immigration office in Miami as Wes had instructed. Minutes later, a black SUV discreetly parked and waiting on the outer edge of the parking lot pulled up to the entrance of the store and picked Olga up. She quickly got in and sent Damon a text message.

"Sorry, running a bit late."

Damon Blackwell had never been so giddy and anxious about meeting a woman in his entire life. Perhaps it was because she was stunningly beautiful, or maybe the thought of consummating an online courtship of compromising photos and flirtatious chats fueled his excitement. Now in his forties, Damon could still charm the panties off any woman he wanted, but he didn't want any other woman, he wanted this one. The thought of her marital status never crossed his mind. Subconsciously, he reasoned that this inconvenient little obstacle would disappear with enough incentive, just like any other hotel development roadblock he's had to deal with in his line of business. He wasn't exactly sure where all of this would lead, but he relished the intrigue of the moment.

As Olga gracefully glided across the foyer of the yacht club restaurant in four-inch heels, she could immediately feel the enchanted gazes of men. Though the white one-piece gown was modest by design, her svelte figure and healthy curves betrayed its modesty. She wore her hair in a stylish bun atop the crown of her head, revealing her angelic, pale-blue eyes. Her delicate jawline was highlighted with a pair of diamond studded earrings, while her face was astutely made up, showcasing her full luscious lips.

Damon had just finished a morning meeting with his culinary director and was enjoying a mid-morning cocktail to take some of the edge off this highly anticipated meeting. He felt his pulse quicken as they locked eyes from across the room. He waved her over to the empty bar stool he had been saving for her with an inviting smile.

They greeted each other with a warm hug followed by nervous smiles and sheepish glances. Sensing the anxious energy floating about, Damon adeptly broke the ice with a bold compliment.

"Do you always come out of a pandemic more ravishing than when you went in?" he inquired.

Acknowledging his witty banter, she returned fire with "I'm not sure, but let's not hope for another one to find out."

Infectious laughter rang out as their moods lifted from her aptly timed response. Eager to foster the good vibes, Damon ordered another dirty martini for himself and a cosmopolitan for his companion. For the next thirty minutes, they went on to retrace their friendship, starting with their happenstance meeting on the dating site and laughed at the cheesy usernames they'd each come up with. As their conversation waded into audacious waters, their casual glances lingered a bit longer, leading to bewitching gazes that brought nostalgia to a few elderly onlookers around the bar. Damon's keen sense of timing led to his next suggestion.

"I've arranged for a private lunch for us aboard my yacht. Shall we?" Damon declared, pointing his index finger towards the restaurant window behind Olga.

As Olga turned to look out the window, she beheld a humongous modern vessel at least 200 feet long moored at the very end of the marina. "Of course," she replied.

Olga tempered her jubilation as the couple walked out of the restaurant onto the marina property. As they strolled along the dock's weathered wooden planks loitered with a few regal pelicans, the shimmering turquoise water soothed their visual senses while creating an otherworldly quietude. White seagulls hovering against a clear blue sky greeted them with melodious "klee-ew" calls announcing their arrival at the impressive modern vessel.

She could see uniformed crew on the top deck scampering about bearing platters of food and glassware as they set a small table draped in white linen. Damon took Olga's hand guiding her across the gangway in her delicate heels, then they ascended in a small elevator to the sundeck for lunch.

"A toast, to serendipity" Damon raised his glass of wine with sincerity, as a bashful smile graced Olga's lips. She obliged his toast with a sip of chardonnay, then, the couple continued the age-old courtship ritual of flattery and boasting over a spread of delectable fare.

"Would you like a tour of the Yacht?" Damon suggested.

"I thought you'd never ask," Olga replied confidently.

As they strolled hand in hand along the railing of the impressive craft, Olga paused and looked out over the graduated hues of the Atlantic Ocean dotted with the meandering white sails of majestic boats and thought to herself:

This is what I've dreamed of since I was a little girl. And now, it is here, and I can reach out and grab it! If this is really just a dream, please, let me keep dreaming until it becomes real.

Damon seized Olga's moment of introspection to assess his own feelings for her. Everything about this woman aroused his desires; her stately presence, her radiant beauty, and her lightning-quick wit. She was different from the bevy of young and naïve heiresses and party girls he's fraternized with in the past. Was she the one to lure him away from the playboy merry-go-round he'd been stuck on for the past ten years? Could she become the Mrs. Blackwell he'd been subconsciously searching for?

Inspiration turned to action as he turned to face Olga and moved in closer for a kiss. He was pleasantly surprised when she anticipated his advance and pulled him in by the nape of his neck, planting a passionate kiss on his waiting lips. Damon lost himself in her kiss, instinctively pulling her body closer to his, as the new lovers felt their unbridled animal urges awaken from months of restraint and anticipation. They hurriedly made their way down to the master's quarters with the urgency of teenagers on prom night and fell into the forbidden throes of lovemaking.

Olga looked down at her wristwatch as she stepped out of the black SUV. It was 6pm when she entered the lobby of the luxury resort. A pang of guilt flooded her conscience as she approached their suite door. She hadn't seen her husband since ten am, but it seemed like an eternity to her. Olga felt obligated to report progress on her search for permanent housing but having spent the last 8 hours in the company of her secret lover, she was woefully unprepared.

Boris greeted her with a sigh of relief, "Olga, thank God you're back, I was worried about you."

"I'm sorry darling, we were stuck in rush hour traffic on the other side of town" she said sincerely.

"Why didn't you answer my calls? I must have called you a dozen times!" Boris asked in a puzzled tone, his relief turning into frustration.

"You did? Ugh, these prepaid phones aren't worth the scrap metal they're made with, I never heard a single ring! We'd seen so many houses; I was too exhausted to call you. Aww baby, I'm so sorry" Olga replied with puppy dog eyes and pouty lips.

"I can't wait till we get settled and meet some new neighbors and friends," Boris declared.

After a moment to settle his anxiety, a self-satisfying grin appeared on his face as he teased "Guess what I have in my back pocket?"

Olga's face lit up with excitement, "Our green cards?!"

On cue, Boris whipped out two freshly laminated green cards for Olga to see. They even had recent photos prominently affixed to the front of the card. Wes had taken the liberty to square every detail with the immigration office prior to their arrival, and now, the happy couple were well on their way to citizenship in only a couple of days after their arrival. Boris and Olga locked arms and danced around their luxurious suite with their free hands holding the cards over their heads in jubilation.

Seizing the positive momentum, the two immigrants scoured the neighborhoods of Fort Lauderdale the next day, in search of an ideal abode. It had to have a master suite with enough closet space to satisfy Olga's penchant for fashion while Boris had to have a separate garage so he could retrofit it into a laboratory for his work. Both agreed that since basements were rare in South Florida homes, they would need a large attic to store odds and ends.

It was only day three of their journey to settle in America, but their determination and tenacity brought them to an ideal patio home nestled in a highly desired suburb of Fort Lauderdale. The one-story, ranch style home boasted three bedrooms, a beautiful master suite with ten-foot tray ceilings, and a huge walk-in closet large enough to host the most extensive of wardrobes. In the corner of the master suite closet, an inconspicuous mechanical access ladder unfolded down from the ceiling giving the owner access to a large attic above. The home had everything Olga and Boris had hoped for, including a separate garage that could be converted into an entomology lab. The only drawback was that it shared an adjoining wall with another home, but the couple was used to close-quarters living back home in Ukraine and Boris viewed it as helpful to better know his neighbors.

An all-cash offer was made and accepted the next day with the closing date scheduled two weeks out.

After that unfaithful afternoon on Damon's yacht, Olga couldn't stop thinking about the billionaire tycoon; his thoughtfulness and generosity displayed the minute she stepped off the military plane, his confident yet chivalrous presence, and of course, his unbridled passion in the bedroom. Judging from the flurry of text messages from Damon that ensued over the last few days, she was assured Damon was equally rapt. Olga had always been able to bewitch any red-blooded man she chose, confident her beauty would elicit their subservience, but to captivate such a brutally handsome and impossibly rich man left her unsure as to her next move, especially in light of her marital status.

Over the next two weeks, while Boris was out interviewing for professorships with universities and colleges, Olga brushed off her inconvenient marriage vows and fostered her secret love affair with the billionaire hotelier. Though Damon had never ventured into secret affairs with married women, he took great strides in ensuring their privacy, directing his inner circle of personal assistants to exercise prudence when planning their dates.

Although they were able to keep their scandalous affair secret from her unsuspecting husband, Damon was the first to profess his unyielding desire for Olga and his hope that she would leave her husband soon. As they strolled along a pristine strip of private beach at sunset, side by side, Damon turned to Olga. Gazing intently into her pale-blue eyes, he avowed:

"Olga, I'm crazy about you. I can't stop thinking about you, about us. Don't get me wrong, I'll always cherish the special time we've had thus far, but I long for the day we can come out of hiding. There are so many adventures waiting for us, so much life to live. I want to share it with you, in the open, and free from this shroud of secrecy"

A rush of euphoria washed over Olga as she replied with a radiant smile, "Oh Damon! You've made me so happy. I feel the same way. If I could leave my husband tomorrow, I would, but it's just too soon. I must make a plan in order for us to have a fresh start."

"Then, Let's make a plan!" Damon exhorted.

"No, I must do this alone," Olga said coldly, her joyous demeanor giving way to melancholy.

Sensing her vulnerability, Damon said in a comforting tone, "I understand Olga, just know I'm here for you and for us." Then, he leaned in and gave her a gentle kiss on her forehead.

Unbeknownst to Damon, Olga had already been racking her brain as to her next move. She missed her period a week ago and confirmed by drugstore kit that she was with child. Olga was overjoyed at the prospect of sharing a child with her billionaire boyfriend, but she couldn't ignore the possibility that it could just as likely be Boris's child she was carrying. Her original plan was to file for divorce soon after establishing residency in six months' time, avoiding the need to disclose the extra-marital affair; but with a baby growing inside her, that plan was rendered moot. She had to come up with 'Plan B' before her pregnancy became evident.

Damon would probably agree to take a paternity test, but would he still feel the same way about her if the child was proven to be Boris's, she wondered? Naturally, she couldn't ask Boris to submit to the test unless she revealed her adulterous affair with Damon. Olga prayed for an answer to her self-inflicted quagmire, then she cried about how life had a way of pulling the rug out from under her feet at every turn, about how life had dealt her another shitty hand.

Her prayers fell on deaf ears, but her cries woke an unspeakable evil in the dark, hellish pit of human depravity...

CHAPTER TEN – A DARK PRINCE

Just as the brilliance of light defined the shadows of darkness, salvation defined the damned. Either light or darkness can blind those who cast aside humility in fervent pursuit of earthly passions. Blinded by darkness, Olga chose to side with the damned. Her indulgent cries for intervention in a dramatized injustice triggered a dark seed sown in every man's heart. Like a persistent echo reverberating through the caverns of hell, Olga's desperate calls sweetly beckoned a slumbering prince.

Travelling at the speed of darkness, Beelzebub hovered over his beautiful foot soldier who was eager to do his bidding. In the bedroom of their new home Boris was sleeping soundly next to a restless Olga when an inaudible voice whispered:

"Look at him! A disgusting excuse of a man, laying there like a gangly rat. Nothing about this creature is deemed worthy of breath, much less your loyalty. He doesn't appreciate your sacrifice. What man leaves his beautiful wife for the comfort of flies?! And now, when his precious swarm of flies is gone, he expects you to bear his child. What audacity! Just start over? Without acknowledging your needs?

You have a chance to finally realize your dreams, what you were always meant to have, a strong man, a rich man, a man worthy of your essence. Damon is ready, now, to make you his one and only, to share his world with you. Sure, you can wait six months to divorce him, but do you think Damon would patiently wait for you? I doubt it.

The only thing standing in your way is this clueless man-child whom the world would never miss. Take what is rightfully yours! Send him back to his maker for some much-needed upgrades."

In the dead of night, Olga slinked out of bed and sneaked into their spacious walk-in closet. Closing the door behind her, she flicked on the lights. A wicked smirk registered on her face when she glimpsed the brown satchel lying by Boris's wardrobe. Still entranced by idyllic visions conjured by the Prince of Devils, Olga pulled out a poison filled syringe and needle from the leather bag and slid it into her pajama pant pocket. Tiptoeing across their bedroom floor towards her husband, Olga glided like the Grim Reaper to Boris's side, her heart galloping with excitement.

With a trembling hand she raised the poison dart to deliver the deadly toxin to her husband's backside, when he abruptly flipped over, adjusting his sleeping position. Still half asleep, Boris glimpsed the outline of his wife standing over him in the dim glow of a nightlight.

"Honey? What are you doing up?" he asked groggily. Then he sat up on the side of the bed rubbing his eyes.

"I can't sleep, I heard some strange noises in the attic," she replied, quickly returning the poison syringe to her pant pocket.

Before Boris could address Olga's concern, a burning sensation on his neck prompted him to rush to the bathroom and flick on the lights to investigate. Standing before the vanity mirror, he noticed that the gash he suffered from shaving five weeks ago festered, showing signs of infection. He winced in pain as he probed the wound with his index finger; then, he loosely affixed a bandage over it, resolving to seek medical treatment in the morning.

Realizing he had unintentionally put off his wife's concern, he hollered from the bathroom "It's probably nothing honey, a new house always makes strange noises. Go back to bed."

"I think there's a rat up there," Olga added.

"Good Girl…" Beelzebub whispered to his obedient foot soldier. Then suddenly, a faint sound of scampering claws scratching against a wooden surface emanated from the ceiling.

Like a good husband, Boris made his way to their walk-in closet where the attic access door lurked in a corner of the ceiling. The springs of the fold-down ladder moaned a warning of impending doom as Boris pulled on a dangling string attached to the access door. A shirtless Boris in boxer shorts started his ascent to the darkened room above, eager to placate his wife's feigned anxiety. When he stepped up on the second rung, he turned and gave his pretty wife a boyish grin and uttered:

"Isn't this great? We are exploring our new house in America."

Olga acknowledged his enthusiasm with a placid smile and said, "I want to see too."

As Boris turned his gaze to the dark opening above, Olga's docile demeanor evaporated, her face now wore a maniacal grin. She crept up following closely behind Boris, ascending each step with malevolent intent. Olga pulled the poison dart from her pant pocket once again as Boris stepped on the tenth rung of the twelve-rung ladder.

Unaware of his vulnerability, Boris reached up into the darkness for a faintly visible light switch affixed to a truss overhead.

In a split second, Olga thrusted the needle into Boris's right calf and squeezed the plunger, emptying the barrel full of liquid death into her unsuspecting husband. Startled by the jab, he scampered up the last two rungs of the ladder in a natural flight response.

A bolt of pain surged up his leg as he stood on the attic floor. Swiftly stooping down and twisting around to investigate, his eyes widened in terror at the harrowing sight of the empty syringe dangling from his calf. A horrified shriek rang out from Boris when he realized the heinous act of his attacker.

With his body now convulsing wildly from the toxins coursing through his veins, Boris peered down from the still darkened attic in disbelief, his heart aching from the sting of betrayal. But, instead of Olga, he beheld a ghastly demon with fiery red eyes and a pair of spiney webbed wings clinging to the fold-down ladder. Succumbing to the powerful synthetic poison, Boris toppled over with a thundering crash and laid shuddering on the attic floor, his eyes rolled back in his head.

Olga woke the next morning to the melodic call of a red cardinal perched on their bedroom windowsill outside. Coming to from a night of restful sleep, she suddenly felt a familiar dampness in her loins. Throwing off the covers, Olga confirmed her intuition that her period had come in the middle of the night as she glimpsed the blood-stained sheets beneath her.

She looked over next to her and found Boris's side of the bed curiously vacant. Taking the opportune time to avoid embarrassment, she quickly bound to her feet, removed the covers from the bed, and made her way to the bathroom to clean herself up.

Devoid of any inkling of the brutality inflicted on Boris the night before, she stood under a warm shower wondering where her husband was. Since it was a Saturday morning, Olga speculated that he must have walked down to the local bagel shop to pick up some breakfast for them.

As the soothing water washed over her, she thanked God for answering her prayers for his intervention into her pregnancy. Although she would have loved to have Damon's baby, she resigned herself to God's timing; then, Olga reasoned that this was a sign that she was still in God's good graces despite her infidelity. She went one step further to posit that just maybe she and Damon were always meant to be together, unwitting to the fact that her illusionary pregnancy was the Devil's ruse.

After her lengthy shower, Olga was puzzled about why Boris had not returned. She wandered around their single-story house calling out for her husband unaware he laid poisoned in their attic.

Boris's eyelids suddenly flung open as panicked gasps of stale musty air filled his lungs. Lying on his back, his head snapped nervously from one side to the other searching for even one photon of light in the pitch-dark attic. Instinctively, he willed his limbs to move, to flee, but they lay paralyzed and heavy on the attic floor. Boris inhaled deeply through his nose in an attempt to steady his nerves but was instantly confronted by the foul odor of decaying flesh, likely emanating from a dead rat, decomposing in the darkness. He tried to call out for Olga, but to his utter shock, only air and bodily fluids ejected from his wide-open mouth, covering his face with dampness. Overcome by his inability to speak, Boris questioned: *Am I still alive? Why am I still alive? How long have I been up here?* His mind waffled between his nightmarish state of existence and the strange demonic creature he glimpsed clinging to the ladder some time ago. Boris realized that this was worse than death, that this was a limbo yet to be adjudicated by a greater force.

Suddenly, a strange luminescent glow dismissed the maddening darkness, bringing a much-welcome reprieve to his living nightmare. The trusses of the roof were now faintly visible, along with open boxes of holiday decorations strewn across the attic. The light green shade of luminescence reminded Boris of the cheap glow sticks his father used to buy him for Christmas as a child. A strange nostalgia washed over him, transporting him back in time to fond memories of his youth and joyful times spent with extended family back in the Ukraine.

As the glow grew brighter, Boris felt a sudden tickle spread across the base of his neck, interrupting his nostalgia. Gripped by the eerie sensation, he hastily pressed his chin against his neck, straining his eyes to investigate the source.

Another whiff of stifling stench assaulted his nostrils when he glimpsed a vile glowing creature crawling over his eyelashes. His eyes widened in terror as the plump maggot which had been feasting on living tissue fell on the cornea of his eye.

Boris's mouth fell agape, and bursts of air and fluids erupted in place of screams. He shook his head violently, dislodging the unwelcome guest, as tears welled up in his eyes and streamed down his cheeks.

"What's the matter? Maggots got your tongue?" Beelzebub teased, then let out a hair-raising chortle.

Petrified by a diabolical presence, Boris fearfully squeezed his eyelids shut and began to recite the Book of Psalm in his mind.

The Lord is my shepherd; I shall not want...

"Liar! You do want. Want is the very essence of your being," the demon chided.

"Look at me!" the demon commanded.

Boris's eyes were forced open by supernatural force, and he beheld Beelzebub's grotesque face hovering inches over his now wide-open eyes. He shuddered with fear at the ghastly sight. Crimson pockmark sores and fluid oozing boils brimmed his goat-like face, contrasting two bulging eyes that were pupil-less and black as coal. Jagged, fang-like teeth flashed under his wicked grin, while long spiral horns jutted unapologetically from his hairless skull, a testament to centuries of underworld rule.

Oh... God! Please, Boris begged for his life in trembling thought.

"He's busy, you know, working mysteriously…or shall I say, remotely…Hahahahaha… Besides, I'm much better looking – don't you think?" the demon jeered.

Sensing his demon form to be too jarring for mortal eyes, Beelzebub transformed himself to resemble a personal injury lawyer dressed in suit and tie. He sat down on a tall wooden stool next to Boris and repeated his rhetorical question, "Don't you think?"

What do you want from me? Boris pleaded inside.

"Well now, that's a bit rich coming from a man who's begging for his life while maggots feast on his rotting flesh. They've already devoured your vocal cords, who knows what they'll go after next" Beelzebub mocked.

Please, let me die, I beg you!

"And squander all the work I've done on these magnificent creatures?" an incredulous look registered on the devil's face.

"Oh, Right, you think it was Bartosh the arrogant midget who created them. You're all the same insolent little pricks who want to play God" the demon admonished.

"I gave that temperamental dwarf a chance to play your role, but he didn't have instincts like you, Boris. In fact, he was so dejected by my decision, he dove off a thirty-foot platform into an empty pool! Who said midgets were afraid of heights!?...Hahahaha."

My role? Boris wondered aloud to the demon.

"We have work to do Boris. Don't you want to save your country from the marauders to the east? You didn't think they would stop at Crimea, did you?"

Beelzebub conjured the depraved images of war before Boris's eyes, executing his centuries old ruse with masterful malevolence.

Columns of heavily armed soldiers as far as the eye can see marched ominously towards his hometown. Their faces were etched with self-righteous determination and devoid of any deference for the sanctity of human life. Boris felt the deafening blasts of guided missiles as they found their mark on utility plants and hospitals, so called prohibited targets of the Geneva Convention. Plumes of jet-black smoke billowed as churches and schoolyards were set ablaze by airborne munitions and a cacophony of rifle fire and agonized cries hung in the polluted air.

Boris gasped. Rocked to his core by the indiscriminate destruction of his childhood haven, tears streamed down his face and his head shuddered in revulsion. But Beelzebub was not done tormenting his recruit.

The cloud of war settled on the scorched landscape revealing the desecrated bodies of innocent civilians strewn mangled and contorted along the roadsides. As the demon brought the images into focus, Boris blinked away his tears struggling to train his eyes on the image of an elderly woman laying on a sidewalk. Gasps of air were met with violent sprays of saliva and mucus as he cried out for his closest aunt who lay dead amongst the carnage.

After what seemed an eternity to compose himself, sorrow and despair were replaced by anger and an unquenchable thirst for vengeance. Boris's eyes became bloodshot with uncontrollable rage and the army of maggots crawling on his neck and face began to glow bright red.

A delighted smile crept across Beelzebub's face as he stared proudly at the glowing maggots.

"Easy Boris, they sense your anger. They are not ready...and neither are you."

Implicit in their new-found partnership, an enraged Boris lay obediently in the dark attic while the devil continued his work on the willing foot soldier. Embellished visions of betrayal committed against the Ukrainian scientist spanning ten years were manifested by the wily devil.

Wesley Walker was complicit with General Valarie in commissioning phase three of the project, feigning ignorance of the ultimate goal of weaponizing the flies and even sharing in the hefty sum of stolen research money. Valarie and Denys Boyko arranged his first marriage to Natalie who was a high-priced prostitute. Valarie and Boyko were on a yacht anchored off the coast of Barbuda enjoying the millions in absconded research funds.

With each distorted vision tethered to an ounce of truth, Beelzebub masterfully wove a web of deceit that ensnared the naïve scientist.

In the final act of his elaborate ruse, Beelzebub could not embellish the vision of Olga's betrayal to include poisoning Boris. Boris had seen his ghastly form clinging to the attic ladder before keeling over. So, the Prince of Darkness, having no inkling about the power of love and sacred vows, apathetically revealed Olga's affair with Damon, hoping to add fuel to the fire.

Instead, the vision cut Boris to pieces. Rivers of tears flowed from his eyes as he was gripped by heartbreak. He turned inward with introspection, examining each interaction, each argument, each act of kindness throughout their seven-year marriage, searching for clues that could have led to her infidelity. *Had he unwittingly hurt her in some way? Was he too harsh when working out their differences? Did he not show her love and tenderness like he should have? Most importantly, how could he win back her love?* These questions burned more brightly than the anger he felt from the previous visions conjured by the slippery devil.

Boris was still very much in love with his wife and getting out of the attic was now top of mind. Having nothing left to lose, Boris declared,

I will do your bidding.

CHAPTER ELEVEN – A NEW YOU

Flashing Blue lights on top of a police cruiser illuminated an otherwise dark intersection of a quiet suburb within the city limits. It was a mundane Monday night as detective Jeremy Epstein pulled up next to the parked cruiser in a black SUV. Stepping out of the vehicle, he glanced back at the street sign on the corner of 5th and 138th, then apathetically rolled his eyes while muttering under his breath,

"One freakin' street over and it would have been the County's problem, now I got to deal with this bullshit call."

Detective Epstein would have been in a better mood if he hadn't been served divorce papers over the weekend by his estranged wife. He actually loved his job. A veteran in the force since 1999, he was nearing retirement before his wife of thirty years had finally had enough and moved out a year ago. Jeremy was a workaholic, never there for the kids, working odd hours, weekends, and even holidays without City pay if the case captured his dogged determination. If she could have held out just one more year, he would have retired, and they could have had another twenty-five golden years together without the stresses of police life. But there was too much damage done, too much water that had passed under that bridge. There was no sense in retiring now;

there was nothing to come home to, except regret and self-loathing.

Probational officer Gomez stood over a sobbing elderly woman. The grieving lady knelt next to a furry animal lying lifeless in the front yard of her duplex. Her neighbors, a middle-aged couple, stood next to the policeman giving their statements to account for their neighbor's misfortune.

As Jeremy approached the scene, the officer walked up to meet him, giving them some space for privacy.

"Good evening, Officer...Gomez," the detective greeted, noticing the officer's name patch on his uniform.

"Hi detective, I was expecting detective Jordan, isn't this his shift?"

"Yeah, well, he got called away, so I'm filling in for him," Peering over the young officer's shoulder, he continued, "I don't normally get called for pet fatalities, so, what's up?"

"This one's pretty gory sir; Mrs. Jenkins and her neighbors suspect torture."

Jeremy walked past the young officer towards the kneeling woman and her neighbors who were standing over the golden doodle. He had investigated numerous cases of animal cruelty in his career and was surprised to glimpse from afar that the carcass was still intact. *Your typical sadistic animal hater would have severed a limb or two, or even a head for shock effect,* he thought.

When he approached the despondent woman, her sobs grew louder, sorrow was now mixed with a tinge of anger. She suddenly stood up and faced the approaching detective. In an angry sobbing voice, she demanded,

"I want the son of a bitch who did this brought to justice!"

"Okay Mrs. Jenkins, let's just take a minute to calm down so we can collect all the facts as to what happened, Okay?" As the woman settled down a bit, the detective politely asked, "May I take a look?"

Jeremy pulled out his flashlight after the distraught lady cleared the path to her deceased dog. A strong biting odor emanated from the carcass as he moved in for closer inspection. It reminded him of the scent of hydrochloric acid he used to handle in his first job as a pool maintenance tech. As the beam of the flashlight crept across the still-warm carcass, it abruptly stopped and lingered over a softball-sized hole in the abdomen of the animal. It was devoid of any bowels or organs. The neighboring couple cringed at the grisly spectacle now made clearly visible by the detective's flashlight and the wife snapped her head away in revulsion.

Undaunted, Jeremy knelt down for a closer examination of the fatal wound, looking for clues that might reveal the instrument used to perpetrate this cruel and senseless act. To his surprise, the edges of the gaping hole appeared smooth instead of cut with a sharp instrument, suggesting it was made by something caustic. Judging from the sour biting smell of acid, perhaps even coming from within the animal.

"Who do you think would have wanted to hurt your dog Mrs. Jenkins?" the detective asked while straining his eyes to peer into the hollowed-out shell of what was once her loyal companion.

"I don't know. The Ukrainian lady on that side vacated her unit a couple of months ago. I think her husband left to go back to the Ukraine. Tom and Jane here live on this side, and I just don't know anyone who would do such a horrible thing!" she replied with a shaky voice.

"People on this block love Teddy, he was the friendliest dog in the neighborhood" the lady continued sobbing as she spoke.

"I let him out the back door in the evenings to do his business in the back yard, and he usually comes right back in, but tonight, he must have wandered into the front yard."

"We heard him barking for just a minute, then he was yelping like he was in pain. He was really loud; it sounded like he was really scared," her neighbor Tom spoke up.

"When we rushed outside to see what was going on, Teddy was already gone," Jane offered.

The detective stood up and walked around the carcass towards the head of the animal. As he trained the beam of the flashlight on the dog's head, the elderly woman screamed,

"Oh my God! What kind of sick person would do this?!"

The eyes and tongue of the animal were starkly absent as the carcass stared vacantly back at Jeremy. He could see right through the dog's eye sockets, revealing a hollowed-out skull. Instead of *'what person?'* Jeremy was leaning towards *'what animal'* could have done this with such precision? No animal he had ever come across could have killed with such speed and stealth, leaving no bite marks or signs of trauma on its victim. Though the use of acid to bore through fur and skin cast some doubt about the veracity of an animal predator. But then Jeremy thought: *Even if the killer were some crazed taxidermist on the loose, he would have claimed his trophy rather than leave evidence for the authorities to find.* The detective was befuddled.

He took some photos and jotted down some obligatory notes on his pad. After promising the woman a follow-up call, he climbed into his SUV and created a reminder on his cell phone to file a report with the Wildlife Commission in the morning. *This was a good distraction from the morass that was his personal life,* he thought. He picked up his pen and notepad again and wrote down the name and phone number of the agent on the for-rent sign prominently displayed in Boris and Olga's front yard before driving off into the night.

Boris felt a surge of energy as each succulent morsel of the golden doodle's bowels was consumed by an army of flies. Unbeknownst to the innocent mortal, Beelzebub created a symbiotic existence between him and the voracious flies. Boris's flesh served as sustenance to new maggot hatchlings, and in return, the wicked flies provided rejuvenation and energy to their host with each feeding. Boris's unconditional agreement to serve the devil was now irrevocable and an exchange of power was implicit. Beelzebub reclaimed his throne as Lord of the flies while Boris had become a vessel for breeding chaos, death, and destruction.

By the dark art of demon hands, a swarm 80,000 strong lurked in the attic of the suburban duplex, coming out each night to feed indiscriminately on animal flesh. With each meal, Boris's human form gradually melded with dipteran form, cementing his ungodly alliance with Beelzebub.

Boris's eyes became pupil-less and glowed an eerie copper hue. Visual stimuli outside the dark attic filled his corneal receptors as they were fed by the sight of each and every fly. His brain grew to understand the signals transmitted by 80,000 spies and Boris felt omnipotent from the new-found power.

His face and neck grew an unruly, grizzly-like beard almost covering his entire mouth. The gash on his neck remained open and invited new members, yet to come.

The same spiky thorns that adorn the assassin fly's legs now sprouted three inches long from his limbs, while the soft flesh of his shoulders and chest hardened into battle armor befitting a dark knight.

His abdominal region was transformed, becoming sectional with a metallic green glow and his muscles became wiry with brutish strength.

The final metamorphosis revealed itself in a pair of iridescent wings that would carry Boris to the edges of the world to seek retribution for the injustices carried out against him.

Though he was not yet strong enough to take flight, Boris continued to hone his powerful vision as the flies gave him an aerial perspective beyond his wildest imagination. Like the tendrils of overgrown vines, the synapses of his brain reached out telekinetically to send and receive signals from his growing swarm; they were now one mind, one body, and one consciousness.

In an expression of triumphant resolve, Boris let out an otherworldly roar by way of 80,000 vibrating wings that shook the trusses of the roof, announcing his impending arrival in the world.

CHAPTER TWELVE – THE ARRIVAL

Over the next two weeks, the emergency line of the Fort Lauderdale Police Department rang incessantly. Though the calls did not amount to actual emergencies, they trumpeted the presence of a stealthy animal slayer lurking amongst the general population. Speculation as to the identity of the perpetrator ran rampant and wide-ranging as images of disemboweled dogs, cats, pigs, and cattle were broadcast across television screens. Some pundits suggested a new strain of virus akin to bird flu may have arrived from Europe, while others believed this to be the work of a depraved soul. Mexican migrant farm workers from neighboring farms claimed this to be the M.O. of the fabled chupacabra, sending panic across the city and neighboring communities. Local news stations cautioned residents to mind their pets and livestock, while the Mayor and Police Chief portrayed an image of calm, adeptly hiding their angst.

Detective Jeremy Epstein picked up his cell phone and dialed the number of the agent renting Olga's duplex. He noticed that the agent was affiliated with Blackwell Residential Brokerage, a division of Blackwell Resorts and Spa, piquing his interest as to why such a large and prestigious brokerage would be dealing with a residence worth less than two million dollars.

A haughty English voice answered the call, "Yes, this is Anna."

"Ms. Mayweather, this is detective Epstein of the Fort Lauderdale Police Department, may I ask you a few questions about the duplex for rent on 138th street?"

"Yes, let me direct you to our website where you can find all the dimensions of the rooms. However, I must caution you, I have an application already in the queue, so you'll have to make haste. Do you have pen and paper ready?"

"I'm sorry I wasn't clear with my question. I'm interested in the owners of the unit."

An awkward pause followed. Before Jeremy could ask his question, Anna interrupted, "Detective Epstein, was it? I must decline your request based on our privacy policy. Of course, if you had a warrant for your request, I would gladly comply. Good day Sir," Click.

Annoyed by the curt response, Jeremy hung up wondering why the agent was so secretive. He had already learned from the tax rolls that the home belonged to Boris and Olga Shevchenko; what he wanted to know was why the couple moved out so soon after buying the home. When he visited the agency's website, the rental-listing included furniture as part of the amenities which supported Mrs. Jenkin's statement that Boris had left the country abruptly. The detective decided to circle back to the Shevchenko's later as an image of a disemboweled horse flashed across his computer screen.

Ashley and Shane were ecstatic when they heard from the listing agent that their rental application had been approved. It was Halloween eve, and the couple had driven the U-Haul truck 16 hours from Nashville to Fort Lauderdale just so they could celebrate the unofficial holiday in Florida this year. Ashley loved the spectacle of five-year-olds parading through the neighborhood, knocking on doors in their cute little costumes with expectant smiles on their faces. In fact, the couple had dubbed it their favorite holiday ever since they found out they couldn't have children of their own.

Ashley made certain the animatronic ghouls and inflatable Halloween decorations were loaded on the truck last, so she could easily access them when they arrived and get right to work in the front yard, leaving the more mundane tasks to her husband. The young couple arrived at the duplex just before dark. Shane ordered pizza to be delivered while Ashley eagerly unloaded boxes of Halloween decorations and began setting up.

As the door to their duplex swung open, Boris sensed the presence of warm blood when Shane staggered in hoisting a heavy storage box full of dishes. He sent a fly out of the roof vent to spy on the intruders, hoping it was another failed showing. He had seen the for-rent sign in the front yard when the flies ventured out each night to feed, and over the last couple of weeks there had been a handful of looky-loos.

Images of the moving truck and young woman staging his front lawn with strange decorations pinged his optic nerve. Boris panicked at the realization that his home had actually been rented this time. He had been confined in his attic by Beelzebub's spell for months, accepting whatever demonic transformation befell him; but now, he was unnerved by his newfound independence. Although Boris knew his faithful swarm was now an inseparable extension of his body and mind, he hadn't had the opportunity to examine his new form in the light. Was he now to just climb down from his dark lair, introduce himself, and walk out the front door in his boxers? Beelzebub didn't leave him any instruction manuals for his new physical enhancements.

I'm not ready, I have to do something... Boris thought.

Ashley stood proudly in the front yard admiring the dramatic lighting that highlighted her eclectic trio of animatronic werewolf, zombie, and bogeyman. After four hours of zealous effort, she was ready to thoroughly impress the Halloween spirit on the little ones she had yet to meet, hoping to ensure their return each year to the most ghoulish house on the block. It was well into the night before the pizza delivery driver showed up, three hours late. The tantalizing smell of an extra-large pepperoni pizza wafted past as the delivery driver hustled to the front door, mindful of his tardiness. Ashley glanced over and saw Shane answer the door, then went about collecting the excess decorations in boxes to be stored another year.

Like a remote-controlled drone, Boris directed his spy fly to follow the scent of the pizza inside. As the buzzing sound of wings whizzed past Shane, an annoyed expression settled on his face. After hours of organizing and setting up their kitchen, he now had to deal with an unwelcome guest insistent on a share of his pepperoni pie.

Ashley walked in, clunking the door with her box of unused decorations.

"Hey honey, shut the door behind you, the bugs are out tonight," Shane cautioned, then went about looking for a fly swatter.

"Welcome to Florida!" his wife teased "Where's the pizza? I'm starving!" she hollered.

As Ashley set the box of decorations on the floor, a flash of vibrant colors caught her eye when she glimpsed the deadly insect cut through the air. She trained her eyes on the pesky devil as it landed on a corner of the pizza box that sat on the coffee table in the living room. Momentarily entranced by its beautiful colors, she inched towards the fly, careful not to scare it away with any sudden movements. Ashley had never seen such an intriguing color combination on an insect before.

As she got closer, she reached for her cell phone snugly held in the back pocket of her jeans and got down on her hands and knees. Creeping ever closer to the fly, she raised her device and snapped two photos in succession before the fly took off again reflecting pink and purple hues off its iridescent wings.

"Gotcha!" she declared with a satisfying smile, then sat down on the sofa to enjoy a slice of pie while searching the image on the internet. Curiously, the A.I. enhanced search engine returned with "species unknown" and "hybrid."

As the fly circled around surveying the living room, Boris's angst became palpable at the sight of storage boxes scattered about his home. Out of the corner of his eye, Boris caught a glimpse of Shane standing over him brandishing an oversized fly swatter, as his messenger fly rested on a storage box.

A blinding bolt of pain erupted in the cortex of his brain as the swatter found its mark, smashing the devilish creature to smithereens.

"AAAHHH!" An anguished cry shook the rafters, startling the couple.

"GET OUT!" An ominous demand followed.

The voice sounded animatronic, akin to the voices of the ghouls Ashley had just finished setting up on the front lawn; except, there was a whirring quality to it, like someone speaking from behind a giant turbine with a megaphone.

Boris meant for his words to be a warning to the unwitting couple as he could hardly control the rage building within him. The swarm hummed like angry wasps in the attic, launching their bodies into the wooden trusses, creating divots resembling errant hammer strikes.

"What was that?!" Shane blurted, curiously looking up at the ceiling, then over at his wife.

A skeptical smirk settled on Ashley's face as she admonished, "C'mon Shane, cut it out. Do you think I don't know all your little Halloween tricks? You startled me, I'll give you that."

Ashley stood up from the couch and started walking over to her husband making kissy noises with her puckered lips, acknowledging his endearing prank.

Shane lifted the fly swatter and repeated the motion on the lifeless blob plastered on the storage box…nothing.

With an unsettled expression on his face, Shane declared with a trembling voice, "It's not a trick, I swear."

"GET OUT!" The whirring voice ordered a second time.

Ashley reached her hand out, expectantly groping Shane's pants pockets, "Where it it?!" she demanded.

"Where's what?" Shane replied, still looking unsettled.

"The remote control to the sound machine you planted, duh?!" Ashley offered, followed by an incredulous eye roll.

"I…I didn't. I swear."

A smug smile registered on Ashley's face as she indulged in Shane's obvious invitation to a game of find the ghost, "OK, is he up there…in the scary attic?" she said in a cute and mildly condescending tone.

She started to wander around the unfamiliar house looking up towards the ceiling in search of an access door to the attic.

Shrugging off his baseless fear of the supernatural, Shane followed his gleeful wife as her enthusiasm rubbed off on him. *It was a perfectly legitimate hypothesis,* he thought; *considering it was Halloween eve, someone must be pulling a prank on them. Maybe the real estate agent planted a housewarming gift in the attic.* In fact, Shane was now certain it was the real estate agent, having shared with her his wife's love of Halloween.

While the unwary couple wound their way around the house to find the attic door inside Olga's spacious walk-in closet, Boris was engrossed in a judicial debate. Charged with sentencing a guilty verdict handed down by his loyal swarm, he had to decide the fate of the murderous couple. Though it was Shane who committed the heinous act, Ashley was guilty by her indifference.

A shadow of his former self reasoned that the despicable act was plainly indiscriminate, emblematic of humankind's intolerance of the Dipteran order, rather than a targeted attack against him or his swarm. Such circumstances only called for a good scare and expulsion from his house. But Beelzebub's demonic flies overruled Boris, and assumed the tyrannical role of judge, jury, and executioner.

Ashley yanked on the cord dangling from the access door with Shane by her side.

Before Boris could give the unsuspecting couple a final warning to flee, the ravenous flies billowed out of the half-open door like soot from a chimney and descended upon the wide-eyed couple who were too petrified to scream. Boris watched in horror, peering down through the cracked opening in the attic. Covered by a shroud of stinging insects, the unlucky couple started convulsing from the effects of the powerful neurotoxin coursing through their veins. It was a helpless feeling Boris knew all too well from his own poisoning at the hands of the demon a mere three months ago.

In a poignant moment of impending doom, the happily married couple reached for each other, engaged in a trembling embrace, then crumpled to the floor succumbing to their seizures in deafening silence.

Borris mouthed a terrified scream, but the flies could not mimic his expression as they were too busy devouring the couple's flesh from the inside out.

With each bite of human flesh, Boris felt a strange energy, a hidden wickedness, pulsating from within. Unbeknownst to Boris, his initiation into the netherworld was now complete, giving him the power to pursue Beelzebub's unholy agenda.

Having been thoroughly satiated by the bounty of human flesh, the diabolical creatures returned to their master still standing in the attic. Boris flared out his long wings running the length of his torso so that the swarm could take refuge on the entirety of his back. Saddled with the weight of his swarm and unsure about his flying ability, he cautiously climbed down from his lair.

As Boris stood there in the spacious closet reorienting himself after months in the dark, a kaleidoscope of images and colors invaded his visual senses. Ignoring the bloody and disemboweled corpses laying on the floor, he moved closer to a mirrored wall opposite the dead couple. His ghastly image appeared in octagonal windows that took a few seconds to decipher. It did not take long for Boris to realize that he now had the visual perspective of a fly, as his orange, pupil-less eyes stared back at him in multiple mirrored windows.

His gaze drifted downwards, and he saw that the gash on his neck festered, hosting a dozen or so maggots soon to become new members of the swarm. When he reached up his hand to feel his unruly beard, his eyes widened at the sight of spiney, three-inch thorns all over his arms. Trembling in front of the mirror, Boris inspected the rest of his transformed body in revulsion, realizing that he had made a deal with the devil without scrutinizing the fine print. A self-loathing tear traced down his bristly beard as he mourned the death of his human form. He was a monster by all accounts…forever a foot soldier in Beelzebub's underworld army.

CHAPTER THIRTEEN – THE DEPARTURE

Between the harrowing spectacle of Shane and Ashley's demise and his clear expulsion from humanity, Boris lost track of time. Twenty-four hours had passed when he detected the sweet scent of chocolate candy permeating the night air; it was Halloween night. Boris sent a handful of spy flies out into the neighborhoods to investigate the festive noises coming through the drafty windows of his house and the origin of the sweet scent.

Meanwhile, his stomach rumbled with hunger pangs he hadn't felt for months. Boris shambled towards the pepperoni pizza, still acclimating to the uncanny signals of his dipteran eyes. After three bites, he casually tossed the half-eaten slice back in the box, uninspired by its flavor.

As he shuffled towards the refrigerator, a tantalizing aroma snuck its way through the seals of the refrigerator door and pinged Boris's hyper-sensitive nose. When he flung open the door, the unmistakable scent of Ukrainian borscht flooded his nostrils. A large metal pot covered with a glass lid was the only item occupying the tidy fridge, suggesting Olga must have forgotten it was there when she vacated the house. Or perhaps she intended for her husband to find it there upon his anticipated return, he fancied.

It was his favorite dish from his homeland and Olga's family recipe called for chunks of pork belly that made the sour soup irresistible. Boris removed the metal pot from the fridge and placed it on the kitchen counter. He lifted the lid to find an overgrown layer of fuzzy, greenish-white mold covering the surface of the coagulated soup.

While his human instincts would have recoiled at the disgusting sight, his dipteran instincts took over. Standing over the pot, he dug his hand into the rotten soup. As his wiry hand broke the seal created by the fuzzy mold, a putrid odor filled the air, and he started salivating in anticipation. Eagerly, he grabbed handful after handful of rancid meat and vegetables, and shoved it into his hungry mouth, alternating hands to keep up with his voracious appetite. When nearly all the gelatinous mixture was gone, Boris lifted the metal pot to his mouth, gulping down the last few drops of spoiled broth.

After he was done gorging himself with spoiled borscht, a strange but satisfying calm replaced the wicked energy he felt when his flies were consuming human flesh. Boris was initially surprised that not a single fly resting beneath his wings vied for a share of the spoiled soup; after all, they did have some genetic traits of the common house fly. After some added thought, his scientific mind posited that the endorphins released by his brain must have been telepathically shared with his swarm, and quite possibly, even the nutritional value of soup was extended as well, rendering their participation in the feast unnecessary.

It was an epiphany Boris welcomed with great relief; a way to keep the devil flies from indiscriminately killing, a perfectly symmetrical symbiotic relationship.

As his crew of spies flew under a moonlit night, caressed by the gentle South Florida sea breezes, images of tiny tots dressed in curious costumes came into view. Though his country did not celebrate the unofficial holiday, Boris was somewhat familiar with the quirky nuances of the tradition, as it had taken root in some European countries that neighbored his homeland.

Elaborate Halloween decorations rivaling the ones Ashley set up on his front lawn registered on Boris's optic nerve. One of the flies landed on the front porch of an upscale home. Boris saw a row of cars lining the street outside the residence while hearing bass ladened dance music boom from loudspeakers within. Out of curiosity, Boris telepathically directed his spy to follow a couple impeccably dressed as vampires inside the spacious home.

Flashes of strobing, multi-colored stage lights reflected off a throng of lively dancers moving rhythmically over a makeshift dance floor. The partygoers' costumes were well conceived and form fitting, suggesting custom tailoring reserved for the affluent. Boris was surprised by the zealous participation of adults in a celebration traditionally reserved for childhood folly.

Laughter and banter reverberated through the halls as guests celebrated eye-pleasing and unsightly costumes alike. Only the wait staff who bore trays of hors d'oeuvres and fancy drinks were not outfitted with costumes, allowing guests to easily spot them for more refreshments.

The jubilant sights and sounds made Boris lament his former membership in humanity, but he quickly snapped out of his defeatism, remembering the reasons he chose allegiance to Beelzebub. If he was to fulfil his destiny, he would need to seize his only opportunity to walk out of his house incognito.

The doorbell of the suburban duplex chimed. Emboldened by the spirit of Halloween, Boris decided to answer the door. He stared at the gangly teenager standing at his doorstep with his orange compound eyes. The boy had a lame tablecloth cape affixed around his neck and the letter "S" sloppily drawn on his dingy t-shirt. He extended a pillowcase bulging with Halloween candy while training his eyes down the street at his next planned stop, not noticing Boris standing before him in dipteran form.

"Trick or Treat, man," the teenager blurted in a sardonic tone, still turned away.

Boris stood patiently, curious as to the boy's reaction to his dipteran form.

As the stoner-kid turned to face Boris, his bloodshot eyes grew wide with excitement, "Whoa...that costume is sick bra, are those real maggots?!"

"No, what do you want?" Boris replied by the wings of his swarm on his back, vibrating his thick Ukrainian accent.

Momentarily stunned by the megaphonic quality of Boris's voice, the teen's mouth fell open, "Oh, dude...does that costume come with a sound machine?" The teen questioned.

Boris stood silent, unsure how to respond to the pesky kid.

"Bra, those spikes on your arms and legs are wicked man!" The teen cheered, giving Boris a once-over.

"Why do you call me 'Bra'?" Boris asked.

"Oh, that's short for 'Bradda' man...you must not be from 'round here. Can I have some candy?"

A friendly smile settled on the boy's face as he raised the open pillowcase towards Boris, releasing an irresistible aroma of chocolate and confectionery.

With lightning speed, Boris snatched the sack of candy from the teen and dug his wiry hand inside. The jagged thorns on his arm tore through the pillowcase and candy poured out of the opening.

"Aww, that's rude man!" The teenager admonished, looking incredulously at Boris.

Before the boy could say another word, Boris grabbed a handful of candy and stuffed them in his mouth without bothering to unwrap them. As he began to chew, popping noise emanated from his mouth as the seal of the candy wrappers gave way to his bite.

The teenager's eyes grew wide again, this time in terror, realizing that this was not normal human behavior. He quicky turned about-face and scampered down the street, haunted by Boris's mischievous and eerie laughter echoing in the background.

Feeling more confident with human interaction, Boris dropped the pillowcase of candy on the doorstep and walked away from the life he knew. He flared out his wings and took off into the night, flying east towards his homeland.

Detective Jeremy Epstein's cellphone buzzed against the hard surface of his nightstand. He was half-way to La-la Land when the annoying clatter woke him from only two hours of sleep. The red numbers on his cheap alarm clock registered twelve am, when he mashed the green button on his phone.

"This better be good" he warned the caller on the other end.

Thirty minutes later, Jeremy pulled up to the driveway of the Shevchenko residence in his SUV. Flashing blue lights from two police cruisers and a forensics van lit up the block as concerned residents milled about the perimeter of the taped-off crime scene.

Officer Gomez was taking statements from the lanky teenager by the couples' moving truck when the detective walked up.

"Detective Epstein, we meet again" Gomez greeted.

"Yes, Officer Gomez, right? What's the current situation?"

Officer Gomez led Jeremy towards the front door away from the teen. "We searched the perimeter of the house, doors and windows, no signs of forced entry. Whoever, or whatever did this was already inside" the officer began.

"What's the estimated time of death?" Jeremy asked.

"Ten pm the night before. Neighbors say they saw the couple decorating the front yard around seven pm. Poor people just got here from Nashville." Officer Gomez advised somberly, then continued, "We secured the scene but we're not sure how much of it was disturbed by the kid. He said the suspect was in some kind of elaborate fly costume…Oh, and he had a deep cut on his neck with maggots crawling around the cut."

"Did you say maggots?" Jeremy questioned.

"Yeah, maggots. He said the suspect had a Russian accent too, like he's heard in old James Bond movies. The fly guy snatched his sack of candy, left the door open and disappeared. So, he came back for his candy."

"And that's when he saw the bodies?"

"Well, the candy was on the doorstep, but he went inside to check out the bad smell and that's when he found the bodies in the closet. He's pretty shook up."

"Any other eyewitnesses?"

"No, but I gotta warn you before you go in, it's the same way all these animals are dying out here. We got a real sicko on our hands."

As Jeremy entered the duplex, the smell of rotten borscht mixed with blood hung in the air. The forensics team equipped with masks and latex gloves treaded lightly about the house

- 134 -

intently searching for clues. Jeremy glanced over at an officer securing a cellphone in an evidence bag, then took out his handkerchief to shield himself from the assaulting stench. As he rounded some storage boxes on his way to the master bedroom, he steeled himself for a grisly spectacle before entering the threshold of the walk-in closet.

What he saw sent shivers down his spine. The desecrated bodies of the innocent couple greeted him with empty eye sockets and wide-open tongueless mouths, as if they were demanding justice for their horrific demise. Jeremy felt an intense vulnerability that turned his stomach, causing an involuntary gag reflex. After a minute composing himself, he pulled out a flashlight and his phone and began collecting photo evidence of his own. The same softball-sized hole in each of the victims, coupled with the stark absence of bowels, coincided with the macabre series of animal killings he'd seen over the last few weeks.

Detective Epstein stood up from his crouched position when he noticed the unfolded access ladder next to the two corpses. He shined his LED flashlight up into the attic, taking note of its capacious quality. Rung by rung, the detective climbed, intent on solving the grisly murders. As his head entered the upper chamber, the pungent smell of urine and feces smothered his nostrils, nearly knocking him off his perch. He quickly waved his light across the attic floor confirming no one was lurking, then climbed down still grimacing from the unpleasant experience.

Jeremy was a veteran of the force and jumping to conclusions wasn't in his DNA; but after perusing the half-completed physical evidence list at the scene, he was confident that the killer would be brought before justice.

It was three am before Epstein left the crime scene. As he hopped into his SUV, he couldn't help wondering about the enigmatic couple from the Ukraine. *Why did they come here? What caused their separation? Where did he go?*

CHAPTER FOURTEEN – THE BIG BREAK

When Damon learned of the double homicide inside Olga's duplex, he became deeply concerned about the public scrutiny he was sure would follow.

Only recently, the couple emerged from the stigma of infidelity when Boris inexplicably left his wife in the middle of the night. Since then, they worked hard crafting a suitable narrative for family, friends, and the general public. The billionaire's publicist made sure the newspapers and tabloids were keenly aware of the couple's fairytale union, allowing them unfettered appearances at high society parties and events.

Now, this appalling development threatened the status quo and could be somehow linked to his live-in girlfriend, whose background he neglected to investigate. Damon knew from experience that any hearsay would make good fodder for the tabloids, potentially marring his sterling reputation and the Blackwell brand as well. To that end, he directed every employee by company-wide memo to avoid engaging with the press about his relationship with Olga, attaching hefty sanctions for any violation.

Olga was a train wreck when detective Jeremy Epstein called her down to the station for questioning. Having been in the United States not even a year, she didn't know what to expect from a foreign justice system. Fortunately, Damon had predicted the police department's call, and after a thorough vetting of the facts with Olga, he sent his high-powered attorney with her down to the station.

Alan Grayson and Olga arrived at the City of Fort Lauderdale police station at nine am on a Tuesday morning. Richly dressed in the height of fashion, Olga drew the attention of a few male officers with the clacking noise of her high heels. Detective Epstein greeted the duo and led them to a private meeting room away from wandering eyes. With her $2,000-dollar-an-hour counsel seated next to her, Olga exuded an eagerness to fully cooperate with the investigation. But Jeremy knew from the stern look on Grayson's face, her statements would be thoroughly sanitized.

"Thank you for coming down to the station Mrs. Shevchenko and thank you as well, Mr. Grayson. I apologize for the short notice." Jeremy began.

"Detective" Grayson acknowledged him with a confident nod, while noticing a voice recorder sitting on the table.

"Please, call me Olga" She replied.

"Ok, may I record our conversation today, Olga?" Jeremy asked.

"Absolutely not, detective." Alan responded for Olga.

"Ok, we'll do it your way." Jeremy quipped.

"When was the last time you spoke to your husband, Olga?" the detective asked.

"The night before he left me…about four months ago." Olga replied nervously.

"I see, I'm sorry to hear that. Do you recall the conversation?"

"Yes, he was excited about an interview with a local college he had the next day. So, we talked about the position and, also, about buying a car. The next morning, he was gone, and I haven't spoken to him since."

"So, you don't know where he is?" Jeremy asked in puzzlement.

"No."

"Did you go looking for him or report him missing? Aren't you worried about your husband?" Jeremy questioned.

Before Olga could reply, the cagey attorney interrupted, "Don't answer that," he said coldly without looking up from his phone.

Sensing he hit a nerve with the last question, Jeremy adjusted his line of questioning, "Did Mr. Shevchenko take any personal effects when he left?"

A pensive expression settled on Olga's face as she thought about the detective's questions, and about her missing husband for the first time in months. *Where had he gone and why hadn't he called? Had he really left her and gone back to the Ukraine, like she told her neighbors? Or was that a convenient supposition she conjured to mollify her infidelity?* Olga stared blankly at her ring finger where her wedding band was starkly absent as an air of consternation hung over her head.

"Olga…Mrs. Shevchenko?" Jeremy gently raised his voice to regain her attention.

"No, he didn't. I had the moving company store his personal belongings in a storage unit down the street." Olga answered.

Jeremy jotted down a note about the storage unit, then continued, "Did you know Ashley and Shane Henderson?"

"No…I mean, not personally, only from the news broadcast and my realtor. They signed a seven-month lease."

Taking a moment, the detective pulled out two photographs of the disemboweled victims from an evidence bag and slid them towards Olga while keeping his eyes trained on her.

"Olga, can you please take a look at these pictures and confirm you don't recognize the couple?"

Olga reluctantly reached across the table and pulled the photos in for closer inspection. As she glanced at the disturbing images of their mutilated bodies, she recoiled in horror, turning away from the ghastly photos. Alan also caught a glimpse of the unsightly images, prompting him to rise from his seat. Placing a large palm over the five by seven photographs, he firmly slid them back towards Jeremy.

"Detective Epstein are we done here?!" the attorney rebuked.

Having confirmed Olga's non-involvement by her startled reaction to the images, Jeremy struck a more conciliatory tone, "I apologize for the gory pictures, Olga. I should have given you an advance warning. We're almost done."

Jeremy reached into the evidence bag once again; this time, he pulled out a large needle-tipped syringe and placed it on the table. Olga's eyes widened like the proverbial deer in the headlights, catching the attention of the two men.

Before the detective could ask, Olga blurted, "Where did you get that?"

"We found it in the attic, Olga…Empty." Jeremy paused to study her reaction.

"That's not possible." she muttered.

The same pensive expression moments ago returned to Olga's face as she struggled to recall that fateful night before her husband's disappearance. Wading through a thick fog of confusion, the frightening face of a cackling demon suddenly appeared, followed by images of her ascending the fold down ladder to the attic, and culminating in her dastardly act of betrayal against her husband. Olga's face turned ghost white, and her head shook in a rhythm of vehement denial.

"No…no, no, no, no…" She bounded from her seat, "I've got to go…we need to go!" and turned towards the door.

Befuddled by her reaction, Alan Grayson rose from his chair and left a business card on the table. "My client has given her statement and now wishes to exercise her fifth amendment rights, goodbye Mr. Epstein," he declared and followed Olga out of the private office.

After the driver dropped Olga home at the B-Well Resort and Residences, Alan picked up his phone and dialed his boss from inside the limousine. Damon was late for a meeting when his cell phone rang. Nonetheless, he picked up when he recognized Alan's number flash across the screen, eager for an update about the meeting down at the station.

"I've only got a few minutes Alan, just give me the Cliff Notes," Damon quipped.

Alan briefed his boss by first assuring him that Olga didn't appear to be connected to the grisly murders of Shane and Ashley

Henderson. He then relayed detective Epstein's notion that Boris was somehow involved.

To which Damon replied incredulously, "How could he be? Olga told me he went back home."

Reluctant to get into a he-said, she-said, debate with his employer, Alan avoided the pointed question. Instead, he recounted the rest of the awkward interview with the persistent detective, including the abrupt ending, highlighting the needle tipped syringe found in the attic, and Olga's strange reaction when asked about it.

"So, where do you think Boris went? Do you think he's still alive?" Damon pressed Alan for the answer to the million-dollar question.

Reticent about his personal suspicion, Alan responded judiciously, "Well, I don't know Damon. What I suspect is that Olga is now a person of interest in her husband's disappearance."

Since Olga had been forthright during their on-line dates about her marital woes, Damon didn't see a need to pry at the time. But now, he wondered about his new lover's mysterious relationship with her estranged husband. Damon never imagined her capable of harming anyone, but her lack of concern for Boris's whereabouts gave him pause.

Perhaps her lack of concern for her soon-to-be ex-husband stems from the excitement of their own burgeoning love story. Or, maybe Boris, having planned to commit such a heinous crime, purposely told his wife he was leaving the country to throw off the police, he thought. Damon mollified his anxiety for the moment and set out to make his business appointment.

Olga poured herself a stiff drink inside the penthouse unit of the seaside residence. The B-Well Resort and Residences also housed fee simple ownership units on its upper floors, and Damon naturally owned the most desirable unit encompassing the entire twenty-fifth floor. She had moved into Damon's bachelor pad only four months ago after Boris had mysteriously disappeared.

During that time, the newly minted couple relished in their newfound freedom. They traveled to exotic locales around the world by private jet and super yacht, enjoying the lavish lifestyle of a billionaire power couple. Damon adored his beautiful Ukrainian companion, wearing her proudly around his arm at high society parties and events, and Olga was finally content having attained the fairytale life she dreamt of as a little girl.

But now, these senseless murders threatened to upend her new life, and Olga desperately wanted to bury the proverbial skeletons in her closet. The skeletons she was acutely made aware of at the police station when she glimpsed the gory murder scene photos, and the empty syringe found in her attic.

Though she flashed back to that fateful night of her husband's disappearance during her questioning at the police station, Olga did not fully trust her recollection of her murderous act. *Besides, if she had actually poisoned her husband, where was his body? Surely, he would not have survived the deadly neurotoxin. And what about the horrific photos the detective insisted Olga see?* If Boris really had something to do with the murders, then he wouldn't be dead at all.

Olga felt somewhat exonerated from her wicked act but could not shake the haunting feeling that if Boris was capable of murder, he would surely return to exact his revenge.

The property manager led the detective through the climate-controlled building, arriving at an orange metal door secured by a flimsy padlock. As the metal roller door clattered on its way up, Jeremy peered into the dark five-by-ten space. He noticed boxes neatly arranged, creating a narrow path into a cardboard maze.

"She's all yours," the attendant said nonchalantly, then left Jeremy to execute the search warrant obtained the day after his brief meeting with Olga and her attorney.

After fifteen minutes of rummaging through unlabeled boxes, he noticed a pile of clothes still bearing hangers piled atop a section of boxes towards the back of the unit. The beam of his flashlight meandered about the pile until it revealed a small handle plainly poking out. Jeremy wound his way around the maze of boxes and excavated Boris's brown leather satchel from underneath his clothes. As the detective gazed into the satchel with his flashlight clenched between his teeth, two syringes identical to the one found in the attic of Olga's duplex lay inside; but this time, they were filled with a milky white substance.

"Bingo," Jeremy muttered under his breath, then placed the satchel inside a large black evidence bag.

Back at the station, the detective sat staring blankly at a stack of papers on his desk. The cover page of the stack cautioned in bold red letters: TOP SECRET – UNITED STATES ARMY – SECURITY CLEARANCE REQUIRED. Jeremy had sent the two syringes to the crime lab for finger printing and chemical analysis, but he purposely withheld the remaining contents of the bag. Well aware of the department's protocol for handling classified documents, he was equally aware of and loathed the litany of red tape needed to view them. Emboldened by his tenure on the force and his apathy of potential sanctions, Jeremy turned over the cover page and began an odyssey into the world of entomology, genetic engineering, and statistics.

Boris's notes were mostly handwritten in Ukrainian, rendering them indecipherable, but his drawings and diagrams combined with Wesley Walker's notes revealed an appalling abuse of science, and quite possibly the missing link to the double murder.

Jeremy opened the top drawer of his desk and pulled out a photo of the enigmatic fly that was extracted from Ashley's cell phone and placed it next to one of Boris's drawings.

"Son of a bitch!" He exclaimed.

"What did you call me?" The police chief quipped, poking his head through the cracked door of Jeremy's office. Jeremy glanced up from the top-secret documents strewn across his desk to find Chief Randall Grady standing at the threshold of his office door. In his eagerness to read the forbidden documents, he had neglected to lock the door. There was no chance of hiding his indiscretion now, only the hope that the chief would act with leniency.

"Sorry chief, that wasn't meant for you...Uh, can I get a minute with you?" Jeremy replied.

"Looks like you're knee deep into it now. I hope your search warrant on the Henderson case bore fruit; the press is all over our asses!" The chief declared as he walked towards the disorganized desk.

"What the hell? Epstein!" Chief Grady bawled as he noticed the classified markings all over the documents.

Perturbed by the detective's disregard for department protocol, he went on a 15-minute tirade. Jeremy quietly received the scolding with the deference due to his superior and good friend. The two men were an unlikely paring of North and South. Jeremy Epstein was a New York Jew from the Bronx while Randall Grady grew up in the rural town of Yeehaw Junction, Florida. Over the years the two men worked elbow to elbow as partners, solving criminal cases with ardent resolve. Although Jeremy wound up separated and on the brink of divorce, Randall climbed the department ranks, ascending to the pinnacle of his law enforcement career in the same twenty years. The two officers had occasionally taken unconventional liberties with department protocols over the years, but now, with the stark contrast in rank, Randall could not condone Jeremy's blatant violation.

After his boss quieted down, Jeremy got up from behind his desk and walked over to his office door. He poked his head out, spooking the usual nosey eavesdroppers who quickly went back about their business. After gently closing the door, the chief started in on him again.

"Now the Feds will be all over us too!" Grady yelled.

Allowing another minute for his former partner to calm down, Jeremy calmly declared, "We got our man."

The two men spent the next few hours poring over the classified documents, using language translation apps on their phones to decipher Boris's notes. After corroborating the treasure trove of information with evidence obtained from the crime scene, they both came to the same conclusion. The Shevchenko's were undoubtedly linked to the gruesome murders and the string of animal killings over the last four weeks, and they needed Wesley Walker's help to bring the Ukrainian couple to justice.

Realizing that lab results would require a few weeks to obtain, the Chief used his authority and retrieved the satchel and syringes from the evidence hold. He figured Boris's partner would be better suited to providing valuable information about the milky-white substance inside the tube.

After a successful morning of backcountry fishing in the pristine waters of Pensacola Bay, the retired colonel was eager to get home to clean his catch. Wes had just pulled his flats boat up onto the trailer attached to his SUV when Jeremy Epstein approached. The detective was smartly dressed in a pair of khaki pants and Hawaiian shirt, attempting to blend in with the local crowd; but the freshly pressed clothes bore hard creases that gave the impression that he was trying too hard.

Jeremy pulled out his government ID from his roller bag as he addressed the colonel.

"Colonel Walker? My name is Jeremy Epstein. I'm a detective with the Fort Lauderdale police department. May I have a minute or two with you?"

"Fort Lauderdale! What time did you start driving…one am?" Wesley quipped in his southern accent.

"It was actually around midnight. Your wife told me I could find you here. Please, it's important that I talk to you." Jeremy explained.

"Well, it's more important I get these fish on ice. Hop in, we can talk on the way."

Jeremy left his vehicle in the boat ramp parking lot and got into the SUV. They drove only a mile down the road, arriving at a combination gas station / diner where Wes could ice his catch. After tossing a ten-pound bag of ice over his catch, the strangers found a quiet booth in the back of the diner and settled in.

"What's on your mind detective?" Wes inquired.

Getting right to the point, Jeremy asked, "Do you know one Boris and Olga Shevchenko?"

Wes's friendly demeanor suddenly evaporated, replaced by a look of concern, "Are they OK?"

"Not exactly. We believe they are connected to a recent double homicide in our city."

Before Jeremy could lay out evidence supporting his bold claim, a dreadful suspicion took over the retired colonel. Either Boris or Olga divulged classified details of the terminated project, or a documents leak led the detective to find him, another participant in the abhorrent secret military project. Seeing as the Ukrainian couple were under suspicion for murder, the latter scenario was more the likely. Unaware that the persistent detective held the brown leather satchel in his roller bag, Wes tried to play it off.

"Nah...I don't believe it. They couldn't hurt a fly. You could have just given me a call instead of driving all this way detective." Wes declared, wearing his best poker face.

"Funny you should mention a fly, Colonel Walker." Jeremy countered with a dead serious look.

Sensing that the jig was up, Wes forewarned the detective in a menacing tone, "I hope you haven't done something you're gonna regret, Jeremy. You have no idea what you're dealing with here."

"We haven't done anything yet, which is why I'm here." Jeremy replied respectfully.

For the next hour, Jeremy shared in great detail the gruesome murder of Shane and Ashley Henderson, as well as the similar fates of dozens of pets and livestock around the city. Photographs of the murdered couple bore the same markings of dead animals spread out over a wide area, suggesting that the killer was indiscriminate and opportunistic. Wes had seen the voracious flies devour prey in a laboratory setting before, but the macabre images of the dead couple sent chills down his spine. He grappled with the thought that Boris would betray his trust after all his efforts to help them forge a better life in this country.

After sharing the photographs and eyewitness accounts, Jeremy pulled out the brown leather satchel from his roller bag and nonchalantly tossed it on top of the table. Then reached inside the satchel and pulled out a stack of classified documents along with two syringes filled with a milky-white substance.

"I really don't know what these documents mean, I'm rusty on my Ukrainian, and those two syringes, I'm sure they're related to these documents somehow," the detective declared in his opening salvo.

Not surprised, Wes said coldly, "Son, do you know the penalties for unauthorized handling of top-secret documents? You could lose your badge."

"Right now, I'm more concerned about losing more innocent lives." Jeremy rebuked.

The detective's words resonated with an ominous possibility. A possibility the now mortified colonel had buried deep in the recesses of his mind, tucked away from his conscience. Now forced to deal with the consequences of his indiscretion and greed, Wes felt remorseful. If he could have walked out of that meeting with the SSU when Boris tried to leave, maybe the innocent couple would be alive today. Maybe the world would not have to deal with another abomination of science. As much as Wes wanted to dismiss the gravity of the situation, he knew he had to collaborate with Jeremy to eradicate the flies.

"Where's Boris? Can I speak with him?" Wes blurted in an anxious tone.

"I was hoping you could tell me; you were his partner on the project, weren't you?" Jeremy countered curiously.

"You don't understand, this project was terminated. Boris was responsible for destroying the flies. I haven't spoken to him in months." Wes explained.

- 149 -

After swearing Jeremy to secrecy, Wes revealed the aims of the ill-intended project, the methods by which the flies were fed, and the unscrupulous people involved. For the next half hour, Jeremy sat in shock as he listened to Wes from across the table.

Since the colonel came clean, Jeremy reciprocated in kind, sharing with Wes the details of his interview with Olga, the empty syringe found in her attic, and the stoner kid's strange encounter with the man in the elaborate fly costume.

"Hold on, did you say maggots?" Wes asked.

"Yeah, I don't know if the kid was telling the truth or if he was stoned out of his mind, but he was really shook up" Jeremy confirmed.

A pensive expression registered on the colonel's face, "He's not lying."

"What? C'mon, it was a great costume is all." The detective dismissed the colonel.

"Have you ever heard of Furuncular myiasis?" Wes continued.

"I can't even spell that. So, no." Jeremy quipped.

"We learned about the ability of maggots to infest live human tissue from my Army training. The condition is common in tropical and sub-tropical climates when soldiers spend days on end in the jungles of Central America." The colonel explained.

"So, you mean to tell me Boris unintentionally brought the flies all the way from Ukraine?" Jeremy asked incredulously.

"It's the only explanation I have." Wes replied pensively.

"Wait till the Chief hears about this. So, what do we do now?" Jeremy questioned.

"We need to finish the job Boris couldn't" Wes concluded, "I'll need time to figure this out. In the meantime, leave his bag and syringes with me. This information must remain confidential."

CHAPTER FIFTEEN – THE NEW PARTNER

A week had passed between the police interview and the search warrant carried out at Olga's storage unit. Olga had expected another request to appear before the authorities, but the police went radio-silent. Even the news stations tapered their coverage of the Henderson murders.

Perhaps they didn't find anything incriminating amongst Boris's belongings. Maybe the movers misplaced the brown leather satchel containing the remaining poison-filled syringes she thought. Even if they had found the satchel, Olga had sworn an oath to her country's government, never to disclose her knowledge of the top-secret project and she intended to uphold her oath.

In the meantime, Damon hired a security team to watch over them, alarmed by the revelation of a killer in their midst. Olga appreciated her boyfriend's concern, but the added precaution only fueled her anxiety as to Boris's mysterious whereabouts and his anticipated return.

She thought of the only way she knew to calm her anxiety, and that was to throw herself back into her profession as a hairdresser. Damon dismissed the idea at first, worried about tarnishing the power couple image they had recently cultivated; but he gave in to his beloved companion's pleading and agreed to compromise. He allowed her to work privately in a newly configured space within the resort salon, and only with overseas clients who were unlikely to recognize her celebrity status.

Olga accepted the restrictions wholeheartedly, grateful for his support. She didn't know exactly where her relationship with Damon would ultimately end up, but she remained hopeful. Hopeful that when they got past this strange series of events, she could finalize her divorce with Boris, and they could become Mr. and Mrs. Damon Blackwell.

Damon and Alan sat patiently waiting in the executive conference room of a modern office tower in downtown Ft. Lauderdale. This would be the second meeting with a joint venture partner on the development of a beachside resort in Singapore.

The first meeting was held between Simon Lim, the patriarch of the Lim real estate empire and James Blackwell, Damon's father. The two real estate moguls were well known to each other over their lengthy careers, partnering on several successful projects on the small island nation.

Although Simon and James had effectively handed the reins to the family business over to their children, the two elderly men insisted on striking the initial deal, relying on their experience and well-honed intuition. If and when they came to general terms, they would leave the final negotiations to their respective deputies. Damon had held that title for some time now, while Simon had only recently bestowed that designation to his daughter Chloe.

Chloe was born with a silver spoon in her mouth and was the youngest among her siblings. She was only a teenager when Damon met her on an overseas business trip with his father shortly after graduating college. She was thin and homely, but assertive and overly confident.

The young Asian girl was instantly captivated by the strapping college graduate, but Damon hardly acknowledged her presence. They never crossed paths again; however, there was the occasional mention of the other by their fathers over the years. Damon and Chloe were unceremoniously kept apprised of key milestones in each other's lives; like when Chloe graduated top of her class, or when Damon was promoted to vice president.

Damon wondered whether Chloe had matured and developed the business acumen to negotiate such a complex deal; after all, she was a spoiled, self-centered teenager when he met her over a decade ago. He did a double take after catching a glimpse of Chloe out of the corner of his eye. Damon was surprised by her graceful appearance as she rounded the corner of the hallway and came into view through the glass partition of the conference room.

Both men stood with smiles on their faces, eager to greet their attractive new business partner. Chloe sauntered in, dressed in a stylish business suit. Her smooth dark hair cascaded softly over her slender shoulders, and her girlish bangs highlighted the subtle features of her beautiful Asian visage. Though her frame was slight, Damon appreciated her svelte figure, which was highlighted by a curvaceous bosom.

Sensing her appeal amongst the two businessmen, Chloe beamed a vivacious smile across the conference table and offered her well-manicured hand for a customary handshake.

"Hello gentlemen" she greeted and took a seat after shaking their hands.

Alan looked out into the hallway of the conference room expectantly and asked, "will your counsel be joining us?"

"Not today, Mr. Grayson. We are still getting to know one another, are we not?" Chloe replied smartly, smiling at the overzealous real estate attorney.

"Of course we are Chloe," Damon interjected, "It's so nice to see you again. The years have been kind to you."

"Thank you, Damon, and you are still as charming as I remembered you to be," Chloe returned.

Damon accepted her compliment as mere pleasantries between business partners, but Chloe spoke with amorous intent.

Chloe had blossomed from the ugly duckling of her teens into the quintessential femme fatale. Her beguiling smile was so much as to make any man crumble at her feet. Coupled with her impeccable timing and wit, she played the field of millionaire playboys like it was going out of style. When she learned about the pending partnership with the princely hotelier from her father, she quickly went to work on her next target. Chloe perused the American tabloids for any gossip or personal tidbits on Damon. She gathered from her research that Damon was already romantically involved with a mysterious Ukrainian woman whose background and history was well-guarded. With their glamorous, red-carpet photos plastered on the front pages of rags, Chloe garnered a good visual of her competition. Undaunted by Olga's stunning beauty, she set out for her next conquest, purposely leaving her attorney out of the meeting to prolong her "negotiations."

"Since we're all here, let's get started" Damon began, "I've prepared a quick presentation for us as a refresher on the project and the terms already agreed to by James and Simon. Alan, can you hit the lights?"

"Just a second Damon, I can't see very well from this vantage point, would you mind if I moved?" Chloe requested coyly.

"Sure thing, Chloe," Damon replied.

As Chloe rose from her seat, both men noticed that her skirt had naturally hiked up her hips, revealing a pair of nicely toned legs. Without a stitch of modesty, the Asian beauty sashayed around the large conference table, pulled up a chair next to Damon and sat down, crossing her tantalizing legs. Alan wore a wide grin, grateful for the gratuitous spectacle while Damon politely averted his eyes while secretly admiring her legs.

"That's better," she declared with a knowing smile.

Damon waded through the first few slides of the well-organized presentation before becoming distracted by the seductive scent of Chloe's perfume. She was sitting so close to him in the darkened conference room that he could almost feel her breath on the side of his face. Damon felt Chloe's glances linger on him every so often after each discussion point, while she hung on his every word, admiring his business savvy.

After the short presentation, Damon was sure he had convinced Chloe that the project would be a home run. But, before he could deliver his final pitch, Chloe lightheartedly suggested they finish their discussions over happy hour cocktails. Since she flew halfway around the world to meet with him, Damon felt it was only proper to accommodate her fancy. Besides, he felt a kinship to Chloe, having each taken the reins of their respective family businesses.

Alan was eager to tag along, figuring Chloe may appreciate his knack for engaging in stimulating conversation. Furthermore, Damon may need to duck out early to be with Olga, and it would be rude to leave a partner, much less a woman, all by herself.

The three suits entered the swanky downtown establishment and bellied up to the bar. It was a busy Friday afternoon as groups of businessmen from nearby offices poured in to celebrate the end of another work week.

"What are you having?" Damon cheerfully asked Chloe as he flagged down the bartender.

"Surprise me!" Chloe playfully returned.

Alan smiled knowingly at his boss, then turned to Chloe, "I wish all of our partners were as agreeable as you," he declared.

Damon whispered his order into the bartender's ear, and she enthusiastically went to fill his order. Knowing his boss was not one to shy away from a challenge, Alan waited giddily for the bartender to return.

The bartender returned hoisting a tray of flaming whiskey shots which elicited child-like anticipatory smiles from the three grown adults.

"A toast, to our new partnership!" Damon declared, as they each blew out the iridescent flame and gulped down the expensive whiskey.

From that drink forward, the evening regressed from a legitimate business meeting to an evening of revelry replete with music and dancing.

The relaxing effects of the alcohol blurred the line between business and pleasure, allowing Damon and Chloe to freely engage in conversation, sharing personal details normally reserved for dates. Details such as favorite movies and types of cuisine were the source of lighthearted banter between the two rich and attractive partners.

Damon and Chloe's friendly exchanges dashed any hope Alan had of engaging with the sexy heiress, making him feel like a third wheel. He was left to entertain himself, ogling single ladies as they passed by the bar while getting totally shitfaced.

As the evening wore on, Damon felt Chloe's lingering glances again, but instead of dismissing her advances like he had in the conference room, he returned her gaze with equal and unflinching intensity. The sexual tension between the two had become palpable, and before long, the bantering and flirting turned into light touching and side-hugs, pushing the boundaries of propriety.

Damon's cell phone chimed a familiar ring tone. It was Olga on the other end of the line. He suddenly remembered he had a dinner date with her at eight pm, leaving him only twenty minutes to get to the restaurant. He didn't bother answering the call; instead, he turned to Chloe.

"I'm afraid we'll need to resume our celebration another time" he said tactfully, then asked, "I trust our time together was fruitful?"

"In more ways than one" Chloe returned sultrily.

"Do you need a ride to your hotel?" he asked.

"You mean your hotel?" she quipped, flashing a smile, "No, think I'll keep an eye on Alan over there. I think he's going to need a friend" she said, glancing over at Alan who was enjoying his fifth scotch on the rocks.

After Damon ducked out of the trendy establishment, Chloe cozied up next to a tipsy Alan at the bar. He was pleasantly surprised that his earlier hope of Damon having to leave early had come true. Now, he would have his chance to charm the exotic foreign beauty sitting next to him.

"I'll have whatever he's drinking" Chloe declared cheerfully to the bartender, exuding her party girl persona.

"I like a woman who's versatile," Alan remarked playfully.

Chloe smiled coyly, then quipped, "Why, how observant of you Alan, I hope you'll find more euphemisms for my many other naughty behaviors."

The newfound drinking buddies erupted in laughter. A woman both beautiful and sharp-witted flirting with me, he thought. Alan could hardly contain his excitement. She was the kind of woman he'd hope to meet someday, and he was certain today was the day.

Alan wasn't physically unattractive by Chloe's standards, but she was not after his affection. She was after information about the mysterious Ukrainian woman in the tabloids; information that might be easily coaxed from her drunken admirer.

Alan was smitten with Chloe and Chloe sensed it. Throughout the evening, she wielded her charm like a finely tuned dog whistle, subtly extracting private details about Damon's relationship with Olga. Whenever Alan threw up a roadblock, she would bat her pretty Asian eyes and order another drink for the two of them to celebrate their new acquaintance.

Although Chloe could not deny Olga's beauty as revealed to her from the photographs in the magazines, she was dumbfounded when Alan told her that they met by chance through an internet dating app. Consoling herself, Chloe reasoned that any man, even one of Damon's wealth and status, could fall victim to fleeting whims, especially if he was couped up long enough by a dreadful pandemic.

It took a few more drinks for Alan to reveal that Olga was still legally married to her estranged husband. To which, Chloe wondered why Damon would choose to have an affair with a married woman? Encouraged by the fact she was better positioned as an eligible bachelorette, Chloe's hopes of getting with Damon grew.

Naturally, Chloe posed the same million-dollar question on everyone's mind; where did Boris go?

With his hopes of an amorous encounter with the sexy brunette impairing his judgement, Alan didn't want to appear uninformed. In his most jurisprudent tone, he embellished, trying not to slur his words.

"The authorities suspect she poisoned her husband and hid his body somewhere."

"Wait, What?!" Chloe became saucer-eyed, "Do you think she did it? Where would she hide a body?"

Frustrated by Chloe's persistent grilling, Alan threw up his hands and replied sarcastically, "I don't know, why don't you ask her yourself? She works in the salon of your hotel."

By the end of the night, Chloe had learned more that she expected to about Olga and how she came to hold the attention of the man she so desired. Alan had practically passed out at the bar before Chloe called him a cab.

Olga was cleaning her hair-cutting shears in the hotel salon. She could have had one of her assistants perform the mundane task, but instead, she opted to clean the tools of her trade herself. Comforted by the daily ritual, she hummed a familiar Ukrainian pop song under her breath while she worked.

It was all part of her effort to gain a sense of purpose and belonging in this new country. In fact, she did everything she used to do at her old job as a hairdresser, except for making the appointments herself. That task she left up to the salon concierge, who qualified her clients based on Damon's strict orders.

Olga wasn't sure she would enjoy serving foreign clientele exclusively at first, but after getting to know the trending hairstyles of varying countries, she gained the versatility and skill to garner raving reviews. She also gained a sense of joy. She assumed an alias to obscure her identity while working in the Salon – Anna.

After cleaning up her workstation, she clicked the icon for the appointment schedule on her computer and saw Chloe Lim's name pop up on the monitor. That name rang a bell with Olga as she recalled the dinner conversation with Damon the night before. She was further informed by Chloe's country of origin that she was indeed Damon's new business partner.

It appeared she was a last-minute entry into the appointment book, having been squeezed between clients just this morning. Olga became nervous about serving Chloe. Even though Chloe was only looking to trim her hair, Olga was made anxious by her status, which probably coincided with lofty expectations.

Damon had spoken highly of Chloe at dinner, highlighting her competency and high business IQ. So, when Chloe showed up at the salon also elegantly put together, Olga felt somewhat intimidated by the five-foot two-inch businesswoman. She put on her flawless public façade and greeted Chloe with a radiant smile.

"Hello Miss Lim, I'm Anna. It's nice to meet you," Olga greeted with a subtle Ukrainian accent.

Anna? Clearly, she's Olga, Chloe thought. Then, flashing a catty smile, she returned, "Yes, likewise," as she sauntered in, surveying the spacious private workspace.

"Please, have a seat so we can discuss how I can help you look fabulous today," Olga followed, pointing to a plush chair in the consultation area.

Chloe sat down and gave Olga's posterior a once-over as she turned to close the partition door for privacy. Olga was dressed comfortably in a form fitting white dress that flattered her tall, slender figure. Her hair was wound neatly in a tight bun on the crown of her head and her toned calves were accentuated by a pair of glittery platform heels. Her face was even more beautiful in person, Chloe secretly bemoaned as Olga turned around and walked towards her. Chloe felt a twinge of envy as she gazed at Olga's radiance.

"You look familiar Anna, where are you from?" Chloe asked, playing along with the charade.

Olga sat in the chair next to Chloe, then replied, "I'm from the Ukraine."

"Now, what is the proper way to say that? Is it 'the' Ukraine or just Ukraine?"

"Either way is correct. I'm old-fashioned, so I still say it the old way." Olga returned with a friendly smile.

Of course, an old-fashioned adulteress who found the pot of gold, Chloe bristled silently within. It wasn't that she felt she was more righteous than Olga, nor did she care what Olga's ulterior motives were; she was simply tweaked by the fact a lowly hairdresser from Ukraine stood in her way of Damon.

The rest of the appointment turned into an awkward cloak and dagger affair with each woman concealing their true identities while unearthing valuable tidbits about the other for future reference. By the end of the appointment, Olga suspected Chloe had been tipped off by someone at the hotel as to her true identity, while Chloe was more determined than ever to wrestle Damon away.

As Chloe exited the salon after her haircut, she noticed an arrangement of business cards offered at the concierge station. She scanned the offering and found Anna's card prominently displayed and picked one up as she left.

CHAPTER SIXTEEN – THE HOMECOMING

The 5,000-mile journey back to his hometown took three days. Boris knew the only refuge for his dipteran form was the secret underground lab he had toiled in for the last ten years. Arriving under the cover of night, he found the heavy metal door leading into the government building secured with a heavy chain and padlock.

Boris snuck around the side of the building searching for the dumbwaiter access. A few pieces of aged wooden boards were clumsily affixed over the opening, allowing Boris's wiry hands to fit through the cracks and pry them free.

The freight platform was lowered to the basement level, thirty feet below ground level. Boris peered down the dark shaft wondering if the mechanism still worked. He found the call button inside the shaft and eagerly pressed it. The gears didn't engage. The power main must be switched off, he thought.

Though he could still manage to see down the dark shaft by the dim glow of a few security lights around the building, his dipteran eyes were severely compromised without ample light. Left without options, Boris summoned his courage and took a leap of faith, fluttering his wings wildly as he descended clumsily down the dumbwaiter shaft.

Boris took a minute to get his bearings as he stepped off the freight platform, feeling his way around the pitch-black room. He felt relieved when the lights came on after he flipped the switch to the power main. The storeroom was neat and tidy, as were the specimen room, the laboratory, and his office. Everything was the same as when he left it a few months ago.

Feeling the lethargy of his swarm, Boris hastened to the specimen room and cranked up the heat and humidity, warming up his corporal extensions. He swung open the door to the caged terrarium, stepped inside, and flared out his wings, allowing the flies to explore their ancestral home amongst the dense foliage. The flies fluttered about the warm humidified air, then took refuge in the leafy trees and surrounding bushes. Boris crumpled to the terrarium floor, exhausted from the transatlantic flight, then fell fast asleep in his new lair.

He woke in the morning next to a few dead flies, casualties of the arduous journey. It had been four days since they last fed on Ashley and Shane, providing them the supernatural energy to fly across the Atlantic. With their energy levels now dangerously low, Boris sent his swarm up the cargo shaft into Fall's chilly air to search for food.

In a wooded patch of the city park, a scurry of squirrels were busy gathering stores of food for the coming winter and the flies took full advantage of their unwary nature, quickly devouring the warm-blooded animals. Within minutes, the flies regained their vitality, as did Boris, through the tendrils of his unique symbiotic form.

With his appetite satiated for the moment, Boris knew he could not rely on the hunting prowess of his swarm much longer. The sub-zero temperatures of the Ukrainian winter were fast approaching, creating an inhospitable environment for cold-blooded insects. Although Beelzebub may have defiled his human appearance, Boris's heart still pulsed warm blood; so, he would naturally become the sole provider in their symbiotic relationship – at least through the winter.

Boris rummaged through his office desk drawers and coat closet searching for accoutrements to dull his harsh appearance. An hour later, he stood in front of a full-length mirror dressed in a long trench coat that came down past his knees. His eyes were covered with a pair of dark sunglasses and a brown Ushanka hat covered the whole of his head. Besides the warm clothes, Boris found a pair of oversized snow boots in the coat closet, and beside the boots he discovered Denys's hidden stash of ultra-fine vodka.

Soon after the swarm returned from their successful hunt, Boris took the freight elevator up to the ground level and stepped out of his new home base with a mission to find food. Though he found some 5,000 Hryvna in a random pocket of his coat, Boris had no intention of buying fresh food from a café; what he sought was the cache of slop tucked back in the alleyways of the finest restaurants in Kiev.

Having patronized all the fine dining establishments near the secret lab over the years, he set out each day to surveil them, dumpster diving opportunistically, but also noting the best day of the week to frequent each one. Soon, Boris had systematically mapped out his route each day of the week to pillage and plunder the slop, keeping the swarm well fed.

After a couple of months acclimating to his new routine, Boris felt a palpable bitterness simmering within. Having suffered decades of deceit at the hands of greedy imposters, he was now ready to deliver retribution to the first charlatan on his list. Becoming a foot soldier for Beelzebub marked the beginning of the end; for Boris, it was the end of his naivety and suffering in that dark attic and for those that aggrieved him, it would be an end befitting their self-serving acts.

Although Beelzebub sprinkled falsity and embellishment over Boris's memories that night in the attic, the demon also supercharged Boris's recollective powers, enabling him to connect random remembrances with scant details. Boris recalled that plane ride home from DEVCOM ten years ago, where careless words were uttered by the drunken General Valarie, Dr. Bartosh, and Denys Boyko. Coupled with Denys's report of her reappearance in the western town, Boris knew where to look for Natalie, the first person on his list. On a cold January day, he gathered a thousand assassin flies in the warm nook of his back and boarded a bus to Lviv dressed in his inconspicuous outfit.

As Boris walked down the city streets lined with quaint shops and cafes, he sent a spy out from under his trench coat into the heated businesses each time he passed one he felt his ex-wife was likely to frequent. They were literally and figuratively his fly on the wall. Soon Boris had covered the whole section of town with his eyes and ears.

Meanwhile, the scent of baked bread and hearty soups permeated the afternoon air, triggering a feeding response too powerful to ignore. Boris snuck into an alleyway behind a well-known café he and Olga liked to frequent and hopped into an open dumpster foraging for food waste.

Boris sat inside the giant metal container chomping on a stale baguette when the familiar tone of Natalie/Kateryna's voice echoed in the alleyway. Boris rose just high enough to peer out of the dumpster and saw his ex-wife walking by hand in hand with an elderly woman graced with white hair.

Natalie carefully guided the unobservant woman around the alleyway corner and into the café. They sat down at a table in the back where it was quiet and where Boris's spy was plainly lying in wait atop a napkin holder.

As Natalie's face came into view, Boris noticed that she had matured gracefully over the decade they had lost. Her long dark hair traced her prominent cheekbones, highlighting her playful dimples as she smiled at the elderly woman across the table. He also noticed the absence of a wedding ring on her finger.

The café was half-empty waiting for the dinner-time crowd, providing a window for Boris to approach his ex-wife. A befuddled look fell on Natalie's face as the tall stranger in dark sunglasses pulled up a chair and sat down at their table.

"Hello Natalie, or do you prefer Kateryna?" Boris greeted, modulating his voice through the buzzing flies on his back as best he could.

Kateryna recoiled in fear of the bearded stranger, then suddenly recognizing the unique character of her ex-husband's voice muttered in puzzlement, "Boris...?"

The old lady placed her hand on Boris's shoulder, then with a disbelieving tone chided, "Kateryna, don't be rude! Your uncle Symon has come to visit us, show him some respect."

"Of course, mama." Kateryna placated her mother then turned her attention to the stranger, "How did you find me? Did Denys send you to find me? What do you want?" she asked nervously.

"Didn't you hear your mother? It's rather rude of you to pepper me with questions when it's you that owes me answers,"

Boris rebuked in an eerily vibrating tone, keeping his eyes trained on Kateryna.

In the three years they were a couple, Kateryna had never seen Boris angry, but she sensed a building tension within him that put her on edge. His menacing words amplified the stark reality of her despicable deceit. She glanced back at her mother and found her staring at a couple two tables away, oblivious to their conversation.

She turned back to Boris and said calmly, "My mother needs to eat, can I get you a cup of coffee?"

Boris sat stoically as Kateryna rose from her chair and walked nervously to the counter. The assassin fly flew stealthily behind her, landing next to the cash register, hiding itself from view.

"I would like a ham and cheese croissant, sparkling water, and two coffees......call the police." she said plainly to the attendant, hiding the panic stirring inside.

The attendant glanced knowingly at Boris, then turned to fill her order.

As those three words transmitted to Boris, the embers of rage he had suppressed for a decade ignited. His muscles tensed uncontrollably, and he felt the frenzied buzzing of the swarm on his back. Boris sprung from his chair and strode over to Kateryna. Before she could turn around, she felt a vice-like grip wrap around her wrist as she was forcefully led out of the café and into the secluded alleyway.

"Please! Please don't hurt me, Boris." She pleaded desperately, as he released his grip on her behind the giant dumpster.

"Like you hurt me!?" Boris rebuked.

"I never meant to hurt you, I never meant to hurt anyone." She offered with tears streaming down her face.

"You're a liar and a whore! You never cared about me, you did it all for money." He retorted, casting his shades aside and staring at her with his orange pupil-less eyes.

"And now, you're going to pay for your greed!"

As an entomologist herself, Kateryna immediately recognized the hallmarks of his dipteran eyes, "Oh my God! Boris...what did they do you?" She cried.

Sensing her sympathy, Boris flung off his hat and trench coat and stood naked in his dipteran form before his ex-wife. His wings suddenly flared out as a swarm of assassin flies hovered, buzzing ominously over his head.

Katerina shrunk back in horror at the sight of his ghastly appearance and the sinister creatures hovering in the air. She grew wide-eyed, covering her mouth in shock, too terrified to scream.

The otherworldly flies flitted about the frigid air forming Boris's pre-dipteran visage over their master's head. The three-dimensional face looked dejected and spoke in a low anguished tone.

"Look what's become of me Natalie, I am a monster. I took on the project so we could have a better life together, so we could raise a family. But now, there is nothing left, no wife, no family, no hope."

Suddenly, his dejected expression transformed into anger, and Boris's voice grew louder and more agitated as he continued.

"I did it for us! You betrayed me Natalie – I will always remember you as Natalie because that's the name you chose to cut my heart out the night you left me!"

Their master's rage threw the demonic flies into a frenzy. They darted menacingly towards Kateryna, feigning attack in random pulses, all the while buzzing ominously with the anticipation of devouring her flesh.

"Wait! Boris, please." Kateryna pleaded, then continued with a trembling voice, "I am not the person you think I am. I am truly ashamed for what I did, and what I said in my letter to you came straight from my heart. I am so sorry for hurting you!"

Kateryna's sincere apology and profound feelings of guilt struck a chord in Boris. Curious as to her reasons for perpetrating such a personal and elaborate scheme, he allowed her to continue.

Kateryna tearfully recounted the plight that led her to her regrettable decision. She revealed that when she was twenty years old, her mother became afflicted with an aggressive form of dementia, prompting her father to abandon the family. Left without the primary bread winner, their financial resources became desperately low. Because she was an attractive graduate student in the field of entomology, the SSU approached her with a top-secret assignment. At first, she rejected the proposal wholeheartedly owing to her conservative upbringing, but as her mother's condition worsened, she reconsidered their offer out of desperation.

In exchange for three years of service, the SSU would provide the supportive care her mother needed and the financial support for Kateryna to continue her education at the university. Denys gave her a new identity and arranged their "chance" meeting at the museum.

Boris listened intently to Kateryna's heartfelt story, crystallizing the cryptic explanations made in her dear john letter some ten years ago.

"If you wish to take my life as payment for my deception, I beg you, take my mother's as well. I cannot leave her in this world alone." Kateryna concluded somberly.

An earthly sympathy washed over Boris as images of her demented mother wandering about the café transmitted from his spy fly still inside. Boris didn't obtain the vengeance he sought; instead, he received closure to a decade-long mystery he had given up all hope of solving.

Without saying a word, he flared out his wings prompting his swarm to return to the nook of his back. As police sirens wailed in the distance, Boris took to the sky and circled the town to collect his spies. When every member of his faithful swarm was accounted for, he flew with the aerial agility of a robber fly back to the secret government lab.

CHAPTER SEVENTEEN – NO ESCAPE

Boris found his collection of music discs sitting on a bookcase in his office. As he browsed through his collection of timeless pieces, he was overcome with nostalgia by that night when he and Olga were serenaded by the swarm. Tears welled up in his eyes as thoughts of her with another man crept into his mind. Why had he been so obtuse when it came to understanding her needs? How could he have missed the telltale signs of her discontent? If he could have kept her happy, she wouldn't have wanted to leave the Ukraine, and they could have raised a family together.

But now, having been thoroughly deceived by the Prince of Darkness, he'd been banished from humanity by his monstrous appearance and left with no hope of ever returning to human form. Boris came to terms that his chances of winning back Olga's love was forever lost, but he still loved her with all his human heart.

Boris moved his boom box and CD collection into the specimen room, curious as to how quickly this generation of flies could learn music. He knelt on one knee, placed a disc in the portable music machine, and played a musical piece expressing his somber mood. George Frideric Handel's "Dead March" filled the cavernous room. Within seconds of pressing play, the enigmatic flies began to mimic the sounds of the different instruments in the classic orchestral piece. Boris stood in awe of the supernatural creatures. It was as if they were perfect reincarnations of their lab-created ancestors, retaining the musical talents of generations past.

As the music got louder, amplified by thousands of pairs of wings, the slow deliberate rhythm of the melancholy song transported Boris back to that fateful night in the attic, the night where his humanity died, where he was duped by the wily devil. Boris wanted desperately to rescind his contract made under duress, and he knew of only one way out.

Boris found a combat knife hanging from a military belt in the office closet. As he unsheathed the seven-inch blade, it rang with a solemn promise. The promise of solace in death. He stood staring into the reflection of the shiny blade, disgusted by the monster staring back.

Boris held the point of the cold steel blade against the underside of his chin and steeled his grip with both hands. With a decisive thrust upwards, he drove the sharp blade deep into his head, aiming for the carotid artery. A few drops of blood trickled down his neck and hands as he held the lethal weapon buried to the hilt against his chin.

Boris's heartrate suddenly slowed to a crawl in an involuntary reaction to the trauma while he felt no pain from the self-inflicted wound. He anxiously pulled the blade out from under his chin and walked over to the full-length mirror hanging on the wall. Boris watched in astonishment as the gaping wound healed itself within seconds, leaving not a trace of trauma on his skin. In a fit of rage, Boris savagely stabbed himself repeatedly in the abdomen, and each time, he was denied the tranquil oasis of death. He sank to the floor and wept, while the Dead March continued to play in his head, mocking the futility of his desperate act.

While General Valarie opted for a warmer climate after absconding with hundreds of millions in project funds, Denys Boyko chose to hide in plain sight, amongst the rich and faceless of Switzerland. Naturally, he dispersed his share of the loot in a multitude of Swiss bank accounts belonging to just as many fake identities; After all, his former SSU colleagues hadn't dubbed him the fixer for his sublime plumbing skills.

When news of Dr. Bartosh's inexplicable demise reached Denys, he promptly applied for and was soundly awarded the leadership position without delay. The powers that be reasoned that the surplus funds remaining from the terminated project were appropriately classified as goodwill between partner nations, and need not be returned, especially if some of that goodwill trickled into their own personal coffers.

With the lofty title of Director of the SSU and millions in his Swiss bank accounts, Denys exuded an air of confidence that attracted a few female recruits eager for career advancement. Even though Denys was a married man, he often crossed the line of casual flirtation, indulging in steamy extramarital affairs with female recruits.

On this particular occasion, he was able to convince Sasha, a recruit who joined the agency six months ago, to enjoy some ultra-fine vodka and career advancement opportunities at the secret underground lab.

After unchaining the heavy metal doors leading into the government building, Denys led the nervous female agent to the hidden elevator and down to the secret lab. The elevator door glided open, welcoming the unsuspecting couple to Boris's new lair.

The ill-fed flies two rooms away detected the scent of humans and darted about the enclosed terrarium in a frenzied state. Alerted by his extra-sensory powers, Boris sent a spy through the cracked doors of the laboratory and into the office to investigate the intruders. Stealthily, his dipteran agent nestled itself in a nook of the bookcase next to two lowball glasses.

The doe-eyed girl's nervousness dissipated upon entering the private office. She glanced around the richly appointed office with an expectant smile, then let her long dark hair fall seductively around her shoulders. Sasha sashayed over to her boss and gave him a gentle peck, leaving a distinctive red lipstick mark on his cheek. Distracted by her beauty, Denys dismissed his surprise that the power to the facility had been left on. He eagerly rooted around the office closet floor until he came across his stash of vodka, then grabbed the lowball glasses from the bookcase, unaware of the dipteran eyes studying him from the shadows.

Boris grew a menacing smile as his unscrupulous former colleague came into view. It was Denys Boyko, "The Fixer" who played the role of callous puppeteer; first, by his indecent proposal to Kateryna in the elaborate ruse, then, creating the misery he endured for years. "Do it for the sake of Country," he and the cowardly General proudly offered, all the while scheming to rob their country blind. He doesn't deserve to live, Boris decided, as his mind raced to concoct an agonizing death befitting the scoundrel.

After Denys poured each glass half full, the sinners sat cozily close to each other on the couch sipping the fine spirit. After a few minutes of small talk, the buxom beauty seductively unbuttoned the top two buttons on her blouse, revealing her deep cleavage.

Suddenly, a sharp note mimicking a violin pierced the air, startling the enchanted couple with their lustful gazes.

"What was that!?" Sasha exclaimed, as the harsh note was followed by an eerie violin solo coming from the specimen room.

Denys sprang into action, pulling his 9-millimeter Glock from its holster. He wedged himself against the wall next to the laboratory room and signaled the young lady to take cover behind him. As Sasha positioned herself quietly behind Denys, the spy fly took its position on her shoulder, hiding underneath her locks of hair. The duo crept into the laboratory room while their heads swiveled nervously from left to right surveying the abandoned room.

Microscopes, glass beakers, and various scientific instruments obstructed his view, prompting Denys to forewarn the would-be intruder.

"I've got a gun! Come out and nobody gets hurt."

The uncanny music grew louder, mocking the two SSU agents.

Denys's frustration grew as he made his way towards the specimen room door with Sasha cowering behind him. When he reached the door to the cavernous room, he peeped through the small window of the door and saw speckles of orange and purple light strangely meandering around the room. Denys's mind raced as he thought about the only people with knowledge of the secret lab; Dr. Bartosh was dead, General Valarie was probably on a yacht somewhere in the Caribbean, and Boris…?

His uneasiness suddenly melted away as a knowing smile replaced his stern expression. He stood up from his crouched position and casually holstered his gun.

Denys turned to Sasha with a wry smile, "It's Boris" he offered, rolling his eyes.

Puzzled by his sudden change in demeanor, "Who's Boris?" she questioned, then also lightened up.

Denys ignored her question, pushed the door open and strolled into the hollow room. Sasha reluctantly followed, while the tempo of the eerie music sped up. Denys immediately recognized the musical piece as The Red Violin Caprices, a haunting violin solo composed to evoke an uneasy mood. He looked up at the thirty-foot ceiling to find the mirrored ball mysteriously spinning, casting haunting hues of purple and orange from the grow lights inside the enclosed terrarium.

"Okay Boris! Show's Over!" Denys shouted over the music, "You got us good, come out and we'll celebrate your return!"

There was no response.

After a few seconds, Denys turned his attention to the dimly lit terrarium and noticed the outline of the boom box sitting on the dirt floor behind the tightly woven mesh.

He turned to Sasha and loudly ordered over the annoying music, "Come on, he's in there. Let's meet my old colleague."

As the unwary couple entered the overgrown landscape, the spring-loaded door to the enclosure slammed shut behind them. Sasha's eyes wandered about curiously, marveling at the elaborate set up.

"What is this place?" she muttered under her breath.

Denys walked over and pressed the stop button on the portable music player, ushering in a much-welcome silence. Annoyed by Boris's silent insistence on prolonging the childish prank, Denys bawled with his newly appointed authority.

"Boris! Stop this nonsense right now and come out!"

Suddenly, goosebumps and raised hairs fell on Sasha's arms as she felt a tickle trace the base of her neck. Before she could address the itch, the stow-away fly that was resting on her shoulder drove its razor-sharp proboscis deep into her neck, delivering a lethal dose of neurotoxins into her bloodstream.

Unexpectedly, the haunting violin solo erupted from the towering trees, this time, much louder and at a feverish tempo.

Startled by the sonic blast, Denys staggered backwards, coming to a halt against the cage. He quickly turned to gauge Sasha's reaction, only to find her shaking uncontrollably with only the whites of her eyes showing and her mouth agape, unable to speak.

"What's wrong? Say something!" He shouted, holding her up by her armpits as her legs grew limp.

Sasha flung her head backwards bucking from the violent convulsions. Her hair flew back, exposing the fiendish creature stuck to her neck. Denys instantly recognized the deadly lab-created fly; he gasped, then released his grip on the young recruit as he foresaw the macabre ending about to ensue.

The loud music abruptly stopped, followed by the thud of Sasha's collapse on the terrarium floor. As she writhed and bucked helplessly in the dirt, Dennis heard the faint rustling of leaves usher in a deafening buzz. The grow lights were suddenly dimmed by a massive cloud of voracious flies hovering overhead.

Triggered by their natural feeding response to Sasha's shuddering body, the voracious flies descended on her with uncanny speed. They quickly covered her body from head to toe, scurrying through the openings of her clothes.

As they tore through her flesh, dissolving a path through to her internal organs with their caustic enzymes, a river of blood oozed from her blood-stained blouse. Her lifeless body twitched erratically, jostled by 80,000 assassin flies vying for a share of her innards.

White with fear, Denys stood frozen, watching as the flies continued their feeding frenzy until Sasha was reduced to a hollowed-out shell.

Realizing his own vulnerability, Denys bolted towards the door. But before he could escape, a shadowy figure leapt down from the tall trees landing in his path with a thunderous thump!

Denys's eyes widened and his mouth fell open as his eyes traced up and down the monster's ghastly form.

Boris's face was wizened and covered with an unruly beard. His pupil-less orange eyes projected an otherworldly glow. His shoulders and chest were covered with a leather-like armored plate, while his abdomen bore a metallic green luster. Jagged spikes jutted out of his arms and legs, and his right hand clasped a shiny seven-inch battle blade.

Reflexively, Denys pulled out his Glock and fired three shots in rapid succession at the dipteran monster.

"BANG! BANG! BANG!"

Boris looked down at his abdomen where he felt the jolts from the penetrating bullets. There was no pain, no blood, only three indentions like those made by fingers on playdough.

"DIE! DIE! DIE!" Denys screamed in desperation, as he emptied his clip in a horrified panic.

Each time, the bullets fell harmlessly to the floor as Boris's supernatural body rejected the bullets' ill intent.

Denys backpedaled, aghast by the indestructible being standing before him brandishing a seven-inch knife.

Boris suddenly flared out his large wings and a swarm of flies formed a three-dimensional image of his pre-dipteran face over his head.

Fearing the same grisly demise that befell Sasha, Denys scampered across the terrarium, ducking branches and hopping over bushes until he reached the far corner of the enclosure. He found a random bush and disappeared behind it, peaking through the foliage.

"Is this any way to treat an old friend Denys?" the eerie face whirred in a strange megaphonic tone.

Terrified by the supernatural spectacle, Denys swore under his breath, "Holy mother of God!." He cowered behind the tall bush, unnerved by the dark forces at play.

"Don't you recognize me? I'm ready to win back our Country...Join me" Boris offered.

Still shaken, Denys summoned his courage and ambled around some bushes towards the fly-like man. He hid his trepidation as best he could and drew on his years of secret service training, hoping to use guile in place of firepower.

Stopping just outside Boris's reach, Denys stammered, "Of, ... Of course, Boris, we never doubted you would be back to serve your Country. I...I sincerely hope there will be no more need to, uh...sacrifice, additional Ukrainian agents, b...b, but I will not question your methods."

Denys paced nervously back and forth, ready to make another run for the door, gauging the unearthly creature's reaction to his initial pitch.

"Sacrifice is a privilege reserved for patriots. Don't you agree?" Boris returned.

"Yes, absolutely! What I meant to say was…that, all the sacrifices we've made have paid off, and our window of opportunity is fast approaching…We have intelligence from our covert operatives inside Belarus that the full-scale attack will occur in thirty days." Denys declared proudly.

Boris appeared to weigh his words, then emoted, "Is that so? Then we have no time to waste!"

A smile crept across Denys's face, pleased his words struck a chord with the ghastly beast. But before Denys could orchestrate his daring escape, Boris moved toward him with otherworldly speed. He seized Denys by his neck with one hand and lifted him off the ground, holding him level with the talking face formed by a swarm of assassin flies. Harrowed by his precarious position, Denys's legs flailed wildly, and his lungs gasped for air. He tried desperately to pry himself free using his hands, but the dipteran creature's wiry hand would not budge.

Boris stared up at the slippery agent whose face was turning blue, while the enigmatic talking face added, "Your country needs you now more than ever."

As if cued by the ominous words, a single fly broke from his eerie hovering visage landing on the base of Denys's neck. Denys felt a sharp sting as the demonic fly delivered a non-lethal dose of neurotoxin through its proboscis.

Boris suddenly released his grip on the poisoned agent, and he fell to the floor like a sack of potatoes. Denys quickly lost control of his limbs as he lay paralyzed on the terrarium floor. A state of delirium crept inside his head, dulling his thoughts and senses. With his eyes still open, he glimpsed a shadowy figure moving over him with a knife. The faint sound of fabric ripping registered on Denys's auditory nerve, followed by the dull sensation of a cold blade dragging across his neck, chest, and abdomen.

Boris made sure there were enough deep cuts on Denys's body to host the next generation of flies, but took care not to sever any major arteries, keeping him alive to endure a long agonizing death. When Boris was finished making the incisions, a swarm of pregnant female flies nestled in Denys's warm living tissue, depositing their eggs in their new human host.

Over the next three days, Denys felt the agony of thousands of maggots infesting his body and feeding voraciously on his flesh as he perished in the obscurity of the underground terrarium.

Boris felt a surge of energy spread throughout the swarm and himself, as if nurtured by mother's milk. His view of humanity was forever distorted by omnipotence and immortality, and wickedness pervaded the whole of his being.

Beelzebub was pleased with his disciple's development, watching from amongst the diabolical swarm. Unbeknownst to Boris, the Prince of Darkness was that single fly that landed on Denys's neck, delivering just the right dose of neurotoxin to set Boris back on track on his vengeance tour.

The wily demon decided it was time to hold tighter reins on his foot soldier when Boris squandered the opportunity to take vengeance on Kateryna / Natalie. Now as an inconspicuous member of the swarm, Beelzebub was well positioned to hold Boris captive to his will.

CHAPTER EIGHTEEN – THE BATTLE

Thousands upon thousands of otherworldly flies emerged from Denys's eviscerated corpse and took refuge among the terrarium landscape. The branches of the trees bowed mightily under the weight of old and new generations alike, while the shrubs brimmed with fluttering wings and prickly legs frenetically buzzing about. Each fly vied for a precious inch of open space in the once capacious environment.

His army was hungry. Boris had timed the hatch of this generation on the intelligence boasted by the now deceased SSU Chief, and it was time to fulfill their destiny. He sent sub-swarms of spies through the dumbwaiter shaft, east to the Donbas region and north to the Belarusian border. The flies transmitted the same images shared by Beelzebub that fateful night in the attic. Columns upon columns of Russian soldiers were marching south towards the capitol. The intelligence was accurate, the full-scale invasion was happening now.

Boris took on the mantle of commander-in-chief, unaware the real lord of the flies laid in wait among the swarm one-million strong. Beelzebub was content to be a bystander in the long-awaited battle, confident Boris's pride for country would culminate in unbridled carnage. Boris was no longer afraid to be called to duty on the front lines, no longer the sickly naïve scientist buried in research. He had become bold, cunning, and powerful, with nothing left to lose.

Led by the dipteran monster, a million assassin flies billowed out of the secret government lab into the cold spring air. As they flew over Kyiv, the massive swarm cast an eerie shadow over the capitol, catching the eyes of nervous onlookers. Sirens wailed as the ominous cloud moved over the populous city alerting soldiers and citizens of a possible attack. People scampered for cover; fearful the invasion had reached the capitol. Ukrainian news crews on the ground captured footage of the strange swarm of flying insects overhead, along with what appeared to be a giant bird amongst them.

It was mid-morning when Boris and his army of flies came across a brigade of 5,000 Ukrainian soldiers. They were traveling on foot and in military vehicles on a wide strip of dirt alongside an ancient forest. The undulating terrain challenged their resolve as they precariously drug heavy artillery over the half-frozen ground. Flanked by a dozen tanks, the convoy moved bravely forward to confront the Russian invaders.

Using his telepathic signals, the dipteran commander ordered his swarm to take cover among the towering trees and overgrown bushes of the old growth forest. Camouflaged by the dense foliage, the dipteran troops moved in lockstep with the Ukrainians just a few feet away. Boris felt a burst of pride as he joined the convoy from high up in the treetops, moving stealthily from tree to tree. This was the culmination of his life's work, and the only worthwhile cause left in his heart.

Suddenly a barrage of missiles whistled past overhead, prompting the soldiers to scamper into the forest to take cover.

Perched atop an ancient oak forty feet in the air, Boris saw plumes of black smoke mushroom in the distance as the deadly projectiles found their mark on random targets. He became enraged by the enemy's brutality and his anger permeated the entire swarm. As the skies were clear again, the soldiers trudged on, moving ever closer to the battlefield.

A husky voice rang out from the formation, signaling arrival at their strategic location. Teams of soldiers took up shovels and began digging ditches around the perimeter of a large swath of land, while officers barked orders mobilizing the remaining troops. Within a few hours, the brigade had fortified their position just thirty kilometers outside a small rural town. It was a small mining town that up until now existed in peaceful obscurity. But not today. Today, it was the next town on the path of Russian conquest, the path to Kyiv.

It was now mid-afternoon. The cold morning gave way to milder temperatures. Temperatures that favored his dipteran troops. Boris knew this was a kamikaze mission for the cold-blooded assassin flies. Many would not survive the precipitous drop in temperature after nightfall, maybe none. He was gripped by the finality of the situation. Without a second to lose, Boris commanded his otherworldly assassins to advance along the dirt path by way of the ancient forest lining its flanks. Using his telepathic powers, Boris stealthily moved his million-fly army towards his objective forty kilometers ahead.

But his message did not reach the entire swarm. Unbeknownst to Boris, there was another field general in their midst, one that was more powerful, more cunning. Beelzebub had cut off the dipteran commander's line to a tenth of his army, commandeering the undying loyalty of a sub-swarm 100,000 strong. After the debacle that spared Natalie/Katerina's life, the Prince of Darkness held back the sub-swarm for insurance, uncertain whether Boris had fully embraced his destiny. Besides, the good soldiers defending their land deserved his protection, the wily devil mused.

Within minutes the dipteran troops reached a hairpin bend in the country road. They came upon a division of Russian soldiers that outnumbered the Ukrainians three-to-one. Boris saw their youthful faces dotting a large clearing surrounded by the forest. Accompanied by killing machines of all shapes and sizes, it was clear his countrymen were outnumbered and outgunned.

The men were enjoying the afternoon sun, lounging about with cell phones in hand and grazing on MREs. Boris could hear their bantering and heartfelt conversations with loved ones over their phones. Unwary of the massive swarm of man-eating assassin flies surrounding their camp, the conscripted soldiers espoused total victory and a quick return home. Some had taken to heavy drinking as empty liquor bottles littered the encampment. Boris relished his moment of opportunity gazing at the undisciplined bunch.

Two conscripts snuck away from their company and lurked along the edges of the nearby woods. They had been drinking all morning, but their fading buzz prompted them to take another swig from the half-empty bottle, away from prying eyes. After a couple of sips, their drunken banter was abruptly interrupted by faint violin music emanating from deep within the woods. Like mice to the pied-piper's flute, the two drunk soldiers stumbled towards the enchanting music. A wicked grin crept across Boris's face as his victims drew near.

Gazing skyward to find the source of the soothing music, their eyes met a dipteran orchestra descending from the treetops like delicate feathers of a bird. The symphony of musical flies fluttered beautifully just over their heads while playing Part I of Vivaldi's Four Seasons with flawless precision.

The young Russian soldier holding the almost empty bottle of vodka raised it to eye-level and stared at the few remaining sips inside. Wondering if it was laced with some kind of hallucinogen, he brought the spout to his mouth to take another sip. But before he could partake in the magic elixir, his companion rudely snatched it away and gulped down the remaining contents of the bottle. The two men stood in awe as they enjoyed the supernatural spectacle.

In the blink of an eye, the music stopped, and the swarm of assassin flies formed a spooky three-dimensional image of Boris's face. In an ominous megaphonic tone, the face shouted:

"ORCS MUST DIE!!!"

Horrified by its angry expression and menacing words, the young soldiers spun around abruptly to escape the ghastly visage, only to impale themselves against the jagged spikes protruding from Boris's outstretched arms. Blood spurted from their necks and their faces turned white with fear as they gazed upon the angry mutant. With a mighty thrust, the dipteran monster flung the two men to the ground.

Clutching their wounds to stem the bleeding, each man broke into a death gurgle as blood obstructed their windpipes, muting their terror-stricken screams. Desperate to get away from the monster, the wounded soldiers began backstroking on the ground with one arm and two flailing legs.

Boris stood before them, cackling triumphantly. He walked over to the flailing soldiers, bent down, and clutched their necks with his large wiry hands. Holding a soldier in each hand, he lifted them off the ground and hoisted them over his head while their legs kicked wildly with fear.

A frenzied buzz began reverberating throughout the ancient forest. It was feeding time. The sunlight streaming through the forest canopy was abruptly dismissed, as the swarm of flesh-eating flies emerged from the foliage, casting an eerie shadow over the men. Like a hard rain, the swarm pelted the Russian soldiers relentlessly, covering them from head to toe.

Still holding the men overhead, Boris stood watching, relishing, tearing up with joy as the flesh melted off the soldiers like wax museum figures left out in the hot sun. Blinded by bloodlust, Boris's wickedness blossomed.

After the two men were reduced to gutted shells clad in bloody uniforms, Bosis fashioned nooses from the thick vines that draped from the ancient oaks and hung the men in effigy from a high branch. Then, he waited.

The sound of a lieutenant's call echoed through the forest. A search party had been assembled to find the missing soldiers; not out of concern for their well-being, but to bring them to reckoning in front of a firing squad for their apparent desertion. Thirty men clutching rifles padded across the forest floor, their heads swiveling intently left and right. Boris was perched high up in the forest canopy waiting expectantly, peeking down at the unsuspecting soldiers. As the lieutenant passed beneath the defiled corpses hanging overhead, the cunning mutant man gingerly dropped a single acorn from the tall tree. It clacked unceremoniously off his Kevlar helmet and landed softly on the forest floor a foot away.

The lieutenant peered skyward, smiling at nature's stroke of serendipity. What he beheld was neither natural nor serendipitous. Fly riddled corpses of the two deserters dangled precariously overhead, staring back at him with empty eye sockets.

"Mother of God!" he muttered. The officer's knees buckled at the ghastly spectacle, as shivers ran down his spine.

Sensing their leader's agitation, the team of soldiers stopped in their tracks and looked up simultaneously. Terror flashed across their faces as expletives flew in the wind. Beads of sweat formed on their brows and their hearts galloped wildly. Itchy fingers caressed the triggers of their rifles as they spun aimlessly about, wary of enemy forces lurking in the woods.

From his hidden vantage point, Boris grinned, then he threw a handful of acorns in the direction of the Russian makeshift camp. The nuts clacked off of woody trunks and rattled the bushes. Restraint was no match against the reflexes of paranoid soldiers, as a cacophony of deafening gunfire erupted from their muzzles. The undisciplined soldiers sprayed bullets in the general direction of the disturbance, holding down the triggers of their rifles in a display of crazed fear.

The die was cast.

While some of the bullets buffeted off trees, a hail of bullets found their way through the thicket, making their mark on idle soldiers lounging about the camp.

Pandemonium broke out as the unlucky were laid to waste and wounded soldiers scurried for cover. Within seconds, the full force of the division returned fire in the direction of the search party. Howitzers, rocket launchers, and tank guns boomed, unleashing deadly projectiles towards the hidden enemy in the woods.

The exploding shells rocked the old growth forest. Hundred-year-old trees toppled like matchsticks as shrapnel tore through their huge trunks. Fiery explosions set the afternoon skies ablaze and plumes of black smoke loitered the forest canopy.

The shelling went on for what seemed like an eternity. The dipteran commander and his troops had long taken refuge in another part of the forest, suffering no casualties in the bombardment. It was grimly opposite for the search party of thirty soldiers. Blown to smithereens, their body parts lay strewn across the charred forest floor, barely recognizable as human remains.

When the dust of battle settled, ten acres of the ancient forest was obliterated while the Russians declared victory against the Ukrainians hiding in the woods. The bodies of unlucky comrades were covertly disposed of in mobile crematoriums, hiding the full cost of imperial ambitions. The commanding officer ordered several soldier companies into the woods to secure the perimeter and to count enemy casualties, still unaware the real enemy lay in wait among the thickets. Boris could see soldiers approaching from all directions through the eyes of his swarm. He estimated their numbers to be three-quarters of the entire division. The others remained at the campsite guarding their equipment. The sun hung low on the horizon as time was running out for the final phase of Boris's battle plan.

Taking advantage of the horseshoe layout of the wooded landscape, Boris moved half of his dipteran troops to the backside of the enemy's camp. His assassins were now perfectly positioned to attack the Russians guarding their equipment. He waited until the smaller group of soldiers were well isolated from the division trekking towards the woods, then, he gave the command. A dark foreboding cloud of ravenous flies floated towards the unwary campers.

More concerned with the prospect of covert enemy forces lurking in the forest before them, they paid no attention to the unholy insects hunting them from behind. Before the conscripts realized their vulnerability, half a million demonic flies enveloped them inside an otherworldly dome of death.

Muzzles flashed with gunfire and bullets riddled the skies as panic-stricken soldiers tried to disperse the massive swarm, but the flies evaded the rounds with uncanny agility. The bullets only agitated the flesh-eating flies; their buzzing became deafening, drowning out the soldiers' voices.

The sound of gunfire erupting in the distance gave the larger group of soldiers pause. They lurched forward into the old growth forest for cover, while turning their heads back towards camp 500 meters away. What they celebrated as a decisive victory moments ago had turned into their worst nightmare. They were faced with the stark reality of being divided and hunted by enemy forces.

As they peered towards the commotion unfolding at the camp, they saw their comrades running for their lives under a strange undulating dome. Though they couldn't confirm the type of weapon the Ukrainians had deployed, the veterans in the group suggested they were incendiary munitions that burned soldiers alive. The young conscripts broke out in tears, sobbing loudly as the brutality of war settled on them.

Trapped under a dome of strange flying insects, some of the soldiers charged towards the wall expecting to break through the pesky swarm. But each time one did, he was met by the sting of powerful neurotoxins that stunned him and sent him convulsing wildly on the ground. The flies descended on the helpless men writhing on the ground, burrowing through the nooks and crannies of their uniforms. As they melted flesh with their caustic enzymes, blood-curdling screams echoed throughout the surrounding forest.

Like a cast net over a school of bait fish, Boris drew the strings taut, and the walls of the death dome crashed in on the terrified soldiers. Within minutes the demonic flies devoured multiple companies of soldiers, leaving each one mutilated and disemboweled under their bloody uniforms. Their defiled bodies laid in pools of crimson while their vacant eyes concealed their unearthly suffering.

After the carnage, Boris commanded his assassins to hide inside the dead corpses. With his bloodlust reaching its peak, he snickered in delight, hidden among the shadowy forest.

After the agonizing screams in the distance subsided, the anxious soldiers emerged from hiding, stunned by the cunning of their Ukrainian enemy. A recovery team was assembled to survey the damage and retrieve the wounded, while the rest of the division clung to the safety of the forest.

Unwary of the swarm of man-eating flies lurking in the corpses, the men approached the campsite with unguarded urgency. Curiosity pervaded the team as they gazed upon unscathed equipment eerily left in place around the grounds. As they got closer, the pungent odor of fresh blood filled the air, prompting the men to cover their noses. Their hopes of rescuing survivors were dashed as they came upon the slaughtered soldiers. There were no signs of life among the mutilated bodies littered about the open area.

The team moved in for a closer inspection. Burn marks appeared all over the soldiers' skin. Some had missing eyeballs and tongues, but save for the blood stains, their uniforms remained curiously unblemished. Clearly their demise was not caused by incendiary weapons, or any modern-day weapons at all for that matter.

Suddenly, the fallen soldiers' bloody uniforms began undulating erratically. Startled by the unnatural spectacle, the soldiers grew saucer-eyed and backpedaled in trepidation. The team of soldiers stood aghast as assassin flies billowed from the lifeless corpses into the afternoon sky. In an instant, the massive swarm organized themselves into a colossal three-dimensional face as large as those found on Mount Rushmore. Except, it wasn't the face of a famous American President, but the face of a Ukrainian patriot. The mountainous sculpted image bellowed with the ferocity of an unholy monster:

"ORCS MUST DIE!!!"

The booming words sent a powerful gust of wind that staggered the shell-shocked team of soldiers. Barely able to keep their feet, they turned and bolted towards the woods in a state of sheer terror.

The voracious flies gave chase with uncanny speed, picking off stragglers along the way. As they administered their gruesome violence, hair-raising screams filled the putrid air, until the last soldier drew his final breath.

The division of soldiers hiding in the woods stood watching helplessly as their compatriots were mercilessly massacred. Suddenly realizing they were battling a dipteran army with supernatural powers, the men glanced nervously around their natural surroundings, wary of the faintest squeak, chirp, or buzz.

As if summoned by the soldiers' hyperactive senses, a faint buzz began to reverberate in the haunting forest. The men looked into each other's fearful eyes as the unsettling hum grew louder. They clutched their useless rifles tighter, trying to calm their nerves. Suddenly, the leaves of the forest canopy began to rustle with foreboding, while the setting sun cast eerie streaks of crimson across the sky. Growing still louder, the hum now reverberated throughout the forest.

The flies came out of hiding forming an ominous cloud over the petrified soldiers. Some of the men took to wetting themselves, overtaken by thoughts of their impending doom. As a deafening salvo of gunfire rang out in the ancient forest, the demonic flies rained down on the division of Russian soldiers, killing every last one.

Totally annihilated, their bloody corpses befouled acres of pristine forest. Instead of bullet holes or shrapnel wounds, their skins were marred by odious sores, and their body cavities were eerily hollowed-out by the genetically mutated flies. Boris strolled proudly amidst the carnage, admiring the efficiency of his dipteran army. His years of tireless toil in the secret lab had culminated in total victory on the battlefield.

Boris's feelings of self-satisfaction were abruptly dismissed by a gust of chilling wind. It was nightfall in the forests of Northern Ukraine, and the temperatures were approaching lethal levels for his swarm of cold-blooded assassins. Boris could feel the lethargy of his troops as darkness colored the skies. He had to move his troops to warmer climes if they were to survive their mission.

He didn't have to ponder the plethora of warm locales to repose his swarm, Barbuda was already marked as a stop on his global revenge tour. Somewhere anchored in the turquoise blue waters surrounding the coral island was a yacht paid for by Ukrainian blood. Boris intended to adjudicate the despicable crime and quash any impunity enjoyed by the silver-tongued general. The mutant man launched himself towards the crescent moon and led his swarm of flies towards the Lesser Antilles.

CHAPTER NINETEEN – THE
DEVIL REVEALED

Meanwhile, back in the United States, reports of Russia's ongoing invasion flooded newsfeeds for weeks. Disturbing images of bombed-out government buildings, factories, and hospitals aired daily on 24-hour news stations. Civilian casualties mounted as imprecise, cold-war era weapons were dusted off and indiscriminately deployed in violation of the Geneva Convention. The World stood appalled over Russia's brazen brutality, disrupting decades of peaceful order on the European continent.

Olga sat crying in front of the television screen as a Ukrainian news program streamed in from Kyiv in her native tongue. Expletives and fiery words flew from the impassioned news anchor's lips as he berated the "Special Military Operation", adding to her grief and despondency. She had been missing her homeland since her unpleasant encounter with Chloe, and now, with war raging in the Ukraine, Olga fell into depression.

Wistfully, she thought about Boris and his love of country. How was he dealing with the war? If he wasn't there already, would he return to defend her? Would she ever see him again?

Suddenly, the news anchor announced that their crew on the front line had some breaking news. An on-location reporter appeared on the screen wearing full personal protective gear and spoke in a somber tone.

"We are reporting to you tonight from a small town just a short distance from the front line in Northern Ukraine. We have to warn you, the images you are about to see are extremely graphic and disturbing, so, we'll delay the transmission for ten seconds to allow for discretion."

After what seemed like an eternity, horrifying images of dead townspeople tainted Olga's television screen. Hordes of dead bodies were strewn across open fields and empty streets. Except for the news team on the ground wearing face shields and yellow gowns, there were no other signs of life. Even the dogs lay slaughtered among the dead. Olga gasped as she stared in disbelief.

Snapping out of her state of shock, she picked up the TV reporter's voice midstream:

"It appears to be some kind of chemical attack by the Russians. The entire town has been wiped out..."

As the camera zoomed in, Olga saw that their bodies had been eviscerated and their eyeballs starkly absent. Strangely, they were met with the same gruesome fate as her murdered tenants four months ago, she recalled. The reporter continued.

"Further up this dirt path some thirty kilometers ahead, an entire brigade of Ukrainian soldiers were also slaughtered..."

The news reporter choked up and paused to compose himself; then he continued in a quavering tone.

"The investigative team there are reporting the same markings on the soldiers' bodies like the ones here, and traces of the same chemical substance were reported among the dead...God, help us all."

Olga's mouth fell open in shock as she recalled the past. After their marriage and her sworn oath of secrecy to her Country, Boris revealed the military goals of the abhorrent project in great detail. Olga learned about the powerful neurotoxins and caustic digestive enzymes of the experimental flies. Boris even told her about their hunting methods, how they paralyzed their prey, how they coveted certain body parts like the intestines, the organs, and the eyeballs.

When he told her that he could actually direct them to attack lab animals and quite possibly human beings, she took it with a grain of salt, privately chalking it up to boyhood fantasy. Even though she saw firsthand their supernatural abilities, like the uncanny ability to mimic violin music, she mused that the lab created flies would likely become another nuisance pest if it were ever to escape the lab.

But now, connecting his words to the gory images on her television screen, she had to consider the possibility that her estranged husband was somehow still involved and that he had failed to destroy the abominable creatures they sought to escape from when they defected to the United States.

There was one thing Olga could be sure of; Boris was no traitor. Even if he could control the flies, he would never turn on his own country. The only person who might have insight into the misdirected attack was Colonel Wesley Walker, who happened to be calling her on the other end of the line. Recognizing the number on her caller id, Olga picked up.

"Are you seeing this? Was it Boris?" Olga asked in a desperate tone.

"Olga, I'm in the car on my way to you. I'm about thirty minutes out. We really need to talk in person." Wes replied calmly.

"OK, I'll meet you downstairs."

Olga was alone in the penthouse condominium. Damon had gone to Singapore to finalize the hotel development deal with Chloe. He told her he'd be back in a couple of days, but it's been a week since Olga has seen him. She was looking for a distraction from his prolonged absence when she flicked on the television, but the disturbing news about the massacre was more than she bargained for.

Olga and the retired colonel had not spoken since that day she and Boris stepped foot on US soil, after the Army plane landed at the Army Garrison in Miami. She was apprehensive about discussing her separation from Boris and matters of the heart, which she was sure would come up. Considering Wes had flown halfway around the world to attend their wedding in the Ukraine, Olga felt he deserved an explanation about her personal decisions. So, for the next twenty minutes she mentally prepared herself to share her reasons with Wes, then she grabbed her purse and headed downstairs to meet her old friend.

"Hello Olga." Wes greeted Olga with a warm smile as he entered the resort lobby.

"Wes! I'm so happy to see you." Olga exclaimed, giving him a warm hug.

They took a couple of minutes to exchange pleasantries before Olga led Wes through the plush lobby, and into her private office of the resort beauty salon.

"I hope you don't mind my sudden intrusion, but I really need to talk to you," Wes began politely after seating himself in the reception area chair.

"Oh Wes, why would I mind? We are like family; you don't need to make appointments with family. Anyways, I see you still have connections in the intelligence community, seeing how you found me so easily" Olga teased.

"Well, sometimes it's more of a curse than a blessing I would say. But I didn't find you by them; detective Epstein told me where you lived," Wes admitted.

After an awkward silence, Olga sighed, then began to address the elephant in the room.

"We just grew apart, Wes. He was always wrapped up in his work at the lab. We rarely even shared a meal together. And when he found out from you that General Valarie and Denys stole the money…"

"I'm not here to judge, Olga." Wes politely interrupted, then striking a serious tone, he continued, "I need you to listen to me very carefully. Something very strange is happening; something diabolical."

"Oh my God, yes! I was just watching the news and saw what happened to those poor townspeople. How could someone do such a thing?! The whole town was massacred!" Olga cried as tears welled up in her eyes.

"They weren't the only ones; an entire division of Russian soldiers were slaughtered the same way. Right now, tensions on both sides are extremely high. Both sides are accusing the other of war crimes." Wes said plainly.

"What?!"

For the next hour, Wes went on to tell Olga the events that led up to his surprise visit.

Three months ago, an American operative working in Lviv was dispatched to interview a lady who had checked herself into a psychiatric hospital. It turned out that that lady was Boris's ex-wife Natalie / Katerina.

She told the American agent about her harrowing experience with Boris, and about how the SSU had turned her away when she sought protection from them. The SSU disavowed any association with Katerina.

Desperate to confirm her own sanity, she sought psychiatric help. She told the psychiatrists about the Robber fly research project, her time spent in Florida with Boris, and the US representative they reported to while they were in the United States – Colonel Wesley Walker. Then, she told them about the frightening assault by her mutant ex-husband and his swarm of assassin flies.

After confirming she was of sound mind, the medical director of the hospital contacted the US Consulate, who routed the information to the CIA.

The dispatched agent conducted an in-depth interview with Katerina, taking copious notes about the strange encounter and the half-man, half-fly mutant that was her ex-husband. Like the myriad of UFO sightings and other unexplained phenomena, the CIA tucked the interview notes away in a cardboard box for future reference.

That was up until a couple of days ago when the CIA obtained a video clip of a massive swarm of insects flying over the Capitol from a Ukrainian news station. Among the swarm was an exceptionally large bird that strangely resembled a flying man. The video clip was sent to Virginia and confirmed by the CIA lab to be authentic.

Katerina's description of the flying monster was on point. Boris had become Dipteran.

When Wes's Senator friend who sat on the Armed Services Committee caught wind of the news, the alarm bells went off and he called Wes in a panic. The indignant Senator demanded to know why Boris didn't hold up his end of the bargain to destroy the flies, and instead, had declared war against all humankind.

"So, are you telling me Boris is some kind of flying monster fighting both sides of the war? C'mon Wes, you don't really believe in monsters and little green men, do you?" Olga playfully chided.

Pensively, Wes pulled out his personal device and handed it over to Olga.

"Not normally, no. But I believe there are greater forces at work here...Take a look for yourself."

As Olga pressed the play button on the video clip, she saw a strange human figure floating in the sky behind a massive cloud of black dots. The clip started off grainy and out of focus; but as the camera man steadied his hand, the enigmatic images came into focus. Olga saw a winged man among a million flies hovering over the Ukrainian Capitol; but rather than the mythological wings of an angel, the humanoid creature bore the wings of a humongous insect. The iridescent wings vibrated at an incredible speed, only allowing her eyes to glimpse the sheen and outline of their motion.

Suddenly, the cloud of flies around the winged man scattered, revealing more of the mysterious creature. Olga's eyes widened as she paused the video and enlarged the image of the repulsive creature. Vaguely recognizing the facial features of her estranged husband, Olga's hands began to tremble and lost its grip on the device, causing it to fall clumsily onto the floor. Her face paled with terror and her pulse quickened.

"Oh my God!" Olga exclaimed, shocked by the disturbing image.

Wes was not surprised by Olga's strong reaction. Unlike himself, she hadn't considered the possibility of otherworldly forces afoot. After Detective Epstein paid him a visit, Wes was skeptical that Boris acted alone, or rather, acted under his own volition. The ghastly photos of the Henderson murders, coupled with the boy's account of a man disguised in a fly costume on Halloween, was all too neatly tied in a bow. Wes knew Boris could never inflict such cruelty on another human being; besides, he wouldn't even know where to buy such an elaborate costume.

About a week after Epstein's visit, Wes learned about Dr. Bartosh's unexpected death through the CIA. He knew the man to be eccentric, perhaps even unstable, but to deliberately plunge to his death off of a thirty-foot platform into an empty pool was baffling. Then, when Denys Boyko's body was found mangled inside the secret lab, Wes could no longer ignore his Christian intuition.

He had long ago accepted Jesus as his Lord and Savior, but it was only in recent days he accepted the existence of the Devil, and the possession thereof.

The colonel saw goodness in Boris as early as their first meeting. He collaborated with the talented entomologist over the years, forming a unique bond. Wes desperately wanted to help his friend, but didn't have a clue about demonic possessions or exorcisms. So, he sought counsel from a Bishop in the Catholic Church who was knowledgeable in matters of the occult. After several meetings, Wes gained a new understanding of the workings of Beelzebub and concluded grim reasons for the mysterious deaths. Reasons that shook him to his very core; not only was Beelzebub intent on destroying the lives of those involved in his unholy experiment, but he was also on the cusp of fomenting nuclear world war.

"God is the only one who can help him now, Olga." Wes returned, then added, "We are all in need of his protection; every one of us who was in the presence of the diabolical flies. We are all vulnerable to demonic possession."

Wes's words transported Olga back to the night before Boris's disappearance. Her fog of confusion over her actions that night suddenly evaporated. She stared blankly at Wes as she realized the mortal sin she had committed, poisoning her husband in the attic so she could be with Damon, so she could bear his child without shame.

Olga began to cry. *She could have easily absolved her sinful actions that night, claiming "the devil made me do it", but what about all the other infidelities? Was the devil whispering in her ear when she fell into Damon's arms? Did he compel her answer Damon's friend request on the dating app?* Olga was not naïve to her sinful nature; she was not about to let herself off the hook so easily. Olga's sobs grew louder as she continued to pass judgement on herself; her brutal honesty rubbing her ego raw.

"I did it! I killed him!" Olga cried, and for all intents and purposes, she had.

"There may still be a way to save him." Wes consoled.

"How?" Olga asked, still sobbing.

"We have to destroy the swarm; they were created by the devil himself" Wes replied. With a pensive tone, he added "Boris is not the only one needing saving, we need to save the world from nuclear war."

Wes went on to tell Olga about his meetings with the Catholic Bishop and the steps necessary to exorcise the demon inside Boris. Although Wes had not come up with an approved plan with the Church, he had some ideas where Boris was headed next. He warned Olga that Boris would likely pay her a visit as well, and that they still had time to strategize about their approach.

The old friends parted with a sense of melancholy and wistful thoughts of Boris.

CHAPTER TWENTY – THE SCOUNDREL

Boris navigated their way across the vast ocean by the stars. His million-strong army of flies had been reduced to just a few thousand by the time they reached the Lesser Antilles. As the temperatures warmed with the changes in latitude, the cold-blooded insects returned to their vibrant state. Although only a fraction of his troops survived the freezing temperatures of Ukraine, he was nonetheless proud of their battlefield performance.

Unaware the townspeople and the Ukrainian soldiers had suffered the same gruesome fate as the enemy, the dipteran commander approached the island of Barbuda to settle another score.

After committing his sinister act of sabotage, Beelzebub escaped his lifeless shell and commandeered the body of another fly among Boris's brigade. He was delighted by his foot soldier's flawless execution of his game plan. Like yin to his yang, Boris had unwittingly aided Beelzebub in sowing the seeds of a nuclear holocaust.

As a reward for his malevolence, the demon decided to allow Boris unfettered discretion to carry out this leg of his revenge tour;

however, Beelzebub remained close by, in case his protege needed some encouragement.

General Valarie was sunning himself on a secluded stretch of pink sand beach. Lying on either side of him were two Brazilian bombshells. The women were topless, their bikini tops strewn across the warm sand. Blissfully intoxicated after polishing off two bottles of champagne, the three lay unabashed under the Caribbean sun.

With his super-yacht anchored 300 meters from the beach, it was well worth the short dinghy ride ashore to enjoy a picnic and a roll in the sand with his voluptuous companions. For the AWOL general who absconded with millions in research funds, it was a typical afternoon of debauchery.

He bought the boat from a Russian oligarch for a song shortly after the international community began seizing Russian assets, railing against their aggression towards Ukraine. It was the perfect hideaway, sailing the turquoise waters of the Caribbean like notorious pirates of old. But instead of a creaky wooden galleon, the general sailed in modern luxury aboard the 120-foot vessel, manned by a dedicated crew of twenty.

Months of indulgent living showed on the middle-aged man; no longer the muscle-clad soldier, the general wore a fleshy tire around his midsection. As he sat up to take in the gentle lapping waves along the shoreline, he noticed a tall lanky figure approaching from a fair distance down the beach. He had frequented this stretch of tucked-away haven for months without seeing a single soul, so he was surprised by the presence of a random intruder. What was even more puzzling was that this stretch of beach was only accessible by boat, and this person seemed to have appeared out of thin air.

General Valarie rose to his feet to get a better look down the sandy beach, rousing the bikini babes from their siesta. The girls picked up their bikini tops that were laying in the sand and hastily covered their bosoms. As they peered out in the distance, they saw the enigmatic man quicken his pace.

Suddenly, the man sprouted wings and took to the air like an alien creature from another world. The three stood frozen for a moment, staring incredulously at the supernatural spectacle.

"What the hell?!" the general blurted.

With uncanny speed, the dipteran monster darted towards its prey, accompanied by his swarm of assassin flies. Now hovering directly over the frightened sun worshipers, Boris spoke by the vibrating wings of the flies.

"Valarie, you fat bastard! What patriotic speech do you have for me today?"

Shell shocked by the monster's supernatural powers and ghastly form, the Brazilian beauties scurried across the sand like ghost crabs fleeing a seagull, making a beeline towards the idle dinghy. Before the general could join them, the menacing flies enveloped him, forming an octagonal cage around the cowering man.

The outboard motor roared to life on the transport boat, and the girls jetted away towards the anchored yacht.

Trapped inside the eerie cage, Valarie glanced up at the hovering monster, disbelieving his eyes and ears.

"What's the matter general, had too much to drink? Here, take a closer look!"

Suddenly, a pair of feet landed firmly on the sand next to the terrified general. As his eyes traced up the lanky beast, the hallmark features of the deadly assassin fly greeted him unapologetically.

The monster's legs were covered in brown bristly fur. Jutting out in all directions were thorny spikes from its ankles to its thighs. His abdomen was segmented like an armadillo's shell with a metallic green sheen, and its arms had similar sharp spikes to those on its legs. As Valarie gazed upon the wizened face of his former colleague, he let out an audible gasp, shuddering at his demonic form.

With his pupilless eyes, Boris started blankly at the petrified general, as a wicked grin crept across his heavily bearded face. Unexpectedly, Boris ostentatiously flared out his iridescent wings to each side, startling the general who jumped back with fright. Bouncing off the living cage behind him, he came within inches of the ghastly monster's face.

"B...B...Boris? I...I...Is that you?" was all the words the silver tongued general could muster.

"No, it's your fairy godmother here to grant you three wishes," Boris chided sarcastically. Then, he let out a sinister cackle, "Ha...hahahaha."

"What...what happened to you?" Valarie stammered, as the hair on the back of his neck bristled.

"It's my new look. Do you like it?" Boris spun around slowly, allowing the general to take in his demonic form.

Boris continued, "How was I to lead an army of assassin flies without the proper uniform? You know all about uniforms, don't you general?"

The general stood petrified, staring at the beastly features befouling Boris's human body. But true to his beguiling nature, he summoned every last ounce of courage in his body and returned,

"This...this is amazing, the way you speak through the flies! The team will be pleased...You are a true patriot Boris; our country owes you a debt of gratitude."

Boris knew the general's words were meaningless; Valarie had always been Bartosh's puppet, just as Wes had said, but he decided to play along.

"Oh? And how shall I be repaid this...debt?"

"Well...I'll put in a recommendation to the President of course" the general pridefully replied.

"Yes...of course, the President is a generous man; after all, he rewarded you with $700 million dollars" Boris remarked in a facetious tone.

His words struck Valarie's facade like a sledgehammer. Momentarily stunned, the general pivoted as quickly as a snake in the grass could.

"You must have been talking to our American colonel friend. I didn't want to say anything before because of your working relationship, but now, I must warn you about the colonel..."

Boris grew tired of his charade, and before Valarie could spew another lie, he drove the thorny spikes protruding from his forearm into the general's neck. The spikes pierced his windpipe and severed his carotid artery, sending him staggering about while gasping for air. As blood spurted from his neck, the flies began closing in around him, anticipating their next meal. General Valarie collapsed onto the sandy beach and the voracious flies divebombed the compromised man. Within minutes, the slippery general was reduced to a hollow shell as his blood mixed with the lapping waves, coloring the shallow waters an eerie shade of pink.

Boris felt a much-needed surge of energy as the flies devoured the man's body, but hunger pangs continued to beckon him. The 200-pound man's flesh was a delectable appetizer, but not nearly enough to sustain his swarm for the next leg of their journey. He suddenly recalled the superyacht anchored just off the shore on his approach to this lonely stretch of beach, and the crew members walking about its deck. They could easily provide the nutritional fuel needed to carry on their journey across the Atlantic.

Just as swiftly as the wicked thought popped into his head, Boris rejected the idea of killing the crew. Although he was considered possessed by the Catholic Church's definition, there remained a smidgen of humanity in his soul. He reasoned that the crew didn't deserve to die. Unlike the Russian soldiers who bombed, shot, and raped innocent civilians, their only fault was serving a traitorous scoundrel.

Boris led his brigade of flies into the Island's dry forest and hunted the deer and wild boars that foraged within, building up the stores of energy they sorely needed.

Operating incognito as a loyal member of the swarm, Beelzebub had a vastly different sentiment, just as he did along the Ukrainian countryside. Once more, he severed the telepathic signals of the dipteran commander, this time affecting half of his swarm, and directed a rogue army towards the fleeing yacht.

Like a tempestuous wind, the swarm of flesh-eating flies blitzed the crew, devouring every last one. Mutilated bodies lay strewn across the decks, hanging over railings, and slumped in private quarters. The diesel engine of the large vessel rumbled a lonesome theme, as the floating slaughterhouse drifted aimlessly about the Caribbean Sea.

CHAPTER TWENTY-ONE – THE BETRAYAL

An air of melancholy surrounded Olga. A few days after Wes's unexpected visit, she still couldn't forget the haunting images of Boris in that video clip. Whether compelled by the devil or not, she alone caused his transformation and suffering. It was she who poisoned him in their attic; it was she who stood to benefit from his demise. Her guilt weighed heavily on her heart.

Despite their agreement to maintain communication and implement a Church-sanctioned strategy to rescue Boris, there were no assurances it would work. *Besides, how could two people alone destroy a bazillion flies?* Olga thought.

Her thoughts shifted to Damon, who had been away for over a week. What she expected to be a short business trip to finalize a hotel deal with Chloe had turned into an extended absence. It was just as well that he wasn't around during Wes's visit. What was she supposed to tell him anyway? That she aided the devil in possessing her husband? The absurdity of the whole situation threw Olga's life into limbo.

She rode the elevator down to the hair salon, hoping to occupy her mind with work. As she sat down in front of the computer in her private office, an email alert popped up on her monitor.

Having served an international clientele for months now, Olga had learned the country codes for most of the world. She recognized the one on the incoming email to be from Singapore, even though the rest of IP address was indiscernible. Hoping it was Damon sharing his homeward bound itinerary, she eagerly clicked on the message.

The entire message was made up of only one sentence that read: "Go home gold digger." Attached to the message was a rather large video file.

Olga grimaced in puzzlement as she read the message. Then, she played the video…

Her jaw dropped as video images of two lovers in bed appeared on her screen. The woman's face was obstructed by the back of the man's head as he moved rhythmically over her naked body. Their passionate moans filled the room. The overhead camera captured his chiseled back, and her manicured nails dug firmly into it. As he quickened his pace the two lovers ended up in a fit of ecstasy. They were breathless, relishing in each other's passionate embrace. Seconds later, the man rolled over to enjoy the afterglow of sex, revealing their pleasure-filled smiles.

Olga wept, screamed, then wept again, as she gazed upon Damon and Chloe's satisfied faces, the unbearable sting of betrayal wounding her deeply. Chloe had gotten her man, like she always did, and Damon had reverted to his playboy ways.

Humiliated by Chloe's sophomoric prank, a tempest of emotions swirled in her head. Humiliation quickly turned into anger when she picked up the monitor and hurled it across the room. Angrily, she stormed out of the salon, drawing stolen glances from her staff on the way out. Olga hastily packed up her belongings while fending off fits of rage.

As she stepped into the cab, she couldn't help thinking about how naïve and stupid she had been, how she threw away a comfortable life with a loving husband for a foolish notion; no, not even a notion, a girlhood pipedream. Olga mused; *did she really do it for money? Was she just a run-of-the-mill gold digger as Chloe had put it?*

She hatefully dismissed the spoiled heiress's slight, owing to the fact that she and Boris had enough money to last them their lifetimes. But Olga could not dismiss the vanity that pervaded her ego. The vanity that compelled her longing for more, more wealth, more status, and even more vanity. She loathed the shallow person she had become.

For the next two weeks, Olga sat in her suburban townhouse and drowned her pain in vodka. Damon's calls to her went unanswered until they ceased entirely, leaving Olga in a state of hopeless depression.

CHAPTER TWENTY-TWO – BELIEVERS

Wes's boat was anchored along a dense patch of mangroves next to his favorite fishing hole. It was his favorite spot, not because it held large schools of fish, but because it was tucked away from busy boat traffic. In fact, there wasn't another boat around for miles, a rarity on a busy holiday weekend.

It was Good Friday, and he was glad the marina was able to fix the outboard motor on his modest flats boat. Though the repair costs were steep, it hadn't exceeded his monthly retirement budget for his lifelong hobby. Sometimes, Wes wondered how large that budgeted line item would have been had he kept the money he earned from the ill-intended research project. He certainly would have bought the forty-two-foot fishing boat he had wanted for years. Instead, he returned every penny of his earnings to the US Government when he learned that the research funds were misappropriated to begin with.

Wes always did what he felt was right in his heart. God always had a way of reining him in, keeping him from wandering too far from His protection. *Is that what happened to Boris?* Wes wondered. Even though that was what the Catholic priest suggested, Wes couldn't fathom how someone as pure in heart as Boris could be allowed to suffer demonic possession. Maybe the virtues of man that glorify God are the same virtues that draw the devil's contempt.

He stared pensively at his bobber floating twenty feet out in the backwaters of Pensacola Bay. As the bobber drifted along the eddies created by the incoming tide, his cell phone interrupted his thoughts. It was detective Jeremy Epstein of the Ft. Lauderdale Police Department.

"This is the second time you interrupted my fishing weekend. Do you have something against fishing?" Wes jokingly chided.

"I'm sorry Wes, something's come up, or, come ashore to be exact." The detective replied.

"Well, since you're calling me from the east coast, I'll assume it's something more than a boat full of Cuban refugees." Wes quipped.

"Worse, much worse."

By the serious tone in Jeremy's voice, Wes dropped his playful banter and listened intently to the detective's words.

"He's at it again...this time 22 people on a yacht. Same M.O." Jeremy continued.

"I'm sorry, did you say yacht?" Wes curiously interrupted.

"Yeah, not just any yacht, a superyacht...registered in Malta to one Mikkael Valarie. Isn't he...?" Epstein remarked.

"Yes, he is. Was he on board?" Wes inquired.

"I'm not sure. From the photos I've seen, it's going to take them awhile to sort out all the identities. Wes, the coast guard, and FBI have taken over the investigation...they came by the station this morning, the chief and I had to hand off the Henderson case. We've been shut out...Damn Feds!"

"Great, that makes three Federal agencies meddling in things they don't understand. We don't have much time, they're probably headed over to talk to Olga now…Hopefully, her billionaire boyfriend will keep her quiet. I take it from your call you want to stay involved." Wes ventured.

"Stay Involved?! What I want is for someone to tell me what the hell is going on! You're not telling me the whole story, Wes. There's gotta be a lot more than just a science project gone bad here!"

Wes sensed Jeremy's building frustration. Although he had shared the details of the secret military project with the detective, he wasn't ready to share what he had learned from his meetings with the Catholic Church. Besides, Wes knew Jeremy was Jewish and would never believe what he had to say anyway.

"You wouldn't believe me if I told you." Wes offered.

"Try me!" he retorted.

Despite his reservations, Wes recounted the multiple meetings he had with the Bishop and described to Jeremy the various stages of demon attack: infestation, oppression, obsession, and possession. Then he went on to tell him about the atrocious extermination of an entire town in Ukraine, the Russian soldiers, the Ukrainian soldiers, and the similar manner of slaughter among them all. Wes hoped he had been convincing enough to enlist the detective's help, but his claim that Boris had transformed into a flying monster possessed by a demon was soundly rejected.

"Get the fuck out of here!" the detective blurted, "You're telling me, Boris sprouted wings and flew to Ukraine with these killer flies?!"

"Look, there are some things that can't be explained by science or the natural world. I didn't expect you to believe me anyway. I'm gonna send you a video clip that's been confirmed by the

C.I.A. lab to be legitimate. Just take a look at it and call me back, ok?"

After Wes hung up the phone, he sent Jeremy the video clip of Boris flying over Kyiv.

Jeremy's report of another mass killing sent Wes's thoughts racing. There were only two people left that Boris had yet to visit: Olga and himself. *Who would be next?* Wes wondered.

Wes had lost an hour of fishing while he was on the phone with Jeremy, losing track of his bobber at the end of his line. As he panned the smooth surface of the water for the floating device, he noticed a large school of bait fish breaking the water's surface on the other side of the cove. Anxious to make up for lost time, Wes quickly reeled in his line and motored his boat over to investigate what was spooking the school of fish. He quickly anchored his boat just outside the school and cast a line towards the frolicking bait fish.

Just before his bobber hit the water, what he thought was a school of bait fish suddenly took flight. To Wes's astonishment, the creatures lurking just beneath the surface turned out to be a swarm of assassin flies. As they shot up to the sky, a giant geyser of seawater traced their path, then showered Wes in an unholy baptism. Wes cowered in terror on the deck of his boat, peering skyward at the otherworldly creatures.

Suddenly, the winged monster appeared from behind the thick line of mangroves, flying over to join his loyal swarm. Wes rose from his crouched position to witness the supernatural spectacle above his head, his mouth fell open in shock as he gazed at the devil's creation.

As if speaking through a giant wind turbine, Boris greeted his old friend by the vibrating wings of his swarm.

"Hello Wes. What phase of the project would you call this?"

Boris's uncanny voice terrified Wes, but his sarcastic reference to the unholy project was even more disturbing.

"Oh my God! Boris, is that you?" Wes called out.

"Tell me Wes, have you spent your share of the 700 million? I'm surprised you haven't bought yourself a yacht like Valarie's." Boris scoffed.

"Boris, you're being manipulated! I returned every penny I ever made off of that project. Boris! I can help you; we have to get you help from the Church. Please, come down here so we can talk." Wes cried out.

"Kill him." Beelzebub whispered...

Boris flinched, startled by the demon's command. Suddenly, he felt the presence of his demon- master among the swarm.

Despite his agreement with Beelzebub to do the devil's bidding, Boris couldn't bring himself to blindly obey the command. He had unresolved feelings towards the colonel. Wes was like a father to him, even attending his wedding in the Ukraine. *But why did Wes stay in that room at DEVCOM if he knew about the diabolical nature of the flies? Perhaps he didn't know. Perhaps he was blinded by greed as well. Was Wes really in on the deal with Denys and Valarie?* Boris desperately wanted to trust his friend again, but his judgement was tainted by the devil's ruse.

Beelzebub sensed the conflict within Boris; so, before Boris could respond to Wes's pleas, he took dominion over Boris's body and soul.

"Boris is dead! I am Diptera. The name suits me better, don't you think?" the devil declared.

Wes sensed a sinister aura emanating from the ghastly creature hovering over him. Suddenly, the dipteran monster urinated on him, drenching his face in a foul-smelling, liquid. Wes gasped for air, reeling from the stench, while Diptera cackled with delight.

The Catholic priest had prepared him for his predicted encounter with Beelzebub. Wes closed his eyes and began reciting passages from an ancient Bible manuscript, rebutting the devil in Hebrew.

An indignant look of surprise registered on Diptera's face. "How dare you speak his name!" the demon admonished in a fit of rage.

Prompted by his angry words, the swarm of voracious flies hurtled toward Wes who was standing on his boat deck below. As they approached within a foot from him, an invisible shield diverted their path around the praying man. The flies circled back around attacking from the other side; but again, was denied access to Wes by a shield of faith.

Infuriated by his impotence, Diptera left the pious colonel and led his diabolical swarm into the swamps, devouring all manners of fur, feather, and fin. Temporarily conceding defeat, Beelzebub relinquished his hold over Boris and reverted to his earlier form as a fly among the swarm. The wily devil grew wary that Wes had enlisted the help of a higher power and decided to bide his time.

Wes's cell phone chimed, rousing him from his trance-like state. When he opened his eyes, a wave of relief washed over him as he gazed at the clear blue sky. Wes took deep breaths, trying to calm himself after that hair-raising encounter.

The caller ID registered Detective Epstein's number. Jeremy had studied the video clip Wes sent over about an hour ago and was calling him back to confirm what he saw.

"I still don't believe there's a man is inside that thing, but I can't unsee what I just saw." Epstein conceded.

"I get it, Jeremy, but I need your help…" Wes replied breathlessly.

"You sound like you just ran a marathon!" Jeremy exclaimed.

"Worse! Much worse. I'll meet you in South Florida tomorrow, we've gotta warn Olga."

CHAPTER TWENTY-THREE – THE PLAN

Wes took an early flight down to Ft. Lauderdale the next morning. Jeremy and Chief Randall Stokes met Wes upon his arrival. The retired colonel traveled light, carrying only a duffle in one hand and Boris's brown leather satchel in the other. They hopped into a police cruiser and headed for the station to discuss Wes's plan to defeat the devil.

The chief had been briefed about the slain soldiers, the dead townspeople, and Boris's return stateside. He also saw the enigmatic video clip of the dipteran monster Wes had shared with Jeremy. On top of all that, the coast guard's horrific photos of the carnage aboard Valarie's yacht left an indelible mark on the police chief's psyche. In his twenty years as a law enforcement professional, he had never seen this level of brutality, leaving him anxious to hear Wes's plan.

Unlike Jeremy, Randall was open-minded to Wes's claim of supernatural forces afoot, owing to his Lutheran faith. Figuratively, Lutherans believe that the devil is a toothless lion; all he can do is roar. He can't do harm to man without man's consent and cooperation; however, Randall believed that consent had indeed been given. First, by the commissioning of the unholy experiment, then, by a man weakened by vengeance and pride.

The three men sat around a conference table at the station. Wes reached inside the satchel and pulled out Boris's research notes. The atmosphere was tense, each fully aware of the dire consequences of failure. As Wes discussed with Jeremy in their first meeting, their first priority was to eradicate the abominable flies.

"I had these notes better translated to English by my contacts at DEVCOM" Wes began, "It took them about a month, there were hundreds of pages, and most of it handwritten. It took another month for me to find the page that mattered the most."

The two cops sat unblinking, hanging onto the colonel's every word.

Wes continued, "the notes depicted several hand gestures Boris used to command the flies to attack..."

With a flair for sarcasm, Jeremy interrupted, "Where are you going with this Wes? Aren't we more interested in fumigating the blood-thirsty pests with a crop duster!?"

"Let the man continue detective!" Randall rebuked.

After regaining their full attention, the retired colonel continued, "Based on his notes, Boris got so good with his hand signals, he stopped using the synthetic neurotoxin all together at feeding time and only used his hands to direct the flies to attack. Most people would have accepted the adaptation and never looked back, but I knew Boris would have wanted to know..."

"Know what?" Jeremy impatiently asked.

"In the last entry of his notes, Boris recorded the results of a little experiment. He wanted to know whether his hand signals were more effective than the neurotoxin in triggering a feeding response from the flies. They were not. The neurotoxin won each and every time."

A light bulb went off in Randall's head, "So, you want to control which prey the flies choose...you want to take away Boris's authority!" the chief exclaimed.

"Exactly, and if that prey had neurotoxin and fly poison coursing through its body, the flies would have had their last meal," Wes explained.

Again, Wes reached into the brown leather satchel and this time pulled out a syringe. Instead of a milky-white color like before, the contents inside now bore a dull brown hue.

"Inside this syringe is a mixture of the synthetic neurotoxin Boris brought over from Ukraine and a powerful insecticide. I had the lab at DEVCOM formulate a pesticide that travels through the bloodstream in seconds. The combination of the two is experimental, tested on lab rats in small doses. There wasn't enough of the neurotoxin to test it on a larger animal. The neurotoxin in this syringe is all that's left from Boris's stock, it cannot be reproduced, it's our silver bullet...our only hope."

"It's got to be a big animal, and how do you propose we get it in front of the flies?" Jeremy asked.

"We won't have to, Boris will find Olga, just like he found me" Wes replied, "If we place the animal near Olga, we just might have a chance."

"Well, you've laid out what we're going to do, the question now is when? And where?" Randall added.

"Tomorrow. We don't have much time. We can't let the Feds interfere, and Boris will not wait either, the flies will need to feed again soon."

"Tomorrow is Easter Sunday," the chief pointed out.

"All the better, we could use a little divine intervention," Wes returned.

Now convinced that the plan might work, Jeremy added, "We need a secluded spot, away from the public eye."

"I know a place," Randall declared.

Growing up in the one-traffic light township of Yeehaw Junction, Randall played with all the local cattle rancher's kids. Those kids had since grown up and taken over the family ranch. He knew he could count on any one of them to help, he was like family to them before moving away to pursue a law enforcement career. Confident his ties to the community were still strong, he assured Wes they would have the venue for their moment of truth.

Wes went by the B-Well Resort and Residences to look for Olga. Expecting to find her styling hair on a busy holiday weekend, he walked into the salon of the five-star resort. To his surprise, the receptionist told him that Olga no longer worked there. After a few probing questions for which he was denied answers to, Wes grew concerned about his friend.

He drove to her suburban duplex and found the driveway starkly empty, the for-rent sign lazily swaying back and forth in the wind, and the window blinds securely shut. A strange intuition prompted Wes to knock on the door, even though the house appeared vacant and uninviting. He knocked and waited, then knocked again. As he turned to walk away from his unanswered calls, he heard the door hinges creak.

Olga stood behind the cracked door with her hand over her blood-shot eyes, shielding them from the mid-morning sun. A strained smile briefly graced her face, then she turned away from the door, leaving it cracked open for Wes to come inside. As he entered the house, he was greeted by clothes and liquor bottles strewn about the floor. Two opened suitcases lay next to the living room sofa, while empty food containers littered the kitchen countertops.

Olga sat limply on the sofa. She was dressed in a modest nightgown and stared blankly at the darkened television screen. Wes surmised that her relationship with the billionaire had gone awry and he felt awkward for having intruded on her grieving process. Sensing she could use a friend right now; he sat down next to her and gently placed his arm around her shoulders. Tears flooded her eyes and Olga began to cry. She buried her face against the retired colonel's shoulder as her sobs grew louder. Wes comforted her in a gentle embrace and waited patiently for her anguish to subside.

When Olga finally calmed down, he reminded her of their conversation a couple of weeks ago about helping Boris. She quickly forgot her pain, wiped away her tears, and listened intently to Wes's words. Wes told Olga about his meeting with Jeremy and Randall that morning, emphasizing the limited window of opportunity they had. Then he laid out their loosely constructed plan.

Olga was to be alone in the pasture with the cows. When Boris arrived at the location, she would engage him in nostalgic conversation, bringing up their history and the happy memories they shared. According to the Catholic bishop, keeping Boris reminded of his humanity will keep the demon at bay.

Upon Wes's signal, Olga would inject the mixture of neurotoxin and insecticide into a grazing cow, triggering the demonic flies to feed on its poisoned flesh.

The Church-approved plan included a team of exorcists lying in wait. After the evil flies are destroyed, they would corral Boris through chants and prayer, neutralizing his ability to fly. Once he was detained, they would transport him to a secret location to complete the exorcism.

Wes's plan stirred a glimmer of hope inside Olga. She had spent the last two weeks examining her marriage to Boris and her actions to destroy it. Each time her ego found an excuse to mask her selfish actions, her conscience deemed her character hopelessly flawed. She could not find within her an ounce of redeeming quality, nor self-worth. Perhaps Wes's plan could finally provide her the opportunity to redeem herself, but more importantly, to save the man she still loved.

Before Wes left Olga's house, he gave her more detailed instructions. He informed her that Jeremy and the police chief would be picking her up in the morning. The four of them would then meet up at the secluded cattle ranch just north of Lake Okeechobee. Working closely with Boris over the years, Wes knew Boris would be active at first light, as would the flies. Dawn was also the time of day agreed to by the Church, and their team of exorcists would be standing by at the tucked away ranch. They parted that evening hopeful that their plan to save Boris would work, and that they would return to some form of normalcy soon.

CHAPTER TWENTY-FOUR – THE TRUTH

It had been a long day for the retired colonel. After enjoying a quiet dinner alone, he checked into an old motel sporting a neon vacancy sign. It was a run-down establishment, probably built in the 1980s, where all the single-story guest rooms faced the parking lot in a simple rectangular configuration. He would have chosen more upscale accommodation, save for the fact it was spring break for the colleges up north, and all the area hotels were booked solid.

Just as Wes climbed into bed, he heard a heavy knock on the door.

"F.B.I.!" a gruff voice barked from outside his door.

"Hold on a sec. Let me get my pants on," the indignant colonel replied.

After flicking the lights back on, Wes opened the door to find two strapping agents standing in the doorway flashing their badges.

"Don't you people have the decency to keep normal hours?" The colonel chided.

"Sorry colonel, may we come in? We need to ask you some questions" the burly agent returned.

"If you must," Wes muttered, as he turned away from the door and sat on his bed.

The two agents put away their badges and followed Wes inside, then sat on the adjacent bed facing Wes.

"I'm agent Santos and this is my partner agent Stacey."

"Well, you already know who I am, so I won't bother with formalities. So, tell me why this couldn't wait until morning?" Wes asked.

In a way, Wes was rather glad the F.B.I. had paid him a visit. He had anticipated their meddling soon after Jeremy informed him about their takeover of the Henderson case and the mass murders aboard Valarie's yacht. Though he would have enjoyed a good night's rest before the big moment in the morning, he knew that the anxiety of not knowing what the Feds were up to would have kept him awake most of the night. Now, they were sitting right in front of him, giving him an opportunity to subvert their investigation, delaying it long enough for Wes's plans to take shape.

"Colonel Walker, we understand through immigration records that you helped a Ukrainian couple to defect to the United States last year. The husband has gone missing. We believe he poses a serious threat to the public's safety. We are a part of task force assembled to find Boris Shevchenko, do you know where he is?" Agent Stacey began.

"Is that so...?" A look of concern registered on Wes's face, "Unfortunately I don't know where he is, perhaps you should ask his wife." Wes offered.

"Mrs. Shevchenko has unfortunately pled the 5th with the police department. We also learned from police records that she has taken up residence with Mr. Damon Blackwell at the B-Well Resort and Residences." Agent Stacey returned.

"Really? I'm disappointed to hear that, they're both friends of mine," Wes stated plainly.

"Just what, exactly, is your relationship with the couple, Sir?" Agent Santos inquired.

"I can't really say, exactly. I'm afraid I'll need to see your security clearances before I can give you that information. You do have security clearances, don't you?" Wes countered.

"Well, not exactly, Colonel. We were hoping you could point us in the right direction or give us some ideas…without violating any security clearances of course. Aren't we both interested in ensuring the public's safety?" Agent Stacey interjected.

"Well, of course I am, and whatever you think is dangerous about my friend, I can assure you that he isn't." Wes declared.

"Now that I'm thinking about it, there may be a place down south we could find him at," Wes continued in a pensive tone, "But I just need to get some shut eye to refresh my memory. I tell you what, if you let me get some sleep, I'll ride with you down south tomorrow morning and see if we can't find Boris."

The Federal agents could not find reasonable objections to Wes's offer. Up until now, they didn't have a clue as to Boris's whereabouts, and much less that their search for a human being was utterly futile. They agreed to pick Wes up in the morning so he could follow through on his generous offer. A sense of relief washed over Wes as he ushered the agents out of his motel room. What he worried about most was a posse of Federal agents stumbling upon the scene, causing harm to Boris or, more likely, themselves. Satisfied that he had just mitigated that risk, he sent a text message to Jeremy, informing him to go ahead as planned without him in the morning.

Olga sat by her bedroom window gazing at the deep red and orange hues coloring the dawn sky. She smiled softly, contented by the inspirational view and the resolutions she made to herself the night before. She would never betray Boris again and she vowed to restore his honor. Olga enjoyed not a wink of sleep, yet her beauty remained undiminished. Dressed hours before, she waited patiently for Easter Sunday to dawn.

Before Jeremy could raise his hand to knock, the front door swung inward, and Olga appeared in the dim morning light. Jeremy's surprised demeanor turned into quiet approval as he was graced with her radiance. Olga was dressed in a simple white sundress that came down to her knees. Embroidered along the hem of her dress were pretty blue and yellow flowers symbolizing her country's colors. The neckline and short sleeves were adorned with delicate lace, highlighting her creamy smooth skin. Two quaint pockets on either side rounded out the perfect Easter Sunday dress. Olga wore no makeup, revealing a healthy natural glow, while her strawberry blonde hair fell gently across her shoulders.

Noticing the beautiful woman approaching the police cruiser, Chief Grady quickly got out, allowing Olga to take the passenger seat. The three unlikely bedfellows sped off in the direction of the secluded cattle ranch, endeavoring to beat the devil at his own game.

"It's so refreshing to be of the same mind," the chief began, breaking the ice from the back seat.

Turning her head around Olga added, "no more secrets," then smiled warmly at Randall.

"The ranch is about an hour and a half drive from here. That will give us time to go over the colonel's instructions. Oh, by the way, he won't be there today," Jeremy announced.

"What the hell do you mean?!" Randall barked.

"Don't worry chief, I took care of everything, the priests have all been told, they are ready work with us," Jeremy assured his boss.

For the next hour, Jeremy went over Wes's instructions to the letter with Olga, while the chief listened in intently from the back seat. When he was finished, the men were left with an eerie foreboding, wary they were about to witness an eternal battle of the ages. Olga was seemingly undaunted, drawing admiration for her bravery from the men.

It was the first time Boris was ejected from his body and sidelined by Beelzebub. Beelzebub's rogue actions against Wes frightened Boris. Despite his accord to serve the wily devil, he hadn't anticipated an unconsented takeover of his faculties. While living his out-of-body experience, Boris witnessed the ferocity of Beelzebub's attack; but he was rather awed by the mercy of the Almighty. Mercy he so coveted now, regretting his unholy alliance made under duress. Mercy, he tried to secure through his unsuccessful suicide attempt.

Perhaps Wes's pleas for him to seek help was prophetic, Boris thought. *After all, Wes's fervent prayers produced a shield of protection against the flies. But how could he seek help now, when Beelzebub can readily take over his being, and was wise to Wes's aims to exorcise him from Boris.*

Despite the burning questions Boris had for Olga concerning her infidelity, he feared for her safety. His quest for answers to the ageless question "why?" turned into a mission to warn his wife: Olga must seek the same protection awarded Wes.

- 231 -

Boris sent his flies out into the surrounding South Florida communities to search for Olga. Hidden within the search party of flies, Beelzebub returned the visual image of Olga standing underneath the canopy of a massive live oak. Half a dozen cows milled about her, taking refuge from the mid-morning sun.

Boris signaled the flies to converge on her location. As he glided over the cattle ranch, he took in a bird's-eye view of the sprawling grounds. A few dilapidated shelters covered with tin roofs scattered across the compound, while a huge red barn stood in the center. Barbed wire fencing stretched around the grazing fields, securing several herds of bulls and cows. Olga stood alone with the cows. Boris did not see another human around. Other than Olga, the ranch was starkly peopleless. Existing in his diabolical form for months now, Boris lost track of the most celebrated religious holiday.

"Look up, he's coming," Jeremy spoke into his radio, transmitting the message to Olga's ear buds.

Boris made his landing fifty yards away. His army of flies quickly formed a three-dimensional image of his pre-dipteran face above his head. "Olga!" the face called out from afar.

Despite sounding as if he were speaking from behind a whirring fan, Olga instantly recognized her husband's voice.

"Don't be afraid, it's me, Boris," he continued, stopping halfway as he approached his beautiful wife.

Olga's pulse quickened as she beheld his ghastly form. Holding back her tears, she cried out bravely, "Boris! I'm not afraid, please, come closer."

Her voice washed over Boris like a warm summer breeze. He felt a connection to her he hadn't felt in months. Eagerly, he moved in closer until he was five feet away. Olga stared up longingly at Boris's life-like face, hovering over his dipteran form.

She saw her husband for the first time since that fateful night. He was clean shaven, and his facial features were more youthful, resembling the young professor she first met in her salon a decade ago. He wore a wistful smile, as if to say: I want to go back, I want to meet you all over again.

Suddenly an unsettled look ushered away his smile. Boris knelt on one knee and bowed his head so that his human face was eye-level with Olga. Then, he spoke in a nervous low tone.

"Olga, listen to me carefully, you are in danger. Go and find Wes, he can offer you protection…"

"Shh…, I am not afraid" Olga interrupted calmly, "I have something I need to confess. I have been unfaithful to you, Boris. I am so sorry!"

Tears welled up in her eyes and Olga began to cry.

"I don't know how we grew apart. I regret not loving you more than I should. You were always so kind to me, always taking blame for my faults, I don't deserve you." Olga admitted.

"Olga, my love. I forgive you. I can only imagine how difficult it must have been for you. I dedicated all of my time to my work when I should have been more attentive to your needs. I am not without fault," Boris replied warmly.

"Do you remember that night we met on the roof-top bar in Kyiv?" Olga asked, smiling at the uncanny image of his face.

"How could I forget? It was the night I first kissed you. My heart almost burst with excitement when it happened," Boris replied wistfully.

"I wish we could turn back the clock to that moment, I wish we could start fresh…"

Just as Olga began reflecting on the past, a large cow wandered between them, interrupting their nostalgia.

"NOW! Now, Olga. Hit the cow with the needle," Jeremy ordered through his radio.

Before she could reach into her pocket for the poison dart, the flies suddenly started moving erratically, distorting the image of Boris's face. Olga hesitated, startled by the unexpected phenomenon. Within seconds, Boris's face was replaced by Beelzebub's goat-like head with two spiral horns jutting skyward. The hairs on the back of Olga's neck stood on end, as she retreated from his ghastly visage.

"I see you've joined the other team!" the devil admonished.

Boris's dipteran body mysteriously rose from its kneeling position, as if moved by puppet strings. He raised his head and stared blankly at Olga, then stood limply before her.

Randall and Jeremy grew saucer eyed as they witnessed the unholy spectacle unfolding. They were hiding in the cupola of the barn peering through their binoculars.

"Holy Shit!" Jeremy exclaimed, while Randall gestured the sign of the cross and began to pray.

Olga recalled Beelzebub's voice as the one that befouled her conscience that fateful night. "It was you!" she screamed, "It was you who stole our lives!"

"Me?! Why do you humans always make me out to be your scapegoat? Did you not summon me for help with your little problem?" Beelzebub chided, referring to Olga's false pregnancy and resulting dilemma. "I merely laid out your options, it was you who…how do you mortals put it?   Oh, right… followed your heart…Hahahahaha"

Unbridled rage erupted inside Olga as she shouted at the devil "LIAR!!!"

She quickly reached into her dress pocket and pulled out the poison-filled needle and syringe. In one fell swoop, Olga jabbed the needle against the side of her neck, squeezing the plunger until the brown-colored poison disappeared into her body.

Before Wes came to Olga with his plan, she had already decided to end it all. She could no longer bear the agony of her shame and self-loathing. After many nights of self-reflection, she concluded that her sins were unforgivable, and her character hopelessly flawed. Wes's plan to defeat Beelzebub came as a beacon of light for Olga, providing her an opportunity to destroy the demonic creatures that ruined their lives, and a chance at redeeming her sins.

Olga's eyes rolled back in her head as the powerful neurotoxin began to take effect.

Jeremy and Randall were flabbergasted by Olga's unexpected act of sacrifice. They stormed out of the barn, hopped over the barbed-wire fence, and ran towards Olga, who was now convulsing uncontrollably. Seconds later, a windowless white van careened through the half-opened barn doors, sending pieces of wood flying through the air. Following the two officers, the van took out a section of barbed-wire fence, as its tires threw mud in its wake.

The two officers stopped in their tracks ten yards away from Olga and the dipteran monster, while four priests dressed in ceremonial vestments scrambled out of the van.   There was nothing any of them could do. They stood and watched the macabre spectacle unfold.

Triggered by her convulsions, the flies darted towards the woman, erasing the devil's hideous visage. But one fly remained hovering over Boris's limply hung head. Sensing the presence of the clergy, Beelzebub remained in the body of the fly for protection, as he watched his demonic creation devour Olga.

Olga fell to the ground as her body continued to writhe and shudder. Within seconds, her face, legs, and arms were covered with the flesh-eating flies. They made their way through the neck and hemline of her sundress, boring a hole through her abdomen. The men watched in horror as blooms of red blood exploded against her white sundress. Olga made no sound, no plea for help, no evasive maneuver to thwart her demise.

Seconds later, the diabolical flies began to die, poisoned by the pesticide befouling Olga's body. The priests began chanting and praying as they approached the dipteran monster. They threw holy water on Boris as they made the sign of the cross, encircling him in a layer of holy protection.

When the last fly on Olga's corpse died, Boris collapsed onto the ground. He began writhing and contorting in unnatural positions, while his skin took on a darkened hue. As the chants and prayers grew louder, Boris's iridescent wings withered like giant flower petals, detaching themselves from his back. In a spectacular display of grace, Boris molted away the devil's garb and emerged anew. Laying naked on the spring pasture wet with dew, Boris wailed,

"OLGA!!!"

Devastated by her self-sacrifice, Boris laid there sobbing, too weak from grief to move. The team of priests brought out a stretcher from the van and quickly carried him away.

As the van sped off in the distance, Beelzebub flew away, defeated again by the power of love.

The End.

www.ingramcontent.com/pod-product-compliance
Lightning Source LLC
Chambersburg PA
CBHW022038240626
47154CB00007B/2463